I0522511

My disguise worked, but Mona was detained. How was I going to get her out of this?

"We have reviewed your papers. You may go, however, we must detain your superior officer a little longer. We have more questions for Interrogator Casola."

"Watch out for yourself. She can be bitchy, and she has friends in high places in Astana."

"Thank you for the warning, Interrogator Arreaux." She returned my identification papers.

"What about my piece?" I asked.

"No firearms are permitted here, not even for interrogators."

"Will it be returned upon my departure?"

"No. Headquarters will have to issue you a new one when you return to Astana."

I was escorted back into the customs area by an NWO guard. "When you exit those doors, you must report to the concierge for quartering assignment. Follow the yellow arrows on the wall. If you get lost, ask anyone with a purple name tag for assistance."

I opened the door and walked down the corridor. It was good that I had to follow a yellow line like some kindergarten kid, because my mind was working overtime with concern for Mona. Why was she being detained longer? What had she done that caused her to be suspected? Would they hurt her? How could I negotiate her release? How could I rescue her?

Dan Arrow and his girlfriend, FBI Special Agent Mona Casola, are on a mission to assist their alien friend Waam in finding out who gave the orders to kill his nephew and steal a secret box—a box like Pandora's that contains something that the world doesn't need unleashed. In the meantime, Mona is also determined to find her missing baby—a human-alien hybrid, called a star child—which has been kidnapped and taken someplace called "the hollow moon." While continuing to discover more truth than fiction in popular conspiracy theories, Dan learns that the New World Order is unfolding its domination plans through the United Nations' Agenda 21, and he has to stop its cogs from turning.

and the NWO is planning to set off a bunch of nukes that will destroy most of the population on Earth. In the meantime, Dan's girlfriend, Mona Casola, an FBI agent, is determined to find the alien-hybrid baby who was stolen from her and taken to "the Hollow Moon." Dan agrees to help and they combine their missions, traveling first to Mars and then to the moon, which they discover to their amazement is hollow and serving as a base for the NWO. Things start out great, but as soon as they get to the moon, everything starts to fall apart, and Dan and Mona will be lucky to escape with their lives. *Dan Arrow and the Hollow Moon* is both intriguing and plausible, despite the fact that some of the subplots appear to be outrageous at first glance. Baker has really done his homework, and he weaves fact and fiction in a way that makes the plot seem completely realistic. A worthy addition to the series. ~ *Regan Murphy, The Review Team of Taylor Jones & Regan Murphy*

ACKNOWLEDGMENTS

Many thanks to Lauri Wellington, Acquisitions Editor at **B**lack Opal Books, for believing in this work and making its publication possible. Thanks, as well, to Faith who helped to polish this novel into its final form. Also, thanks to Jack, whose work on the cover design added character to this work's presentation. And, finally, many thanks to Black Opal author Dan Barrett for his continuing support and advice. Also, a large chunk of appreciation goes to my good friend Larry who, several years ago, fell on his noggin and got me writing again.

DAN ARROW

AND THE
HOLLOW MOON

Edward S. Baker

A Black Opal Books Publication

GENRE: SCIENCE FICTION/THRILLER/SUSPENSE

DAN ARROW AND THE HOLLOW MOON
Copyright © 2018 by Edward S. Baker
Cover Design by Jackson Cover Designs
All cover art copyright © 2018
All Rights Reserved
Print ISBN: 978-1-626949-51-5

First Publication: JULY 2018

Published by Black Opal Books **http://www.blackopalbooks.com**

DEDICATION

To my wife Edna, who supports my writing, even though it draws me away from her at times when I should be near.

Also, to all you believers who know that the Dan Arrow novels are rooted in more truth than fiction.

Chapter 1

When our debit card was denied at a gas pump outside of Newport News, I knew that it was time to head home. Mona and I had been on a two-week vacation, compliments of Mack, Mona's boss and head of an investigative unit at the FBI in DC. We had traveled all over the east coast, well, from Deerfield Beach to Virginia Beach, following the local coastal roads, sleeping in the best hotels, dining in mom and pop's, and just enjoying getting to know each other again.

"I guess the party's over, baby," I said to Mona, "unless you want to call Mack and ask him for an extra couple of grand."

"Slide it through a second time, Danny."

I did, and this time it worked.

"That's Mack's way of letting me know that it's time to come back to work," she said.

With a full tank of gas, we found our way to I-95 and pointed our rented Escalade north to DC, and on Monday we were back in our respective offices. Mona got to park down the street in a federal lot and hike a couple of blocks to 935 Pennsylvania Avenue, that concrete building with all the windows and a distinctive line of American flags. I, on the other hand, got to park on a side street near Stan's Used Cars and walk uphill half a block to a door with a "Moving Sale" sign taped to it. Yup, it was good to be back at the old grind.

As I climbed the stairs to the second floor, I couldn't help noticing the distinct odor of an old building. It was so different from the smell of the subterranean snake holes where I had spent so much time over the past two months. Yeah, it smelled like home.

Another moving sale sign was taped to the door of my office. I pulled it down and walked in. Hal was bent over, rummaging through a small cardboard box on the floor. Across the small of her back was a Harley Davidson tattoo that I had never seen before. Of course, she had never shown me that side of her.

"I'm back, Hal."

She turned quickly and tugged at the bottom of her tee shirt. It was nice to see that her modesty was still intact. "So you aren't dead after all," she said with a look of mild disappointment. "I suppose you're wondering what's going on here."

"Where are we moving?"

"Out of here, unless you come up with some dough. The landlord has been here three times inquiring about his rent. You're two months in arrears."

"I'll take care of him," I replied, although I wasn't sure that I could come up with more than one month's rent in cash.

I looked around the office. Hal's desk was cluttered with empty paper coffee cups. Cardboard boxes bore hand-scrawled messages like *2 for $1, make an offer,* and *free.* I walked into my office. My desk and its old executive chair were gone. It was definitely a moving sale, and I already had been moved out.

I walked back into the outer office. "So what's been going on?" I asked Hal.

"Listen, Danny, I've had to sell this stuff in order to feed myself and keep a roof over my head. I haven't had a paycheck in over a month. You just forgot about me."

She had a point. I guess that I had been so engrossed in being with Mona after the Powers case that I had forgotten to check in with Hal to let her know that I was alive and to see if she needed help with anything. "What about Willie? Didn't he give you the two grand that he owes me?"

"Fine upstanding guy, Willie. I called his number, but somebody there told me that he was doing eighteen months for bookmaking."

"Oh."

The phone rang.

"That's probably the electric company telling us that they're going to shut off the power," Hal said, picking up the receiver. "Dan Arrow PI. How can I help you?" She handed the phone to me. "It's some guy named Juan."

I took the phone from her. "Dan Arrow," I said in a firm and official voice.

"Mr. Arrow, it's me, Waam."

"Hi, my friend! How have you been these past two weeks?"

"I've been good enough for most of these past two weeks, but I need your help. Do you have time to see me?"

"It looks as though I have plenty of time on my hands. My assistant is having my office redone, and all appointments are on hold." Waam probably knew that I was lying through my teeth. I figured that if I didn't get a client in the next day or two, I'd be signing up for public assistance.

"Good. Can I come by at dark?"

"Sure, I can be here then."

"See you then, Mr. Arrow."

I hung up the phone and told Hal, "We have to clean up this place because we have a client coming after dinner."

She sighed. "Listen, Danny, you won't be able to use the conference room for your meeting because I've sublet it for six months to an alternative lifestyles counselor. You'll have to use my desk."

"What the hell is an alternative lifestyles counselor?"

"She's a therapist who is helping men and women cope with issues of transgender transformation. Nice woman. You'll like her."

"Did you get a name?"

"Sam something or other. I have it in my datebook."

I rolled my eyes at Hal.

"What's a girl gonna do when she needs money, Danny? The lease is only for six months."

"Well, you could go out on the sidewalk and strut your moneymaker."

Hal gave me a stern look. "Watch what you say, Mr. Smartmouth. You could be running your ass straight into a sexual harassment charge at the Human Rights Commission!"

I made a cross with my two pointer fingers. "Whoa. Sorry. I was just kidding." I made a mental note to buy her a bottle of wine as a peace offering.

"And you'd better watch what you say to Sam La-Femme when you meet her," Hal warned me.

Aha! We have a last name. Great, I thought. *Samuel or Samantha LaFemme. That sounds possibly transgender in itself.*

I opted to change the subject. "Can we find a sofa someplace?" I asked. "This client is a really big man, and he isn't going to fit in a normal chair."

"Fat guy, huh?"

"Tall and broad."

"He isn't one of those creepy dudes with the sunglasses, is he?"

"No, he's nothing like that. He's an Ummite. They're very tall and very peace-loving people from the planet Ummo. He saved my life. Now he needs my help."

"He's a space alien, and you owe him a favor? He's gonna expect you to do it for free," Hal said with her hands on her hips.

"We'll see."

"Well, I think there's a sofa in Sam's office. Maybe you can drag that down here after she closes up for the day."

"Did you keep a key? Maybe I can simply use her office for my meeting."

"I'll ask her when she comes in."

ﻌﻌﻌ

Waam showed up at seven-thirty p.m. His eyes told me that he hadn't slept in a couple of days. I escorted him to Sam LaFemme's office. Waam bent down so he could pass through the door and into what had been my conference room. "Interesting décor," he said. "This is very non-threatening, almost feminine. I did not expect it."

When I closed the door, Waam broke into tears and, still bent over, laid his massive head on my shoulder. "Doroo is dead," he sobbed.

"Aw, noooo," I said softly, patting his bicep. Doroo was Waam's nephew and had become a good friend in the short time that I had known him. "I'm so sorry, Waam."

"I haven't told his mother. She's my sister, and I don't know how I can tell her. He was her only child."

"Can you tell me about it?" I asked.

Waam sat down on the sofa. Sitting, his head was only a few feet from the ceiling. Hell, he was nearly ten feet tall on a short day. I handed him a box of Sam La-Femme's tissues.

Waam wiped his eyes and then began. "As we had planned, Doroo carried the electrical essence of His Excellency for a date with your star. As he approached the point where he was to jettison the magnetic storage device into the molten plasma, his tureen was intercepted and overtaken by the Draconians. His Excellency and the toroidal device which contained him were taken. All on board were killed. My tureen received a distress message but, by then, it was too late, and all was lost. The video devices in Doroo's tureen automatically continued to transmit signals."

Waam pulled a cell phone from his coat's breast pocket, touched the screen a few times, and then handed it to me. The video displayed the door to Doroo's tureen being blasted open, probably by some sort of laser weapon. As the reptilian soldiers began to shoot liquid light at the crew, Doroo held up his hands and stood in front of them. I couldn't understand what he said, but his physical motions translated to me as, "Stop!" He was unarmed, and he was instantly cut in half. There were more blasts and many sparks.

When the video ended, I handed the phone back to Waam. "I'm so sorry for your loss, Waam. Doroo was a good friend."

"His tureen's automatic tracking devices continued to send messages indicating its location. However, the tureen was within the gravitational pull of your star and, as it plunged into the solar fire, transmission ceased. There is no more to tell. I have lost a nephew, and my sister has lost the light of her life."

"What can I do to console you?" I asked.

"Find the one who issued the order to kill Doroo and his crew, Mr. Arrow!" Waam replied. "The order may have come from officials on your garden planet."

"I owe you and Doroo that much," I told him, "but things are going to hell here. I have to stay local and earn a little money in order to keep my office open and my assistant employed. Give me a few weeks to get my affairs in order, and I'll get on it."

Waam pulled a bar of gold from his pocket and handed it to me. I had to grasp it in two hands in order to keep from dropping it. "Surprisingly heavy," I said.

"That bar weighs ten of your Earth pounds. It's pure gold that was recovered from Galactic pirates by an Ummite patrol. The pirates claimed to have pilfered it from a shipment that was heading to the Draconians from the Chinese."

"The markings are clearly Chinese," I said, turning the bar over in my hands to examine it.

"Will that bar help to settle your local affairs, Mr. Arrow?"

"Are you giving me this gold, Waam?"

"We Ummites have little use for it, except to trade for resources from other planetary systems. They, in turn, trade it for resources from the Draconians, who have a great need for gold. Finding Doroo's murderer is much more important to me than that bar of gold. If it will help you to get on the track of the individual who gave the order, then it is yours."

I did a quick estimate in my head: Sixteen ounces to the pound times ten pounds was 160 ounces at about $1200 per ounce. *I think Hal can probably get by on that.* "I'll begin in the morning."

Chapter 2

It was after ten before I got home to Mona's apartment. Mona was in a snit because dinner was cold. I apologized profusely, but my assurances didn't match her level of expectations about what life should be like when a man and a woman decide to move in together.

The apartment was full of the heavy aroma of cooked beef. And a beef was what Mona intended to discuss with me.

"Okay, you called me and told me you'd be late, so I'm figuring maybe eight o'clock," Mona said angrily. "I started cooking your roast when I got home at five. It's been in the oven since then. Take it out now, if you want."

The oven was set for 500 degrees. "Uh, the meat is going to be a little overdone," I said. I removed the roast and turned the oven off.

"I increased the temperature to five hundred at eight-thirty, so it would be just the way your goose was gonna be when you finally found your way home."

I already knew that there'd be no chance of getting

lucky tonight. "I'm sorry, baby. I had a client, and it simply ran late."

Mona crossed her arms and huffed. She stood looking at me for a moment and then went to the liquor cabinet, pulled out a bottle of scotch, and poured herself three fingers full. The glass showed signs of previous use, so I knew she had been into the scotch earlier. She was definitely pissed at me.

"So, how was your first day back at the office?" I asked.

"Fucking long, Danny. I do better in the field than in a damn office."

"So what kinds of things did you have to deal with?"

"Many reports are coming in from all over the country about loud booms and rumbles that rattle houses. Military authorities, local police, and fire units have no idea what's causing the problem. Frankly, neither does the FBI or the CIA. We don't know what to make of it."

"That's interesting. I haven't heard any booms or felt any rumbles."

She gave me a look like I was going to feel a boom at any moment.

Mona took another swallow of scotch. "Look, there's more. Like you already know, some of the higher-ups in the Bureau are supportive of this New World Order thing. They hold me suspect because of my presence at the arena that day and my possible involvement with the collapse of the facility at Livermore. Frankly, they may suspect me of complicity in the sidetracking of the emergence of the New World Order. I feel like everyone is pointing at me and whispering behind my back."

"I'm sure that not everyone is whispering about you. That's simply paranoia. Is Mack any help? Are there others in whom you can confide?"

"I told Mack what I'm feeling. I told him that because many FBI higher-ups support the NWO, it feels unsafe for me to be in Washington. I asked him for a field assignment."

"What did he say?"

"When one comes along, he'll let me know about it, and we can discuss it."

"Well, we'll do whatever is best for you, baby. I don't like seeing you this way."

"So who was your client, anyway?" Mona asked. "Seven-thirty seems awfully late for an office visit."

I had to be straight with her. Besides she knew my client. "It was Waam," I replied.

"Oh? How is Waam? Did you take him out for drinks?"

"You know that he came after dark because of his tremendous height. He wanted as few people as possible to see him. And you know I could never have taken him out for a drink because he would have been seen as an oddity, and we couldn't have been inconspicuous."

"So, how is he?"

"Not good. He was very distressed. He came to tell me that Doroo is dead."

Mona's expression changed from anger to concern. "This isn't good. Was it an accident?"

"No, the Draconians did him in. They cut him in half and sent his tureen into the sun."

"Oh, god…"

"There's more bad news. They took Miss Hitler's container with them when they left for home. So, Hitler may still out there somewhere cavorting with the lizards."

"We should have killed that motherfucker when we had the chance."

"Waam has asked me to help him find the person or persons who gave the order to kill Doroo. He thinks the orders may have come from someone here on Earth."

"You told him that you would, didn't you?"

"Yes. It's going to be a field operation. Do you think Mack might assign you to assist me?"

"Actually, I'm not going to ask Mack to assign me. I'm going to tell Mack that I'm going on this field assignment. In fact, I will insist on going along with you. It's the perfect field assignment. Besides, Waam is Mack's friend. I wonder if Mack knows about Doroo's murder?"

In spite of the late hour, Mona called Mack and told him about the field assignment. He wasn't yet aware of Doroo's death and was very distraught at the news. "Of course," he said, "you should go with Dan on this assignment. I'm afraid that he's going to dive into some treacherous waters. He'll need someone he can depend upon."

"Thanks, Mack," Mona told him.

"I'll take care of the paperwork tomorrow. Please keep me abreast of what you two discover."

"Will do, Mack."

☙❧

I was starting to undress for bed when the cell phone rang. It was Waam. He had heard from Mack and had learned that Mona would be joining me on this assignment. He asked if we could meet him in an hour at a baseball field outside of DC in Potomac River Park. I suggested one a.m. "There's something I've got to do before we get started," I said.

I told Mona what was going down, and she begrudgingly climbed out of bed and into her jogging outfit. We both put on shoulder holsters and wind breakers to hide our pieces.

Before we left our apartment, I jotted a quick note to

Hal, telling her to sell Waam's gold bar to a gold dealer, pay all the bills, including her own rent, and put the rest of the cash in the safe in the office.

I put the note and the gold bar in a small canvas bag.

Since I had returned the rental Escalade, and I had no idea where my car had been impounded six weeks ago, Mona drove. On our way out of DC, I asked Mona to stop at Hal's place. I got out of the CRV and rang her bell. Three times.

Finally, she came to the door with a crowbar in her hand. "I thought you might have been one of those tall creeps," she said. "What are you doing out so late, Danny?"

I told her that I was going on assignment, and that I would check in with her when I could, but not to expect anything too regular. Then I handed her the bag and explained about the gold bar. She put the bag on the table nearest her door and removed the gold bar. "Damn, this is really heavy. How much do you think it's worth?" she asked.

"A hundred and sixty ounces at twelve hundred dollars an ounce means about two hundred thousand dollars, less commission and fees. Get what you can for it, but don't give it away. This could keep us in business for the next year or two."

"Way to go, Danny!" she exclaimed.

I wished Hal good night and told her I'd see her sometime in the future, but I wasn't sure when. She had a big smile on her face when she asked me to give her love to Mona.

"Yeah. Sure," I replied.

⁓⁓⁓

Mona and I headed west out of DC, along the Potomac River. The road was very smooth and curvy. Trucks were not allowed on this stretch of road, and the Parks Commission kept it in primo condition. We wound through the tree-studded landscape for almost ten miles when we came upon a sign that let us know that we were close. As we slowed near one of several ball fields, I saw a red light flash three times beside a tree to our right. I told Mona to drive toward the tree. She bounced over the short concrete curb and, as we approached the tree, a giant of a man stepped from behind its trunk. "There's Waam!" Mona said.

Waam greeted us warmly and showed us an iridescent line in the grass. "Follow this line," he said. "It will lead you to my tureen, which is presently cloaked."

"Our military should have this technology," I told him.

"We can't give it to you because it will afford you great advantage over your enemies. Your generals will use it to annihilate thousands and put their families in chains."

"He's right, Danny," Mona said.

At a T in the iridescent line, Waam told us to stop and to feel in front of us. Yes, there was something hard. In my mind's eye, I could see a thin handrail. "Step up," Waam told me, "and you'll feel the ramp under your feet."

I did as instructed and was soon ascending the ramp. Mona followed close behind. "This is incredible!" she told Waam.

Of greater interest to me was that once we reached the top of the ramp, we could see everything inside Waam's tureen. Only from the outside was it invisible to the human eye.

"Please be seated," Waam told us, pointing to the circular area near the middle of his tureen, where we had been seated during the trip out of Livermore. As we sat, one of Waam's crew got up and closed the ramp.

When he sat back down, I felt a slight jiggle in the seat. I assumed that we were hovering above the ground in case we needed to escape discovery. I stood for a moment and looked through the outside shell of the tureen. Yes, we were above the surface. I could see the dome of the US Capitol Building below us, about fifteen miles to our east. I sat back down.

"Thank you for joining us, Agent Casola," Waam began. "I would like to show you what we know of Doroo's fate."

I knew this was going to be ugly, especially on a full sized video monitor.

As the video began to play, we saw the crew inside Doroo's tureen, all busy at various controls to ensure a safe voyage toward the sun. "They were between Mercury and your star when they were fired upon. Watch the reaction of the crew to the unexpected warning. Doroo slowed his tureen to keep his crew safe from attack. They were in an unarmed transport vessel. Now, watch the door." Suddenly the door began to glow red and then it exploded inward. The crew dived for cover. Four reptilian guards entered, pressing their chest plates and sending bursts of liquid light at the crew members. Doroo put his hands into the air, motioning for the reptilians to stop shooting. "He is telling them that he and his crew are unarmed and will offer no resistance," Waam said. A reptilian touched his chest plate, and a burst of light severed Doroo such that his upper torso fell backward and his legs crumpled to the floor.

"Enough, Waam. Enough!" Mona cried.

"Wait, Agent Casola. You must see that they take His Excellency."

We watched as the reptilians killed everyone on

board, even those who pleaded for their lives. Then they ransacked the tureen until they found the box in which the electrical essence of Miss Hitler was stored. The lizard who found it roared and held it aloft for the others to see. They all then exited the cabin.

"They were all lizards, Waam," I said. "Nobody from Earth was there."

"But we believe that the message to board the vessel and take the toroidal container came from the garden planet. The Draconians may even have launched from the garden planet. You must find the one who gave the order. If he is human, you must terminate him. If he is any other race, please give me the pleasure of the termination."

I nodded. "An interesting question is whether the lizards got their orders from the NWO or whether they planned this on their own."

"I don't think it makes a difference, Danny," Mona interjected. "They both stand to profit from Miss Hitler's migration into a new body and from the reptilians' emergence from the underground. From what we know about the NWO's plans, aren't most of us already supposed to be dead when that happens?"

I had to concede that Mona had a point. The most important thing for us to discover was who it was who gave the order that caused Doroo's death. And then we had to find Miss Hitler before she migrated out of Pandora's Box and into a younger human body.

Mona changed the subject. "Waam, before Danny and I go home, I have a question for you. The FBI has received hundreds of reports of booms and metallic scraping sounds from all over the country. Sometimes the booms shake houses and rattle dishes. Do you know anything that could shed any light on these reports?"

"I think it may be the Chinese, Agent Casola. The Draconians are seeking as much gold as they can. It is common knowledge that the Chinese government is buying up as much gold bullion as it can get its hands on. I think they may be purchasing it to trade to the Draconians."

"What would they trade it for?" I asked.

"Power. Maybe new technologies that would give them military advantage over the USA and Russia. Maybe medicines to keep their people safe from any pandemic that might be unleashed upon the world. There might be a dozen things worth the cost of the gold that they have been hoarding."

"What about the rumbles and explosions?" Mona asked again.

"I think the Chinese may be involved in global subterranean gold mining," Waam replied, "perhaps as far as a mile below the surface, basically stealing the gold from beneath countries that don't even know that they are there. Especially since your military and homeland security forces don't know the origins of such sounds."

I stood to say good night to Waam and was struck by what I saw through the tureen's walls. We were in outer space! "Mona! Stand up!" I said, pulling her to her feet by her elbow. "You're not going to believe this!"

When she was fully erect, Mona's eyes widened in awe. "Help me with our bearings," she asked Waam. "Where's the Earth?"

Waam pointed at the floor. "It is twenty million miles behind us."

"My god, Danny, it looks so different from space. It's not really round. It's sort of oval. And the moon is so big!"

"Your lunar orb appears so large because it is so much closer to us at the moment than your garden planet," Waam told us.

I saw two tiny white objects leave the surface of the moon and quickly disappear around it. "What were those?" I asked

"Later…" Waam replied.

I couldn't believe what had happened to us. Mona and I had been so engrossed in our conversation with Waam that we had been completely unaware that his tureen had left the Earth's atmosphere and was whisking us an incredible speed toward some unknown destination.

"Where are you taking us, Waam?" I asked.

"To an Ummite fortification on your red planet," he replied, pointing to the outer wall behind us.

We turned. Sure enough, we were headed toward Mars. Even a school kid couldn't miss its reddish color and the lines that were for so many years thought to be canals.

"We have traveled twenty million miles thus far, but we have one hundred and twenty million more to go," Waam told us. "Enjoy the journey. It will take a couple of hours."

Chapter 3

"What about my car, Danny?" Mona asked. "We left it on the grass at that ball field."

"My guess is that the national park police will find it in the morning and have it towed to impound. Then they'll run a license plate check and discover that it's registered to a federal agent."

"Yeah, and then they'll call the Bureau and be directed to Mack. He'll tell them that I'm on assignment, but the park police will report me as a missing person anyway because of the suspicious circumstances."

"I think you're right, baby. And then your family will be interrogated, and your mother will get upset that you're a probable missing person, and your father will be even more pissed that you're involved with me again. I can't win."

"This isn't about you, you chauvinist asshole. I've got to get a message to Ma somehow that I'm okay. I don't guess that we have any cell towers out here, do we?!"

I squeezed Mona's hand. "Waam will help us get a message to your mom."

"Yeah, well, he'd better not deliver it himself. If she opened the door and saw him standing there, she'd shit a brick, and we'd be burying her the next day."

I chuckled at the image.

We had been traveling in space for almost two hours. Mars was looming ahead, getting larger and larger as the minutes ticked by. As we studied the planet, it was clear that several areas rose like mountain ranges from its otherwise flat surface. We could see at least one canyon that rivaled the Grand Canyon, and ice caps that clung to both poles. Also, we could see small white or grey objects occasionally lift from the surface and fly into space. There was definitely activity of some sort going on.

"How much longer before we land?" I asked Waam.

"We'll slow as we approach so the others can identify us and know that we belong and have business here. We should land in about twenty minutes, your time."

Even though we were slowing, motion inside the tureen was virtually imperceptible. How that was accomplished was beyond me, but I felt some consolation in that it was probably beyond the grasp of most of our physicists and engineers, too, because if they could have figured it out, our astronauts wouldn't have to be subjected to vomiticious spinning in a centrifuge as part of their training for riding in the space shuttle.

"Incoming!" shouted one of Waam's crew, in English. Then, a beeping alarm sounded, somewhat like the signal of my microwave when my popcorn is finally burned.

"Hold on!" Waam told us. The tureen began rolling quickly and raced toward the Martian surface. The rolling images projected on the interior walls were like a ride in a theme park. When I closed my eyes, I felt nothing, but when I opened them, the images caused a little nausea.

As we rolled, however, I saw three Nazis bells pursuing us.

"Look, Danny," Mona exclaimed, "those are the same flying saucers we saw in Bill Powers's notebook. They're German!"

"They're Nazis," I reminded her.

"Aren't they old technology?"

"These seem to have been updated," Waam said. "They're more maneuverable than I'd have expected!"

The beeping alarm turned to a squeal.

"Shields raised!" the same crew member shouted.

Suddenly we were rocked by a blast of liquid light. Then we were struck again.

"They have new weaponry!" Waam exclaimed.

Our pilot caused the tureen to suddenly spiral upward, it did a roll, and then it dived. As it did, the alarm squealed again. We were hit again, and this time sparks flew from one of the control panels. I could see smoke billowing from behind us.

Waam sat in a second pilot's seat and took over the controls. "Keep the shields up!" he cried. "Perhaps we can deflect any other shots."

Mona squeezed my hand.

The tureen seemed to be rolling counterclockwise again. Waam was struggling with his controls. The alarm squealed again. He dived to the left, and the shot missed us. Then, we were rolling again, this time in a clockwise direction. Waam finally seemed to stabilize the tureen. I could see the three bells in hot pursuit. Then one suddenly exploded. A ball of light blazed between the two remaining bells. They gave up the chase and quickly maneuvered away.

"What happened?" Mona asked. "Why did they stop shooting at us?"

"Ground support," Waam told her. "We're nearing the Ummite fortification."

Below us, I could see a small opening with antiaircraft weapons pointed skyward and following our tureen. Behind the opening stretched a hose-like tunnel with crystalline walls that hugged the contour of the surface for an unknown distance and then plunged underground. Waam guided the craft into the small opening, and we shot down the Habitrail. "The tureen is on autopilot now," Waam told us. "The controls will bring us in from here. We've arrived safely."

It was difficult to judge how fast we were traveling, especially since this was only our second time traveling in a tureen. But once inside the walls of the crystalline tunnel, I could see that it was close to a mile in diameter, which was much larger than I had estimated from the air.

When we finally came to rest, Waam stood and asked how we were. I could tell that Mona was a little shaken, so I put my arm around her shoulder and replied, "It's obvious that we were in very good hands."

"We were lucky to have lost only one stabilizer. They have a weapon that I haven't seen before. It was like liquid light on steroids. I'll have to report it to our commander and hope that our technicians can modify our shields to protect us from it."

"That was quite a reception, Waam," Mona said.

"In truth, I hadn't expected it. This is the first time we've been fired upon in Martian skies."

Waam's crew began shutting down the tureen, closing small hatches, turning dials, and inspecting the panel that had sparked when we were hit. "The repairs should be accomplished easily," Waam's co-pilot told him.

"Thank you, Munno," Waam replied. "Say hello to your life's partner from me."

After Munno opened the ramp and walked out of the tureen, I asked Waam if Munno was gay.

"Gay?" he asked. "Why would you ask that?"

"I have much to learn about your species," I replied. "On Earth, when you refer to a life partner, it usually means someone of the same sex."

"Do you mean gender?"

"Yes, gender."

"On Ummo, we do not have wives. The term itself means that one is subservient to the other. In our union ceremonies, we join life's partners, regardless of gender. And, gender is almost obsolete. We don't procreate in the same manner as you, for penetration of one by another is seen as a form of assault, although some still practice that act. Procreation is accomplished in a laboratory. The female receives the fertilized egg and carries it until she begins to show. At that point, our physicians remove it surgically, and the final stages of development are accomplished in specialized growth chambers. If the fetus is judged to be defective in any manner, it is destroyed."

"And in same sex couples?"

"If the same sex couple is male, the couple employs a female to carry the egg. It is an honored occupation. If the same sex couple is female, the egg is fertilized by inserting donated sperm into the egg, and one of the life partners carries it."

"I think we're headed in that same direction, Waam, although we don't have your technology yet," Mona said. "Some among us will destroy a fetus if it is defective, but others will not."

"I know it is that way," Waam replied, "but eventually your governments will mandate destruction of a defective fetus as a matter of course, especially if the NWO's progressive agenda is implemented. To their end, the cost of maintaining a defective entity is an excessive waste of resources that the greater community should not be required to absorb."

Waam checked a few devices and then suggested that it was time to exit his tureen. As we walked down the ramp, I noticed that the spot on the tureen that had been hit by the liquid light was still smoking, although, to my untrained eye, I could see nothing on the tureen's structure that I could identify as a stabilizer. The tureen's skin was simply smooth, with the exception of the small rumpled area which was still smoking.

Waam sensed my curiosity and told me, "The stabilizer on a tureen is electromagnetic because it's for use in the vacuum of space. It's integrated into the composition of the outer shell. The stabilizers on your primitive flying machines extend from the fuselage because they utilize passing gasses to keep your machines aligned.

"Oh," I said, as though I understood how an electromagnetic stabilizer might work.

"Come. Commander Omer is anxious to meet both of you."

Mona took my hand, and we walked alongside Waam through the hangar area where his tureen and many others were hovering about three feet off the ground, as though suspended from the roof by an invisible wire. My mind drifted back to when I was a kid. I remembered seeing a long pendulum hanging in the Museum of Science and Industry in Chicago. It swung perpetually because of the rhythm of the Earth's sidereal action. And by the checking the markings on the ground beneath the pendulum, it was possible to tell what time it was. I wondered if the tureens would be caused to sway in the same way, but then I realized that they weren't hanging by a wire. They were simply hovering by magnetic levitation. So much for daydreaming! What the hell, I guess I was really tired. I mean, Mona and I had left DC around eleven at night, then we had driven to Potomac River Park, then chatted with Wham for a while, and then spent three more hours traveling to Mars. It must have been about four in the morning, our time.

It also struck me that we were underground again, walking in a huge facility that had been hollowed out under the planet's surface. Lighting was artificial. A persistent low hum told me that air exchange was controlled mechanically, just like at home. "Are all alien facilities underground?" I asked Waam.

"Alien?" he asked. "Here, you are the aliens!"

"But Mars is not your species' home, is it?"

"No, but we have had a presence on the red planet for more than a thousand years. Are you the alien in your own country, where you have had a presence for fewer than four hundred years?"

"We may have been in North America for only four hundred years, but our ancestors created a civilization where there wasn't one."

"Mr. Arrow, your perspective is too narrow, and your knowledge of your own planet's history is amazingly devoid of factual information."

"So, educate me."

"Those who search your country for evidence of past civilizations have found artifacts which prove your historians wrong. But those artifacts don't fit into the commonly accepted story of your beginnings, so they're hidden away because they cannot be explained. The truth is that several civilizations have called your country home for several millennia each, and the evidence of their past presence is still visible from the air. Your species has the tools to look for that evidence but chooses not to see."

"Tools?" Mona asked.

"Yes. A recently advanced one, Google Earth, is all you need to use to explore the garden planet's surface for evidence of past cities. At one time, a large city existed in what is now the swamps and lowlands of Florida. From the air, evidence of its roads and the foundations of its skyscrapers are clearly visible."

"What happened to those civilizations?" Mona asked.

"They went the way of most human enterprises. The inhabitants destroyed their own civilizations. The few survivors returned to primitive animalistic lifestyles. Over two or three generations, all knowledge was lost. Stories of the great civilizations that once had flourished became the foundation of folklore and myths. Have you heard of Atlantis?"

"Isn't that a myth?" Mona asked.

"My point exactly!" Waam replied. Then, he turned to me. "And, the answer to your question is 'no.'"

"No, what?" I asked.

"No, not all of our installations are underground."

I had forgotten that I had asked that question.

"We build many of our outpost facilities underground for protection against the severe weather outside," Waam continued, "and also to protect against potential attack from other races, known and unknown. We did not build this facility, however. It was built by those who came here before us."

"So outer space is not all peace and quiet?" Mona asked.

"Not at all. All species from all planets compete against each other for a finite amount of mineral, animal, and vegetable resources in order to sustain their civilizations. Although we enjoy trade agreements and sign peace treaties, not every species is trustworthy or peaceful by its nature. Wars are inevitable."

"Like the lizards?" I asked.

"Like the lizards…"

We came to a doorway, which Waam opened by pressing his hand onto a chrome plate. The door simply vanished, and we walked through the opening where it had been.

Within a few seconds, I heard a slight whooshing sound, turned, and saw that the door had reappeared. I imagined that someday we would enjoy the same technology in our secure facilities and, perhaps, as front doors on our homes.

A guard greeted us by raising his right hand. "Muhoo, Captain Waam."

"Muhoo," Waam replied, giving the same hand signal. "The commander is expecting us."

"Yes, sir, he is. Permit me to announce you."

The guard entered a room momentarily and then returned. "You may go in."

Waam led, followed by Mona and then me. The office was Spartan. No carpets or amenities were visible; however, communication devices and several monitors were mounted or perhaps molded into the walls to the right of a desk. The commander was shorter than Waam, probably only nine feet tall. He was dressed in a deep purple jumpsuit with no distinguishable evidence of his rank.

"Welcome, Captain!" The commander said, grasping Waam's shoulders in his hands. "I am glad that you reached us safely."

"Ours was an eventful entry, Commander."

"It is an unfortunate turn of events, Captain, that the Draconians have escalated our relationship into a cold war."

"I think you're being generous in describing their actions. It was clearly a direct assault upon an announced Ummite tureen, flying on a diplomatic mission. There was nothing cold about the liquid light which almost disabled my tureen and possibly could have injured two human passengers."

"I will report this incident to the high command, and I will send a formal message of protest to the Draconian ambassador. But you should know that Commissar Nargas has put a price on your head. In videos of the disaster at Livermore, you were identified as one of the two Ummite conspirators. Nargas himself claims to have seen you helping his concubine to escape. "

"Thank you for this important information, Commander. This bounty will limit my ability to interact with NWO officials."

"And, Captain, I wish to express my deepest sorrow for your tragic loss.

"Again, it was at the hand of the Draconians, Commander, that my nephew Doroo and his crew were terminated and their tureen was sent into the solar fires."

"I vow to you, Captain, that I will do what I can to seek justice for this unwarranted incident, but, as you know, I have limited power in this part of the galaxy.

"That's why I've brought Mr. Daniel Arrow and Agent Mona Casola to our fortification, Commander."

"Yes, I see," Commander Omer said, turning his attention to Mona and me, the small guests who stood beside Waam. "Could it be that they're free to do things which would mean immediate termination for the rest of us?"

"Yes, Commander. The garden planet has yet to become a member of the Galactic Federation. Thus, they are not bound by the rules and protocols that bind those of us who have taken the oath."

"It is indeed a pleasure to meet you, Agent Casola," the commander said, extending his large hand toward Mona. She offered her hand, which he shook gently. "And Mr. Arrow," he said, turning to me, "I trust that you will share with me the plan that you have begun to develop to assist the captain in his quest for justice?"

Before I could answer, Waam asked, "Commander, what have you learned about the human that the Draconians call 'His Excellency,' the one stolen from Lieutenant Doroo's tureen?"

"Unfortunately, nothing. Our sources have learned nothing."

"This is unacceptable to me, Commander. I ask that you continue to press them for information. Surely our spies know where His Excellency has been taken."

Commander Omer gave Waam a stern look but then relaxed his gaze. "You must be very tired and stressed from the events of the past few days, Captain. We can talk later, perhaps when you have had time to sleep and to reflect further upon our role in this star system."

Waam clearly realized that he had overstepped his bounds by challenging his commander. "Yes, sir. You are wise, and I have not slept since learning of Doroo's death. Undoubtedly I do need rest."

"Very well, Captain. Why not show our guests to their quarters so that they, too, can rest. It's been a long day for us all. Perhaps you and our friends will join me for dinner this evening?"

Waam nodded, obviously knowing that dinner was a command, not an invitation. He saluted the commander and then gestured that we should follow him out of the commander's office. Once we entered the corridor and were out of ear shot, Waam whispered, "I don't believe our commander. Draconians are boastful. Those who have done this deed will brag about it. I'm certain that our spies know where His Excellency has been taken."

Chapter 4

The Draconian facility was constructed underground to protect its inhabitants from the rays of our solar system's star, as well as to hide the activities of the Draconian Guard from the six other species which had established outposts on the red planet. Entered from two directions by winding tunnels, the facility itself seemed like an underground continent. Hollowed out to ten miles in height, its diameter measured almost forty miles across. It was lighted and heated artificially so that its warmth and humidity mirrored that of the Draconian home planet, known to human astronomers as TrES-2. Quartering almost five thousand reptilians, it was an oasis of sorts in this part of the galaxy, so very far from friends and brothers at home.

In Sector Nine of the facility, the Draconians had established their new migration laboratory. It was state of the art. From the outside, it appeared to be a large hill in the middle of a plain of solid rock. However, inside was a well-equipped series of seven migration chambers; two dozen toroidal storage stations; container fabrication, growth, and maintenance rooms; and three generators dedicated to ensuring continuous power in case of potential outages from unanticipated causes.

It was here that the Draconian Guards brought the small, black toroidal storage unit that they had found hidden in Doroo's tureen. The storage unit was carefully inspected for damage by migration technicians, and it was weighed to ensure that its contents had not been removed by the Ummites. When all was found to be in order, a coded message was sent to Queen Igua that His Excellency had been returned and that his abductors had been terminated.

Immediately after receiving the message, Queen Igua ordered that an unmarked tureen be readied for departure, and within the hour she was en route from TrES-2 to the red planet's outpost. In order not to alert spies or to draw unnecessary attention to the outpost, her travel was labeled as a routine excursion. Her arrival at the outpost was unannounced, and she traveled incognito to the migration facility in a standard military transport.

Dr. Laskey, the chief designer of the next generation containers and the enhanced migration process, was no longer available to oversee the migration of His Excellency into his new container. Now seen as a traitor, Dr. Laskey had a price on his head and was rumored to be in hiding on Ummo or at one of its outposts somewhere in the galaxy. The commander of the Draconian Guard was confident that his location would one day be determined and ultimately he would be apprehended for termination, along with those who were hiding him.

This day, however, Dr. Laskey's able assistant, Dr. Angelo Cassini was fully prepared to oversee the migration of His Excellency into his new container. It was he who had studied Dr. Laskey's field notes and had conducted numerous test runs until the process had been perfected. All systems were fully operational, and he awaited only Her Majesty's arrival before commencing the procedure.

"Dr. Cassini?" the queen asked when she entered the migration room with two huge body guards.

Dr. Cassini bowed deeply and presented his hand to Queen Igua. "Your Majesty, I am honored that you will be present for today's procedure."

"Doctor, it is I who am honored to be in the presence of the man whose knowledge and skills will set the course for our ultimate destiny. Your name will be recorded boldly in the history of the emergence of the New World Order and the dominion of the Draconian Empire."

Pointing to a stainless steel cabinet, Dr. Cassini said, "We have moved Der Fuehrer's toroidal storage unit from the magnetic vault to the migration unit. His electrical essence sleeps in the small black box which you see inserted into its center portal. We have attached the necessary wires and will begin as soon as you are ready."

"I have been ready for several decades, Doctor. I also was ready a month ago at the Livermore facility. You should be grateful that you were not present at that catastrophe. It was a horrid affair, where many died under the feet of those who ran from the arena. Let's finally get this done!"

"We are ready," Cassini said. "The young container that is awaiting its master is fully functional and operationally efficient. It should serve Der Fuehrer well for many years."

Cassini showed the queen the head piece and belt that had been placed into position on the container. Eight thin, colored wires ran from the headpiece to the belt. Three thicker wires hung from the belt to the floor. Cassini retrieved them and snapped their ends into ports on the migration machine.

"The migration machine will create an electrical vacuum, or void, inside the container," Cassini told us. "When we discharge the toroidal storage unit, Der Fuehrer's electrical essence will rush into the container to fill the void. These wires will ensure that all electrons are properly situated. When the light on the migration machine turns green, we will remove the headpiece and belt, effectively trapping the electrical essence within the container."

"And His Excellency will then live?"

Cassini nodded to two technicians who stood beside the migration machine. They began flicking switches. "We will induce two brief electrical impulses to start the container's heart and the brain. At that point, Der Fuehrer should begin to breathe on his own and will shortly thereafter awaken, fully alert and ready to begin his dominion over humans."

"Oh," Queen Igua said with surprise, "the light has already turned green!"

"Yes, Your Majesty, Der Fuehrer has already passed from the toroidal storage unit into the new container." He nodded to the technicians, who removed the headpiece and the belt. Within a few seconds, the young body twitched and arched its back. Then it relaxed against the table on which it rested. Using a stethoscope, Cassini listened to the chest area of the container. He smiled. "His Excellency soon will be with us again."

"This process is indeed intriguing, Doctor. I had anticipated that it would take much longer."

Cassini nodded and smiled. "The ability of the new containers to accept an electrical presence far surpasses that of used containers. We no longer need to worry about rejection, and the new containers will feed as humans do. They no longer need to endure protein baths, the way our greys and humanoids must. It is, as we humans say, a whole new ball game."

A cough and moan interrupted the conversation. The new container was evidencing small movements. Its eyes opened and blinked several times. Each grasping an arm, the technicians assisted the container to rise into a sitting position. To accelerate alertness, one technician held a small triangular oxygen mask over the container's nose and mouth. When the container pushed the mask away, Dr. Cassini smiled and told Queen Igua, "He is now with us!"

"Your Excellency!" The queen exclaimed. "It is so good to see you again!"

"Where am I?" Hitler asked, unaware of his nakedness.

"You are safe within the Draconian facility on the red planet," replied Dr. Cassini. "There is much to tell you, but it can wait until you have regained your sense of bodily containment."

"Much seems like a dream," Hitler said, "but I remember that Dr. Laskey finally migrated me out of that old woman's container. He planned to give my electrical self to the renegades. Did you foil the abduction?"

"No, but yes," Queen Igua replied. "Your toroidal storage container was, in fact, taken by the renegades, but they were apprehended by the Draconian Guard."

"And what of the renegades?"

"They were terminated."

"Excellent." Hitler paused for a moment, recollecting the recent past. "And Dr. Laskey, as well?"

"The doctor has eluded us thus far. He is in hiding, but he will be found."

"The renegades included two Ummites," Hitler recalled.

"Among those who were apprehended were three Ummites. All have been consumed by this system's star."

"Good. I want a full accounting of who they were, and if they were under orders from the Ummite Command or if they were acting independently."

Hitler stretched his arms and rolled his shoulders.

"Is your new container stiff, Excellency?" Dr. Cassini asked.

"On the contrary, the energy I feel in this new container is exhilarating. May I see it?"

The two technicians assisted Hitler to his feet and escorted him to a full length mirror. His mouth opened in surprise at what he saw. "I'm brown-skinned! Who ordered that I be brown-skinned?"

"Your Excellency," Dr. Cassini entreated, "the original container intended for you was destroyed by the renegades. Other than its race, this alternative container is actually stronger than your original and will serve you for many more years. It's not only human but has hybrid elements that offer you enhancements beyond your expectations. Within a few days, you will learn how to look into eyes and read minds like the reptilians and greys. You will also enjoy the superior agility of the Antarians and, with luck and much practice, you may have the ability to shape shift."

"I am not pleased with this color. I may lose supporters among my Nazi regulars."

"They are but a small portion of the human condition," Queen Igua reminded him. "The racial balance on the garden planet has moved steadily toward people of color. Within a decade, there will be more people of brown complexion than white."

"But this color will continue to be looked down upon by those of white and yellow castes."

"Surely, your leadership skills and superior intellectual and physical abilities will win supporters from among all human races," the queen contended. "And when you emerge to coalesce the leaders of those who remain after the pandemic, bringing with you the advanced medical aid of the garden planet's reptilian brothers, you will be hailed again by all the peoples as the chosen emperor of your orb."

Hitler turned to the left and then to the right, gazing upon his new container. "There is a certain exotic allure to this container, Doctor. Its youth is almost hypnotic, like a siren's song that causes me to want to experience its sensuality. I will dwell in it, for the time being, Doctor." He turned again toward the two technicians and said, "Bring me the raiment of a military general. I am ready to inspect my troops."

Chapter 5

Waam sent a greeting that woke us up. "Time to rise, my friends," his hologram told us, hovering above the foot of our bed. "Breakfast begins in thirty minutes at the officers' mess. You will find a bag containing human grade toiletries in the bathroom."

He's been watching too many movies, I thought.

"How long have we been sleeping, Danny?" Mona asked.

"I think about two hours."

"Jesus, how's a girl supposed to keep her beauty?"

Mona dragged herself out of bed and into the shower. Our quarters had all the amenities of a three star hotel. Nothing was too fancy, but what more did we need than a bed and a bathroom, anyway? At ten by ten, the bed was big enough for a family of six, like something Lily Tomlin would use for a skit. The mirror over the dresser was mounted too high on the wall to see anything but the ceiling and the wall behind us. A television might have been nice, so we could have caught the morning news, but so much of today's news bordered on propaganda, and it certainly wouldn't have meant anything there on Mars.

And, I guess there might have been some sort of video device built into the molded plastic walls of this room, but I didn't have the technical savvy to know where to find it or how to turn it on. I made a mental note to ask one of the bellhops. In the bathroom, the toilet and sink offered us similar size issues. Fortunately, management had ensured that we had a footstool to use to climb reach the necessary height to sit on the john or turn the faucets on the sink.

When Mona came out of the shower, a towel was wrapped around her head, and she was wearing a guest bathrobe that looked like it belonged to somebody twice her size. I figured that even the shortest Ummites who found their way to Mars would be tall enough that a size small robe would still look big on a seven-footer.

When it was my turn to shower, I found the hot and cold knobs were mounted eyeball-high on the wall, but they weren't too inconvenient to use. The water temperature was easily adjustable, and the warm water felt great as it ran down my face from the nozzle that was mounted at the ten foot mark above. Mona had left the soap and shampoo in the stall for me to use. Then I found disposable razors in the bag of toiletries that was perched on the back of the toilet. Good old Waam had thought of almost everything, except shaving cream and a styptic pencil. I shaved using bar soap and the razors, which must have been Russian-made because they looked sharp but tore my face in several spots. I used small pieces of toilet paper to try to stop the cuts from bleeding.

"Jesus, Danny," Mona complained when I walked out of the bathroom with an Ummite sized hand towel wrapped around my waist. "Didn't your little sister teach you how to shave?"

"Naw, baby, my family wasn't Italian."

Mona threw a pillow at me. I grabbed her by the arm,

pulled her to me, and planted a big kiss on her lips. Her robe slipped to her waist, and I could feel the warmth of her breasts against my stomach. "You know," I said, "I'd let you shave me if you wanted to be sure it was done right."

Mona smiled and winked. "I don't think you'd want me near your throat with a straight razor."

"Good morning, my friends. Breakfast begins in five minutes in the officers' mess. Directions to the mess are posted on the wall outside of your room." It was another hologram from Waam.

Mona pulled her robe up to cover her breasts. "Do you think maybe those things are two-way communications?" she asked.

"Who knows? You'll have to ask Waam."

☙❧

Per the directions on the wall, after we dressed, Mona and I followed the green line on the corridor floor to the officers' dining hall. Small white arrows were cut-out of the line every ten feet or so to let us know which direction we should be walking. St. Mary's Hospital back in DC used the same strategy. I wondered who thought of it first.

Waam was waiting for us when we arrived. He raised his hand and waved. Mona saw him first and pulled my arm in his direction.

"Greetings, my friends," he said.

"Listen, Waam," Mona asked immediately. "Are those holograms two-way things?"

Waam laughed. "I can assure you that they are pre-recorded projections. We respect our guests' privacy."

"Then good morning to you, too," Mona replied.

We sat across from Waam at the table so we could

talk. I noticed that approximately thirty other Ummites were seated, but the room was half empty.

"Small crowd today," I noted, nodding to a table of three who had turned to look at us.

"Many of us are on assignment, mostly to our garden planet facilities in Italy and Switzerland. I fear that our forces here are too few, but that isn't my decision."

A tall woman approached us and asked what we cared to drink. They didn't offer coffee or tea because Ummites didn't use stimulants, so Mona and I opted for jubwat juice, a delicacy of some kind from Ummo. It was citrus in taste but otherwise unidentifiable. I didn't ask Waam to elaborate.

He lifted a small device from the chair beside him and placed it on the table so all three of us could see it. He tapped the screen in a few places, and a video began playing. The audio was something we couldn't understand, so Waam turned the volume down and began to explain what we were watching.

On the screen was a planet much like Earth—white clouds, water, and land, but the land masses were clearly different. "This was the red planet during the first age of man," he explained. "Like the garden planet, it was a paradise with many species of flora and fauna. Man brought many of the species here to inhabit this world. Some unexpectedly dominated the planet, feeding on the native species and causing their extinction. Balance of nature was difficult to achieve, but after several centuries, means to harmony were eventually discovered. Then, when resources began to be diminished on the home planets, Man began to mine the minerals on the red planet. Large smelting facilities were created. The atmosphere and bodies of water became impure. It was an experiment gone wrong. Mining persisted, however, and to assist in the mining, Man created humans. Humans were genetically inferior, with shorter life spans, diminished mental capacity, but greater muscular ability. Human containers were modified to tolerate the impure atmosphere. Humans were a slave race, and genetic misfits were tolerated."

The images on the video turned to another planet, devoid of water and plants. Waam continued his lecture. "Man was at first not aware that another planet beyond your ten planets was in orbit around your star. This one, called Nibiru, passes through the orbits of other planets once every twelve thousand of your years, in a long elliptical orbit. As it passes through the others, its gravity causes upheavals on the surfaces of the others and modifies their orbits in small measures. Once it was discovered, Nibiru was monitored closely. On one pass, it collided with your tenth planet, obliterating it. What remains of that planet is now known by your astronomers as the asteroid belt between the red planet and Jupiter."

"After the collision, Man left the red planet to mine on another planet in a neighboring solar system. Humans, however, remained. Some among them had knowledge of smelting and machinery and passed that knowledge along to others as generations came and went. Other beings from other solar systems found the red planet, stayed for a few centuries to take what resources they wanted, and interbred with female humans, causing great diversity among the types of humans that inhabited this orb."

"Why are you telling us this stuff, Waam?" I asked.

"It is always good to know something about the history of the planets you visit. It's especially important that you know about the history of the red planet because it's the beginning of the history of the garden planet."

"Let him finish, Danny," Mona said. "This is interesting. It may help us to understand some of the things in Powers's notebook."

"Yeah, you're right, baby," I replied.

Powers's notebook was something that I received in the mail from Billy Powers, a guy who had been strangled the night before he was supposed to meet with me to explain his theory about a huge government conspiracy that involved space aliens. That was how I learned about the plans of the New World Order and eventually met Waam. It was the reason that I was here on Mars with Mona.

The waitress came back to our table carrying breads and cheeses. They were from Earth. In fact, Mona recognized one small loaf of cranberry nut bread as coming from Sticky Fingers, a vegetarian bakery that she likes in northwest DC.

"Some things on the garden planet have become favorites of ours," Waam told us. "Your poppy seed bagels with cream cheese are like nothing else in the galaxy. They are so basic, but so good, especially with a cup of black coffee."

We both nodded. But I asked, "I thought you guys don't drink coffee and tea because of the stimulants."

Waam had been discovered. He leaned forward and smiled. "Well, I do enjoy a few vices."

The video had continued to run while we had been talking, so Waam backed it up to a scene we had already watched. He tapped the screen, and it began again. While Mona and I ate, Waam said, "On its next passage through the planets Nibiru caused a shift in the orbits of several planets. The red planet slipped into the orbit further from your star, causing daytime temperatures to vary so radically that that life could no longer be supported on the planet's surface. We Ummites came to the rescue, transporting much of the surface water to the garden planet, expanding its own seas and diluting their salt content. Our largest vessels, called arks, carried purified water first, followed by sea life and plant and animal species to enhance the species already there. Other waters were directed to underground caverns on the red planet, where they still exist today."

The video shifted to images of several alien species. "Six species officially inhabit the red planet today. Its surface and sub-surface have been cordoned off into six sectors, where each species maintains an outpost facility, which serves as a rest, refueling, and maintenance station for our vessels and arks on missions to other solar systems. Between all six species, we have arranged peace and trade treaties, even several alliances. However, we Ummites and the Draconians have never been on good terms."

"Why is that?" Mona asked.

Waam paused the video. "We see different futures for the garden planet. We have different agendas."

"Yes, you've been on Earth for many years, but have not truly made your presence known. What role do you play on Earth?" Mona asked.

"We're gently pushing you humans toward self-realization of your place in the universe," Waam replied. "We're preparing you for membership in the Galactic Federation."

"I feel like we're some sort of backward culture living on the same planet as major technological civilizations, but almost totally unaware of their existence, like those Stone Age people in the Philippines," Mona said.

"In a very real sense, you are. As you're given small pieces of new technology by our race and the others, we Ummites try to help keep you from destroying yourselves and destroying your planet, as your creators did to the red planet."

"How so?" I asked.

"Most notably by reducing the damage caused by your misuse of nuclear technology, like what happened at the Three-Mile Island, Chernobyl, and Fukushima power plants. Only through our efforts was radiation contained. Some Ummite Tureens were sighted by those on the ground as we negated the effects of radiation leakage, but the presence of our tureens was hushed by the respective governments. What we did was similar to adding baking soda to acid. The acid still remains, but its destructive nature is diminished."

"Powers's notebook had some stuff related to UFO's being sighted over Chernobyl," Mona said. "I don't remember what the article said. I just remember the headlines."

I moved us back to the subject of Waam's video. "So Mars was really once a planet somewhat like Earth? What is it like now? From Earth, it looks pretty much like a desert."

"Your university scientists see only what NASA wants them to see. Photos are air-brushed to remove anything that shows signs of life existing here, past or present. Look at the video again." Waam tapped the screen, and the video started once more. Now the video showed pictures of Mars from the air, maybe a hundred miles above the surface. "See these odd looking dark images that look like snowflakes? They're the remains of a huge redwood forest. The trees are but skeletons of their former selves, but hundreds of them hug the mountains at the eighty-first latitude. Their descendants are the giant redwoods in the northwest of your country, brought to the garden planet as seedlings by Ummites many years ago." Waam waited for a moment until the video changed to a desert scape. Then he said, "If you'll look closely, you'll see the foundations of buildings that stood here ninety millennia ago. It was the site of one of the original smelts, when humans were casting iron and aluminum for their own purposes."

I was intrigued. Maybe Waam was telling me the truth, but maybe not. I didn't know him well enough to be certain. I've seen squares and rectangles like that on Earth that I've been told are natural formations. But how would I really know? If Waam was telling me the truth, most of our anthropologists have been taught a lie, and they are continuing to teach the same lie to future generations. But hell, if you believed most of Earth's scientists, Waam didn't exist either!

"Will we have an opportunity to actually see the things that you've shown us in the video?" Mona asked.

"Perhaps I can arrange visits to some sites, but not all. For example, the famous face on Mars is in a friendly sector. The trees, however, are not. I will see what the commander can arrange."

A young Ummite soldier approached us and saluted Waam. "Sir, a communication from the commander."

"Thank you," Waam replied. He opened the letter and read it quickly. "There will be no response at this time. Please inform the commander that I will speak with him when our guests are preparing for their mission." The young soldier turned and left the dining hall.

"It is bad news?" I asked.

"It's not good news, but it's important information. The message conveys news from our spies within the Draconian forces. It confirms my suspicions that the Chinese are to blame for the loud booms and scraping sounds that are being heard around the surface of the garden planet. There is clear evidence that they have been mining gold under all continents, using laser moles and small nuclear devices. Apparently one of their moles burst through a wall in our facility in the Canadian Rockies. There has been a skirmish, and they have been defeated. Our spies inform us that the Chinese have struck a deal to purchase your moon from the Draconians, who want two million tons of gold for the purchase. From your moon, they will be able to use Draconian weapons to strike anywhere on the planet."

"That doesn't make sense," I replied. "Aren't the Chinese also in the coalition that plans to establish the New World Order?"

"Supposedly, but this news also puts them in direct conflict with the one they call His Excellency."

"Do you mean with Hitler?"

"Yes, with the electrical essence that was stolen from Doroo's tureen."

"So," Mona chimed in, "maybe the Chinese issued the order to steal Hitler from Doroo, so they be could be sure that Hitler was out of the way and they could take control of the NWO!"

"Perhaps," Waam replied, "but if Hitler's essence has not been destroyed, then there will be conflict within the NWO and perhaps a full scale war on your planet, a war to dominate the human element."

"I don't trust the lizards," I said. "A war on our planet, especially if it was to occur after a pandemic reduced the Earth's population by ninety percent, would create the perfect opportunity for the Draconians to assume total control. There would be no NWO. There would be only lizard law."

"I fear you may be correct, Mr. Arrow. They and their hybrids would rule your world."

Mona's expression turned to anger. "I hate those scaly bastards, especially Nargas! He impregnated me and then stole the baby."

Waam looked surprised. "I wasn't aware—"

"It's something that I don't like to talk about," Mona told him. "I'm not even sure when it happened, but when I was his captive, Nargas kept talking about my container carrying our child—his and mine. When you dropped us off in Denver, Danny took me to an abortion clinic, and they confirmed that I was pregnant. We scheduled an abortion for two days later, but on the day of the abortion, the baby was no longer there!"

"Yes, Waam," I added, "We heard the baby's heart beat and saw it on the screen during an ultrasound test. Mona was clearly carrying a hybrid child on the day of the examination, but two days later it was gone!"

Mona's eyes filled with tears. "The night before the abortion, I had a dream in which Nargas was looking down at me, telling me that everything was good and that I would be okay. I'm now convinced that he abducted me and stole my baby."

"It was most likely no dream, Agent Casola. It was probably a repressed memory of the abduction. In 1953, the Draconians and their greys entered into an agreement with your government that in exchange for certain technologies, they would be able to abduct humans for research. Although the number of humans they were permitted to abduct was very limited, over time they have violated that agreement. It has been estimated that up to forty percent of all humans have been abducted at least once during their lifetimes."

"What makes it worse is that it's a two-edged sword," Mona replied, her eyes now tearing. "I wanted that lizard hybrid out of my body in the worst way, but I wanted it gone under my own terms. Nargas simply took it out without even asking. I was used as a lab rat with no voice in what happened to me."

"Draconians are that way. All members of the Galactic Federation have the technology to do what Nargas did, but few of us do such things. We Ummites have the technology, but we would never have helped you to remove the fetus because we have sworn an oath not to harm humans, and the fetus was at least half human, and maybe more. Nargas did what he did because he doesn't respect humans as Galactic equals. To him, you are less than greys."

"What do you think Nargas did with my baby, Waam?"

"If the child survived, I cannot be sure. If it's a good specimen, he may raise it to maturity. Otherwise, he might use it for experimentation or other more grisly outcomes."

Mona jumped from her seat. "Where is there a bathroom, Waam?"

"Just outside this room, on the left."

Mona turned and walked away, wiping her eyes. She was clearly upset, and I thought she would probably want to be alone for a few minutes.

After Mona was gone, I turned to Waam. "This has been a difficult time for Mona. Her mothering instincts are strong. As much as she hates the thought of a hybrid being placed inside of her without her consent, she recognizes that the hybrid is partly made up of herself, much like any baby would be partly its mother. She feels a great loss."

"I sense that she would like to know what happened to her child."

"I haven't told anyone this, especially Mona, but the morning after we learned that her baby had been taken from her, I received an anonymous telephone call. The caller told me that Mona's baby is alive and well."

Waam looked over my shoulder. His face showed concern.

"You bastard!" Mona cried. She had come back quickly because the bathroom door was locked, and she had overheard what I had said to Waam. "You knew that my baby is alive, and you didn't tell me! How could you not share that with me?"

"I was going to tell you, baby, but not until I thought you could handle it."

"You're like Nargas, Danny! You're making decisions that affect me, and you don't even have the decency to include me in the decision. How do you know that I couldn't handle it? Who made you God? All you males are motherfuckers!"

"Honestly, I was going to tell, you, Mona, but I had to figure out what the guy told me."

"What's so difficult about learning that a baby is alive and well? It means that my baby is alive and well."

"It's not quite so simple. I asked him where the baby was. I figured that maybe we could go get it."

"And what did Mr. Anonymous tell you, dick brain?"

"He said that your baby was in the 'hollow moon.'"

"What the fuck is the hollow moon?"

"That's what I needed to figure out."

"Can I get separate accommodation?" Mona asked.

Waam gave her a look of disbelief and then turned to me. "It can mean only one thing. It's the moon that revolves around your garden planet."

"Is there a facility under its surface, Waam? Something like this facility?" I asked.

"No, Mr. Arrow, the entire moon is hollow. It's not a natural formation. Your moon is an artificial structure that was brought here by Man several hundred thousand years ago. It's now occupied by the NWO and the Draconians. Several of your governments and several races from other star systems have constructed facilities on its exterior, but its interior is occupied entirely by the NWO and the Draconians. It is that structure which the Chinese intend to purchase from the Draconians."

"Then my baby is within reach?" Mona asked.

"Yes, your baby is within reach, but getting to the interior of the moon will require returning to the garden planet and traveling to your moon in a Draconian tureen. The entrance to the interior is on the dark side of your moon and is heavily fortified. There is no other way."

Mona stopped crying. All she could focus upon was getting to her baby, if only to see it, to see what kind of beast it truly was. "Motherfuckers," she muttered.

Chapter 6

Queen Igua was seated at the end of an oval table. Around it sat ten other reptilians, all dressed in garb signifying their status as leaders among the Draconians. At the opposite end sat a young dark-skinned man, barely thirty years of age. "Your Excellency," she began, "thank you for joining us today. My royal council is interested in your plans for the first phase of the new emergence of the New World Order. Is everything ready to begin?"

"Your Majesty, let me begin by thanking you and your staff of scientists for providing me with this excellent container. Since the late 1940s, I have been moved from container to container, each with varying strength and health levels. Some have rejected my presence almost immediately. In others, I have felt trapped, as though handicapped in some manner. However, your newly developed containers and the expedited migration process are worthy of Galactic applause. I feel more energetic and mentally alert than I have in fifty years."

Queen Igua nodded and smiled. Her royal council members seemed pleased at the young Hitler's praise of his new container. Certainly, no other race had accomplished so much in managing to extend the lives and work of individuals who were important to their goal of Galactic dominance.

"Your Majesty, the plan has already been set into motion. In fact, preparations began twenty-five years after my reign over Germany was brought to an end. Then in 1992, the anvil was struck by the endorsement of Agenda Twenty-One by the United Nations at its Conference on Environment and Development. Under that plan, wealthy nations will give resources to poorer and ultimately all will have access to the same levels—"

Hitler was interrupted by an aged reptilian. "I well remember how much we all were enthusiastic about your first attempt to establish the New World Order. We could not wait to emerge from our subterranean existence. But you failed. What makes this attempt any different?"

"In my first attempt, we tried to use force to establish the NWO. We know now that such a tactic was an unfortunate mistake. We were close, but the unanticipated development of the atomic bomb by our adversaries caused us to lose valuable allies, and we were outnumbered and overwhelmed. Force is not the answer. We must be allowed to assume control because the people of all nations desire it."

The reptilian hissed. "And how will that be accomplished?"

"Let me attempt to paint the bigger picture for you. Agenda Twenty-One involves all aspects of life on our planet: education, health care, energy, food production, transportation, and government. It has been shown that, with the proper education and indoctrination, the Earth's population groups will gladly give up their individual freedoms, accept limitations on their choices, and sit idly by while their money is devalued and while their voice is taken away."

"How does this Agenda Twenty-One fit into the domination plans of the NWO?" asked another aged reptilian.

"The overarching goal is to create obedient, dependent people, who will accept what they are told to do by the government without reservation. The key begins with education, where standardized propaganda is established for all grade levels, from nursery school through graduate school. Earth Day and Global Warming are two of our most successful initiatives. The recently developed Common Core Curricula in the Americas is another ingredient. So are the gun control initiatives that we have implemented in Australia, Europe, and the United States. The preaching of the Social Justice philosophy is yet another. We have come at the goal from many directions. By changing the way education is provided, those with the greatest mental capacity learn only the basic propaganda and nothing more. The propaganda that all humans receive comes from many directions at one time, such that the people have no option except to believe it to be the truth. Over time, an entire culture can be re-socialized."

"And how about efforts to relocate the population?" asked another reptilian.

"The effort has been entitled Sustainable Development. Again, it is a United Nations initiative under Agenda Twenty-One. The plan empowers local governments to take the control of land use away from private property owners. Under the plan, local governments have been charged with the task of ensuring that the larger portion of the population is relocated to cities and zones of human habitation where individuals can be controlled and their mobility limited. Already most communities now have the power to seize properties by eminent domain. Seized properties are torn down, and apartment buildings and condominiums replace them. Thus, properties that once housed a single family may now house hundreds of families. Eventually, people currently living in rural areas will be relocated by their governments into zones of habitation which are close to employment and mass transportation centers. Newly vacated land will be reclassified as Wildlife Zones, seen as important for the ecological preservation of the planet. Once reclassified and off-limits to humans, those zones will be available to you for your purposes."

"Excellent!" Queen Igua hissed.

"And why will your people give up their properties and go into these centers willingly?" asked the aged reptilian who had hissed earlier.

"First, the population will be decimated through a carefully orchestrated pandemic which will eliminate ninety percent of the Earth's humans. Food, medicine, and ammunition will become scarce. The NWO will emerge as the best form of government to protect the world's remaining masses. People will be encouraged to migrate to population centers where supplies will be distributed by friendly NWO officials."

"And what of those who refuse to leave their lands?"

"They will be terminated by NWO guards disguised as each country's own national troops or, in some cases, as lawless rebels. People will plead for safety, and protection will be available only in the population centers."

"And how will you protect your own troops and NWO leaders during this pandemic?"

"Through vaccines and protective shelters. We have carved many subterranean fortresses where our loyalists will hide in safety while the pandemic ensues. The last of the facilities are being completed now and should be ready within several months. Once everything is prepared, we will send word that the chosen ones should migrate to sites selected for them. Once the doors are secured, we will release the virus."

"Certainly there will be others in the Galactic Federation who will oppose this initiative," huffed Commissar Nargas, seated to the left of the queen.

"The greatest threat to our success comes from the Ummites. As you know, they have sworn an oath to protect humans and to promote human evolution until such time as they are seen as being fit to join the Galactic Federation."

"Yes, Comrade Nargas," Queen Igua added, "were you not at the Livermore facility where His Excellency's televised migration was disrupted by two Ummite subversives and several human rebels? Many dignitaries were trampled to death, and our huge arena was destroyed because of that incident. We cannot allow anything like that to happen again!"

"I do not trust that the two Ummites were subversives," Hitler continued. "They may have been acting under a directive from their leaders. Until we are certain where the Ummite Grand Council truly stands, we must ensure that they cannot interfere with our plans!"

"Yes, let's drive them from this solar system!" hissed a reptilian.

"Yes! I agree!" said another, raising a single claw toward the sky.

"As you wish, comrades. I will order a strike against them," said Queen Igua. "The message must be clear that the Ummites are no longer welcome in this part of the galaxy.

Chapter 7

"O uch!" I complained. "It feels like you're putting nicks all over my head."

"You're such a baby!" Mona replied. "Suck it up! I'm doing my best. I think you have only one real nick. The others were just pulls."

Mona had been shaving my head for the past half hour. It was slow going using the dull razors that we had been provided by the Ummites. We had no scissors, so Mona hadn't been able to trim my hair short before starting in with the twin-bladed razor. She was sitting on the toilet so she could rinse the razors clean every stroke or two. I was kneeling on the footstool with my head on her lap. It was almost comical, but my back was beginning to hurt, and my knees were growing numb from lack of circulation.

"There we go, Danny. Stand up and let me look at you."

I did as commanded.

"Oh boy, you weren't made for this kind of look—Danny Cue-ball, private eye! Ha, ha!"

I scooted the footstool to the front of the sink and

stood on it so I could see myself in the mirror. My newly shaved head bore streaks of red and blue, and I saw that my scalp had veins closer to the surface than I had realized. "I look like a fucking Easter egg!"

"It's not that bad, Danny. The important thing is that I don't think anybody is going to recognize you. Hell, I'm not even sure who you are! It might be fun sleeping with somebody strange tonight. I mean, I've never been in the sack with a bald man before!"

From her words, I ascertained that Mona wasn't still harboring anger at my not telling her about the location of her baby. But Mona wasn't helping my ego at all. Not that I'm anything to look at, but I've always had a full head of hair that I could flaunt in a bar full of bald guys who were trying to pick up chicks. Now, though, I felt conspicuous. This was going to take some getting used to.

It was Mona's turn. She sat on the stool with her back to me, and I sat on the toilet, squeezing some kind of thick shit from a tube and combing it through her hair.

"Be sure to get the roots!" she instructed.

"Yeah, yeah! Just let me do my work," I replied. "Hell, I ain't no damn beautician."

"Ouch!" Mona said. "You're pulling my hair!"

"You know, Mona, this shit is burning my fingers. Are you sure it's safe for your hair and scalp?"

"This is Mars, Danny. We've gotta use what they have. Waam says it's safe, so I have to trust the guy."

I continued squeezing and combing. I knew one thing for sure: when God handed out hair, he made sure that the Italians got the thick stuff. Mona must have a thousand hairs per square inch, and maybe more. Those ladies in the circus, the ones who hang by their hair and spin a hundred feet in the air, they have to be Italian.

"Okay, baby, I think that's all of them," I told her.

Mona stood up, moved the stool, and looked at herself in the mirror. Her hair was soaking wet and combed backward on the top and both sides. "Nice ducktails," she said. She asked for the tube of bleach and used a small brush to apply bleach her eyebrows. When she was finished, she turned her head from side to side and tilted it downward so she could check the crown. "Are you going to like me as a blonde?" she asked.

"I'll tell you after I make love to you tonight. Who knows, the sex might be better with a blonde!"

"Give it up, Arrow. You look like a stranger, and I promised my boyfriend that I'd never cheat on him with a stranger."

"Does that mean you'd cheat on him with a friend?"

"Maybe…"

"You know, Mona—"

There was a knock on our door.

"Who is it?" I asked.

"I have a message from the captain."

"I thought he sent holograms."

"The captain asked me to deliver this to Mr. Arrow."

"Just slide it under the door. We are indisposed at the moment."

A white envelope appeared from under the door. I opened it. "It's from Waam," I said to Mona. "He wants to share some information with us about the moon, so we won't be surprised by what we might see while on our mission. Dinner at thirteen quid."

"Okay. I can be ready by then. I have to wait an hour before I wash this stuff out of my hair. Then I'll have to blow dry it."

Time is a funny thing. I guess all Galactic races have some sort of measure to mark the passing of linear time. On Earth, it is the clock with the minute and second hands, slowly revolving around a circle, the way our

planet revolves around the sun, or the way the moon revolves around the Earth. It's different on Mars. The days
and nights are about the same in length as the Earth's, but
a year is almost twice as long. It's especially different in
an underground facility where the only things that tell
you what time it is are bodily functions. When you're
hungry, it's time to eat. When you're tired, it's time to
sleep. When your bladder sends the message, it's time to
take a leak. So, to make sure everybody meets at the
same place at the same time, the Ummites have divided
the day into eighteen quids. Each quid is the same measure of time, calculated by digital clocks that operate according to some formula that I haven't been able to understand. Waam says that it's attuned to the shifts in the
polar axis of the red planet. When the axis shifts a specific number of degrees, a quid is clicked off. Portions of
quids are measured by subsets of degrees. Basically,
though, a quid is about an hour and twenty-four minutes,
Earth time.

While Mona's hair was bleaching, we sat watching
one of a stack of DVDs that Waam had brought back to
Mars from the Earth. It was a complete twenty-four-
episode serial in black and white of Buster Crabbe as
Flash Gordon. In today's episode, Flash's girlfriend Dale
Arden was being held captive by Ming the Merciless. She
was forced to wear a ball gown of some sort.

"Turn it off, Danny!" Mona told me. "It's hitting too
close to home."

I looked at her, and Mona's eyes were watery. I
pulled her to me and kissed her. "It's okay, baby. I wasn't
thinking."

"It reminds me too much of that bastard Nargas and
how he had me dress for the ceremony at the Livermore
facility."

"You're right. I'm sorry." I shut off the DVD player.

When an hour had fully elapsed, Mona hopped into the shower. A few minutes later I heard the blow dryer going. *This is going to be interesting*, I thought.

When the bathroom door opened, out came a blonde with Mona's face. She actually looked pretty nice as a blonde, and I told her so.

"You're just saying that to make me feel better. I don't think I like it."

"It kind of gives you that Marilyn Monroe look, like you're walking down the sidewalk and your dress blows up." I meant it as a compliment.

"Don't get used to it, Danny. I'm going back to chestnut brown as soon as this mission is over."

"That's okay," I said. "I fell in love with a brunette, so why would I want to hang with a blonde?" I didn't know what else to tell her. I mean, I kind of liked her as a blonde, but I was just as happy with her as the dark-haired Italian princess that I always accused her of being.

☙☙☙

Waam met us at exactly thirteen quid, give or take a couple of clicks, at a small alternative eatery in the underground Ummite facility. This place specialized in meat dishes, which was somewhat out of the norm for the dining hall, or 'mess' as Waam referred to it, where almost all dishes are vegetarian. At the Omo Cree, which loosely translates into the 'Flesh Fountain,' it was possible to sample a variety of flash-frozen meats and sausages imported from around the galaxy. Once I found this place, I became an affectionato of smoked sausage from the planet Serpo. It was a blend of several different birds and beasts, and it was flavored with a strange spice that nobody seemed able to identify. One grey from Zeta Reticula—a shorter, friendly type of grey—told me through his eyes that the spice was a ground insect glue, similar to honey bee propolis, the stuff that bees used to glue their hives together. He also told me that he liked it when the protein baths included some of that spice because of the scent that it left on his skin. I had never heard of bee propolis before, so I made a mental note to check it out the next time I was back on the farm in the US of A.

"Your beard is coming along nicely," Waam told me when we joined him at the table. I had been growing a beard for almost ten days, as part of a disguise that I would use to implement the plan that we had concocted. My shaved head and Mona's blond hair were additional elements of disguise. "Permit me to introduce Dr. Ian McCloud. He is a research specialist on loan to us from the University of Sydney in Australia. Dr. McCloud, this is Dan Arrow and Agent Casola."

Mona and I took turns shaking Dr. McCloud's hand.

"Dr. McCloud has spent several days conducting background research on the hollow moon," Waam continued. "You will probably find it interesting." He saw me look at the menu and suggested, "But perhaps we should order something first."

I nodded. Hell, I was hungry and hearing some long treatise from an egghead was the last thing on my mind. A small grey came to take our orders. I looked him in the eye and asked, "I thought you guys didn't eat. What are you doing here?"

"This is a great part-time assignment for me, besides I don't pilfer food. The chef is concerned about employee theft of expensive meats."

His answer made sense, but if he really needed extra money, he could have made a small fortune by pilfering rare foods and selling them to meat eaters like me.

After our meals came, Dr. McCloud started to tell us about the moon. But before he could get out the first word, Mona asked, "Hey, we went to the moon in the 1960s, but we haven't been back. I thought going there was a good thing. Why did we stop going?"

"Yes, you Americans did go to the moon in the 1960s, and you *have* been back," McCloud replied. "However, you're correct that you haven't been back, at least as far as John Q. Public knows. Why? Because it is already occupied and has been that way for fifty thousand years. The moon is littered with empty buildings and abandoned equipment. From a public relations standpoint, there was no reason to go back to somebody else's ghetto. At least none of the astronauts has been back. Your government has sent no more rockets with capsules into space because the technology is too old, too costly, too dangerous, and too slow."

"You're blowing my mind, Doc," I said.

"Your world governments have known about the hollow moon for many years, and they have known for a very long time that the moon is occupied. In fact, about one thousand dome-like structures of diameter around eight hundred feet have been witnessed both by astronomers and by astronauts. If we look backward, we find no records of these structures until the 1950s, when the Germans arrived in their bells after escaping from the collapse of their government at the end of World War II. They are credited with building the first modern structures and bases on the moon. However, they weren't the first to build there. In fact, when they arrived, they discovered many crystalline structures in decay, as well as neighborhoods of stone-made houses in disrepair. The Germans received assistance in the construction of their own facilities from the Draconians and the Zeta Greys.

"Every moon mission launched by you Americans involved either UFO sightings or interactions with UFOs. In 1968 the astronauts inside Apollo Eight spotted a very large extraterrestrial vessel, which was no longer visible when they made their next pass over the crater in which it was parked. They took pictures, but none were released to the public. In 1969 Buzz Aldrin witnessed two UFO's hovering close by. As he watched them, they merged into a single object and flew away. And, when Apollo Eleven was landing on the moon, the astronauts reported an entire squadron of UFO's lined up along the wall of a crater."

"The government didn't report any of this, did they?" Mona asked.

"Nope. If they had reported it, the public would probably have panicked, like they did during Orson Wells' famous radio broadcast."

"There's much more," Waam told us. "Go on about the hollow aspect of the moon, Dr. McCloud."

"Back in 1969, Buzz Aldrin and his crew set up special equipment to send signals to Earth about seismic activity within the moon. When they returned to their orbiter, they released their lunar module, which fell back to the surface. What do you think happened?"

"It went thud," I said.

"Then it probably bounced several times," Mona added.

"Actually, the seismic instruments recorded a continuous reverberation that lasted more than an hour! The moon was ringing like a bell or a crystal glass!"

"No shit!" Mona said in disbelief.

The doctor noted that Mona used a man's vocabulary. "Then, in 1970, when Apollo Thirteen jettisoned its third stage, the impact caused the moon to ring for almost three hours!"

"Incredible!" I said.

"Many astronauts claim that the moon gongs like a grandfather clock when it's hit by meteorites." Dr.

McCloud took a long sip of water. "But there is more. At least two Russian scientists, Vasin and Shcherbokov, claim that the moon is possibly a hollowed-out planet and that it was brought to the Earth specifically to provide a base for those who brought it here, or to influence the tides of our oceans. They also postulate that it could be entirely manufactured as an artificial satellite for our planet. They believe that intelligent life has occupied the moon for thousands of years."

"Have American scientists chimed in on any of this?" Mona asked.

"Only Carl Sagan, and he came at it through the back door. He said that if the moon is hollow, it is artificial because a naturally formed planet or moon could be only a solid object. He didn't have any evidence that the moon is hollow, except for the unverified reports of the astronauts and the wild claims of the Russians."

Mona looked at Waam. "So my baby may be inside this hollow moon?"

Waam excused Dr. McCloud and thanked him for his research on the subject. Once McCloud had departed, Waam said, "Dr. McCloud is aware of our presence on the red planet. He does not believe that the moon is hollow. His expertise is in library science, and his skill is research. The veracity of what he finds is left to the recipients of his research reports."

"So you think the stuff he told us is a bunch of hooey?" I asked.

"On the contrary, I know that your moon is hollow. I have flown close enough to see the ruins on its dark side. There is a city of crystal that would rival anything that you could imagine, and it is entirely deserted. When the moon was brought to the garden planet by Man, they may have destroyed or displaced the inhabitants of that city." Waam paused for a minute and then added, "Or, Man could have found the hollow moon elsewhere, drifting like a ghost ship, and brought it to the garden planet like a reclaimed piece of space trash."

"And what about my baby?" Mona asked.

"I have seen tureens entering and leaving several heavily guarded entrances to an underground facility. Our spies have been to this facility. They say that the crust of the moon is about two miles thick. Its interior is completely hollow. Extending from its north and south poles is a giant pillar that contains hundreds of facilities and garages for tureens of all sorts. Perhaps as many as twenty thousand reptilians inhabit this pillar. Several thousand individuals representing eleven races from other planets, including your Nazis and NWO forces, are also quartered there. I am convinced that Commissar Nargas has taken your baby there to be raised as a Star Child."

Chapter 8

"My superior officer?" I asked.

"Yes," Waam replied.

Mona chuckled. "It's about time that somebody recognized who's really the boss around here!"

"There are very few females in the outposts and the underground facilities," Waam explained. "We suspect that the same will be true for the hollow moon. If Agent Casola is not in the role of your superior officer, she would have to travel as a nurse or food service worker, neither of which would give her access to the information that we hope to acquire."

"You know, things don't appear to be any more equitable for females in space than they are on Earth," Mona said. "We are always the ones getting the shaft because we get pregnant."

"Actually, Agent Casola, females play a role equal to that of males among the planets of the Galactic Federation. Reproduction in the Federation is conducted outside of the female container, where growth of the fetus can be monitored, and any anomalies can be rectified."

"You mean that imperfect children may be terminated," I replied.

"Most often."

✃✄

The plan was now set and would soon be in motion. Traveling as NWO interrogators, Mona and I would return to the subterranean facility beneath Dulce, New Mexico to see if we could learn who had issued the order to overtake Doroo's tureen and terminate its crew. If we learned nothing at Dulce, we were to travel via underground shuttle to Denver, Livermore, and Four Corners, in that order, for the same purpose. As Waam had told us after the meeting with his Commander, the Reptilians are boastful, and someone in one of those facilities would know who gave the command and who carried out the orders. Especially important to our plan was what we had learned at Livermore when Nelson and I entered that snake's den as interrogators: nobody fucks with an NWO interrogator, not even the lizards. While we were investigating Doroo's murder, Waam would be working on a strategy to get us to the moon to rescue Mona's baby, if it was still alive.

Mona put the finishing touches on my beard with a razor, shaping harpoon points at the top, beside my ears. I thought it fit well into the interrogator role. I had asked her earlier about maybe shaving everything except the moustache, but she thought that someone might recognize me from my visit to Livermore a month ago. She was probably right. Given my bald head and the beard, I don't think that my Aunt Martha would have recognized me if I knocked on her front door. That was definitely a good thing.

Waam had supplied us with new uniforms, each emblazoned with the NWO phoenix and the interrogator stripes on the sleeve. Unsure of her size, he had given Mona two pairs of trousers. She tried on the first pair, but they were a little baggy. "Are these better?" she asked me when she had the second pair on. They were a little tight on her butt, which I definitely liked.

"Turn around," I said spinning my pointer finger. She did. "Yeah, baby, I definitely like the way that pair shows your figure." I should have lied because she immediately decided on the first pair.

૯૭૯૭

Waam sent a hologram at six quid, directing us to a small conference room down the corridor from the Omo Cree. It was marked by four over-laid triangles. We donned our uniforms, including dark brown leather jackets which ensured that our pieces were obscured from view. Then we marched in official cadence to the conference room. Inside, we were greeted by Waam and a sharp-chinned grey. His face was the elongated type, not the gentle child-like face associated with the greys here at the Ummite facility. His eyes were less rounded, and they swooped upward at his temples. He was dressed in a baby blue jumpsuit that I had seen before in the caverns at Dulce and Livermore. I shot Waam a look of concern. "Does he understand English?" I asked, pointing at the grey.

"No, he doesn't have to. He can read your thoughts through your eyes."

I looked the grey in the eyes. I distinctly understood his comments to me, as though they were spoken, yet no words were exchanged. *'You recognize that my species generally works with the Draconians,'* he told me. *'But I am here to assist the Ummites in avenging the death of Waam's nephew.'*

I looked at Waam, who said, "He is one of us."

I looked back at the grey. "What is your—"

Before I could finish forming the words, he told me that his name was something that I could not pronounce because it is not within the human voice range. *'You may call me Grau. That is what the Germans call me.'*

"Why would you—"

'For the same reason that you and Agent Casola are here. Commissar Nargas terminated two of my closest friends. I want to see him removed from power.'

I turned to Mona and told her what the grey had said to me. Mona looked him in the eye and asked, "Aren't you afraid that—"

Again, Grau answered before her words had been formed. *'I am what you would call a double agent. I work for the NWO, but I also work with the Ummites. I could be terminated at any time by either one. My goal, however, is to undo the commissar.'*

Mona told me what he had conveyed to her. I nodded. This seemed good. So far, Waam hadn't screwed us, so he seemed trustworthy. If he thought that this grey was on the level, I would have to trust his judgment. Besides, we were on Mars, and there was no way home except at Waam's pleasure.

"What is Grau's role?" I asked Waam.

"He's your pilot." Waam touched a panel on the table, and a screen lit up on the wall at the end of the conference room. Mona and I sat down. Grau followed our lead. A picture of an old Nazi bell came into focus. "This is how you will be traveling back to the garden planet. Grau will command the bell."

"Where did you get that antique?" I asked.

"We found three disabled bells in a cave in the Swiss

Alps. We used parts from all three to construct this one. It works well, but will only reach three-quarter speed. Most important, we have the codes necessary to gain access to the NWO underground facilities."

"Waam, we can't just show up at Dulce and expect to be greeted warmly," Mona said.

"We have thought of that. The bell will have three other passengers as well, three greys who were injured at the Livermore incident. When you arrive, you will tell the facility commander that you exchanged a dead Ummite for these three greys. He will believe you because it is widely known that we Ummites honor our dead through long ceremonies, and the loss of a dead Ummite soldier is almost unbearable for those left behind unless the body is recovered and a cremation ceremony is conducted."

That made sense to me, especially as I reflected on Waam's excessive grief over the loss of his nephew, Doroo. I tried to think of something to say, but Waam continued, "My sister is still in mourning over Doroo's loss. I fear that she will never be able to live a normal life again."

I nodded in understanding. "Then this plan is good. What about the three greys? Will they tell a different story?"

"They have been put through a memory erasure procedure. They will remember nothing of their past. Memories will have to be artificially constructed for them by the Draconians, including everything they have ever learned. As a precautionary measure, they will be drugged so that they will offer you no resistance during the journey, and so they cannot read your thoughts by accident."

"When do we depart?" Mona asked.

"As soon as we're finished here. The greys are already strapped aboard the bell. Technicians are prepping it for launch as we speak." Waam turned to Grau, "Is there anything else you need before departure?'

'Only your assurance that Mr. Arrow and Agent Casola will not disclose my double role if they are captured and tortured.'

"Mr. Arrow," Waam repeated, "Grau would like your solemn promise that you and Agent Casola will keep his dual role confidential at all costs."

Mona and I nodded at Grau. He turned toward the door and opened it, signaling that it was time for us to leave.

"Have a safe and pleasant journey back to the Garden Planet, Mr. Arrow," Waam told me. "And when you discover who it was who gave the order that resulted in Doroo's termination, if he is not human, remember that he is mine. It is the only gift that my sister could want."

"You can count on me, Waam."

"I know."

Chapter 9

We followed Grau down twisting corridors, all looking the as though they had been constructed of the same light brown plastic material. I thought it was probably some sort of liner that hid wires, ducts, and pipes from view. I wondered if the cavern had been constructed using standard moles or laser moles, or perhaps something else. Then I remembered Waam telling me that the Ummites had found this facility vacant when they had arrived on Mars, so nobody probably knew exactly when or how it had been constructed.

Grau pushed open a door and waved us inside. Mona was first to walk into the hangar. "Is this thing flight worthy?" she asked.

I saw what she was concerned about. We had ridden to Mars about ten days ago in Waam's beautiful tureen. It had smooth lines, smooth surfaces, and looked like it had been designed in a wind tunnel to be especially aerodynamic.

This Nazi bell, however, looked like it had been made of cast iron in the 1940s and had taken a few hits from artillery rounds at one time or another. It was generally a dull black in color, with a few newly welded cracks, and it was literally shaped like the liberty bell.

"You've got to be kidding," Mona said into Grau's eyes.

'*It is perfectly safe*, he replied. *I had it out yesterday for several laps around the red planet. Its responsiveness is not as keen as a newer tureen, but it will get the job done. Certainly, a journey from the red planet to the garden planet will be easily accomplished, unless our path intersects an asteroid zone.*'

Mona's face turned to one of concern.

Grau chuckled. '*That was a piece of humor, Agent Casola. Everyone knows that the asteroid belt is between here and the ringed planet.*'

"I didn't know that, and I don't see anything humorous about it, anyway."

Grau continued to chuckle as we walked under the bell, which was hovering about nine feet off of the ground. The hatch into the bell was open, and an iron ladder, similar to the steel ladders that led into the underground facilities at Dulce and Livermore, extended from the hatch to the concrete floor.

I climbed up first then turned to offer Mona a hand as she climbed into the bell. When she was in, Grau leapt up the ladder as though he was a little kid who was excited to be off on an adventure. Mona and I watched him seat himself and then we looked around. Seating was different from the modern tureens, in that it was attached to the outer walls instead of an interior core. Also, the seats consisted of simple, basic webbing attached to fold-down aluminum frames, like the seating in the old C-130 transport planes of the Vietnam era. Three of the seats were already taken by the greys that Waam had drugged and had strapped in for the flight to Dulce. Waam had them placed on one side of the bell, giving us the opportunity to sit opposite of them to balance the load a bit. I imagined that all three greys probably didn't have a combined weight equal to Mona's, which isn't to say that she's chunky. Those little guys weigh like they're made out of Styrofoam. I took a moment to feel an arm on the biggest of the three. His skin was cold and just didn't feel like skin. It was more like some kind of synthetic material that you'd find on a soft-skinned doll, and it smelled funky, probably from the liquid they bathed in. "Here, feel this," I told Mona, offering her the grey's arm.

"That's okay. I'd rather not."

Mona found a seat across the bell from the three drugged greys, lowered the frame, and sat down. "This contraption is like a jalopy. I hope it can actually get us back to Earth."

I pulled down the frame beside her and sat down. "I guess I can't disagree with you," I replied. "It is probably held together with chewing gum and coat hanger wire."

The inside of the bell was basic, sort of like the inside of a submarine. There were simply no amenities. Metal surfaces were painted either black or grey. Markings on gauges and switches were in German and some form of alien cipher. Only a few video screens were mounted where the pilot sat, so I was pretty sure that only Grau would have a view of where we were headed. And, it was a sure bet that there was no ladies room. Thank you, Waam, I thought.

I heard a noise outside the bell. A head popped into the hatch. It was another grey in a baby blue jumpsuit. Grau turned his head and signaled to the other grey, who then entered the bell, pulling in the ladder and closing the hatch. What interested me was that Grau knew he was there and they communicated to each without speech. So, I guessed that in order to communicate with humans, they must look into our eyes and verbalize telepathically, but they can telepathically communicate with each other without the necessity of looking into each other's eyes. I wondered if they were connected in some way. Like, maybe any grey can communicate with any other grey at any time. That would make them similar to ants. Is there a limitation on distance? Could they be some form of ant and alien hybrid? I made a mental note that these were some things I would have to find out.

I felt some uneasiness in my stomach and realized that the bell must be in motion, so I stood and looked at Grau. Over his shoulder, I could see images of the interior falling away beneath the monitor. We were not exiting via the long transparent tunnel through which we entered the facility. Instead, we were exiting vertically, through the ceiling of the hangar.

The second alien came up to me and looked me in the eyes. *'Please sit, Mr. Arrow. We wouldn't want you hurt if we need to make a sudden change in direction.'*

"I haven't had the pleasure," I said back to him.

'You may call me Rachel. I am the co-pilot and navigator.'

"Rachel? Are you female?"

'Yes. But not in the same manner that Agent Casola is a female. I am not a breeder.'

"Breeder?"

'On Draco, some females donate eggs for fertilization. Other females are impregnated and carry the fetus for two months, until it is large enough to be sustained in a birth tube. Those who are impregnated are called breeders. And some females do neither. I am among the latter. Those of us who are not breeders fulfill responsibilities for the good of our civilization.'

"What sorts of things do you do?"

'*Whatever we are assigned. We do not have choices the way your species currently does. But that is changing for you. As your kind evolves, you will assume our enlightened practices because they will be good for the survival of your species. The free will that has fostered the demise of your species will go the way of all primitive practices.*'

I sat back down, as Rachel had initially instructed, and I whispered what she had told me into Mona's ear. "You're shitting me," she said. "How enlightened can it be to grow a child in a Petri dish and then raise it without the warmth of a mother's touch? These greys have a lot to learn about nature and nurture. They remind me of termites with their big round heads and spindly arms and legs."

"Shhhh," I reminded her softly. "Who knows if they can understand our thoughts or our language? We have to be careful about what we say and think."

Mona nodded, then she crossed her arms and sighed. It was going to be a long trip, and we had no idea how we would be greeted when we got to Dulce. This was another mission with a high probability of our winding up in the soup.

Rachel's advice to sit down was definitely in my best interest. Riding in the bell through the Martian atmosphere was rough. We were buffeted and twisted like a small boat in a storm until we broke out of the atmosphere and into the calmness of space. Once we became weightless outside of the planet's gravity, the ride became smoother, more like what we had experienced in Waam's tureen. Still, it was not a quiet ride because whatever sort of engine the Nazis had engineered to drive that buggy made humming and electrical arcing sounds that reminded me of the sound effects they used for the

space ships in the old Flash Gordon series that Mona and
I had been watching back on Mars.

We hadn't been weightless for more than a minute
when Rachel jumped up from her seat and came back to
us.

She pushed our heads together so we could both look
into her eyes and she told us, '*Stay seated and remain
quiet. We are being approached by two Draconian tureens. They will probably scan us for contraband. This
will give us an opportunity to test the codes we have ob-
tained.*'

Mona gave me a look of concern. "I hope they don't
board us," she whispered.

I nodded. I was certain that this was not a good thing.
With six different races occupying Mars, why would they
be singling us out for harassment, unless they suspected
that we launched from the Ummite fortification—or unless Grau or Rachel had ratted us out?

Grau halted our forward movement and hovered the
bell in space. The two Draconian tureens came alongside,
one on each side. I could see Grau making hand gestures
as he conversed telepathically with someone on his monitor. At one point, he gestured in our direction. When he
did, Rachel turned to look at us.

Our bell was swaying as it hovered. At one point, it
banged gently against one of the Draconian tureens.
Grau's hand gestures became more animated. The Draconian tureen banged back against us, sending our bell into
the other tureen and delivering a harder blow to that one.
Rachel's face grew worried. Grau continued his hand
gestures. I felt like we were being bullied. However, after
a long minute, the two Draconian tureens backed away
and sped toward the surface of Mars.

I stood up, walked over the Grau, and tapped him on the shoulder. He was obviously shaken. "What was that all about?" I asked.

'Draconian guards on a scouting mission. They wondered what this bell was doing off of the garden planet. I told them that you recovered it from the Ummites and that we are transporting you two interrogators and the three former captives back to the Dulce facility. Once they learned that you are NWO interrogators, they decided not to conduct an interior inspection of our craft.'

I told Mona what Grau had told me. "Do you think we'll be safe for the rest of our trip?" she asked.

I was growing tired of relaying messages, but I asked Grau, anyway. He told me that he thought so. Most important, the codes seemed to be recognized by the Draconians.

"They think so," I said to Mona.

Rachel sat back down beside Grau. Within a few moments, the bell began moving again. Acceleration seemed slower when compared to Waam's tureen, at least it looked that way on the gauges that I inspected, but we were making progress toward Earth and home. About twenty minutes later, I noticed that Mona's chin was resting on her chest. I could tell that she was asleep because a thin thread of drool was hanging from the corner of her mouth and was slowly descending to her blouse. I reached down with my finger and swiped it away.

The major problem with the bell was that its interior walls didn't let the passenger see the outside at all. Only the crew had monitors. You've got to credit the German technicians for being first out of the starting blocks with retro-engineering crashed tureens, but their designers had given no consideration to passenger comfort. Imagine designing a bus with no windows. What you would have is a closed container like the trailers that the eighteen-wheelers pull. I guess that's what riding in a bell is like—riding in the trailer end of a tractor-trailer. It rode rough, it offered no entertainment, the view sucked, and there were no restrooms.

My bladder was starting to ache when Rachel touched my shoulder, rousing me from a semi-sleep. I looked into her black eyes. She said, '*Mr. Arrow, you and agent Casola should prepare to disembark.*'

"Are we there? Dulce?"

'*Yes. We landed five minutes ago. Our bell has been rinsed down to cool its exterior and to remove any hazardous microbes that we might have picked up in space. They are about to open the hatch.*'

I shook Mona. "Gotta get up and look official, baby. We're already in Dulce."

"How long have I been out?"

"I don't really know. Maybe six hours. Maybe eight. It's so damn hard to tell."

"Why am I so tired?" Mona asked.

"That's a good question for Grau or Rachel."

Mona got up and walked over to Rachel, who was busy helping to shut down the bell's power system. When Rachel turned to look at her, Mona asked, "Why am I so tired? Did you guys drug us or something?"

'*It is the nature of the bell on humans. The magnetic field that it develops causes your bodies to secrete L-Tryptophan. Actually, the result eases the boredom of long flights.*'

"How long was our flight?"

'*In your time, close to fifteen hours.*'

When Mona told me what she had learned, I understood why my bladder was aching. My tanks were definitely overdue for an emptying. When I got the chance, I complained to Grau. '*Yes,*' he told me, '*bells were intended for use on the garden planet and not for extended deep space travel. Captain Waam gave us plastic containers for you to use for elimination, if necessary. Didn't we tell you about them?*'

I turned away from him and muttered, "Who are you working for anyway, the NWO?" I realized that if I had asked about a bathroom during the flight, he or Rachel would have given us the containers and we'd have figured out a way to use them without embarrassing ourselves. I made a mental note to remind myself that if you don't ask, you're forced to suffer in silence.

A tapping sound on the hatch prompted Rachel to open it and hand the ladder to someone below. Rachel was first to descend, followed by me and then Mona. As Mona stepped onto the smooth stone floor, two large men in NWO uniforms climbed into the bell.

A third and fourth stood below. Soon, one of our passenger greys was handed down to those below.

He was followed by the second and the third. One of the NWO guards saluted Mona and said, "The base commander thanks you for negotiating the return of this bell and the three Zetas. He regrets that he could not be here to thank you in person."

Mona returned his salute. "We've had a long trip. Would you please direct us to your restroom facilities?"

"Yes, sir." He pointed to two doors on a wall about fifty yards away. "That would be what you are looking for."

"Thank you," Mona replied. We both quickly walked away to relieve ourselves. Well, Mona told me that she needed to "freshen up."

After she did her business, Mona met me outside the restroom door. "Have you checked your cell phone?" she asked.

"No, I've had it on buzz."

"My ma has called twenty times. I could probably spend half an hour listening to her voicemails. And Mack called, too. He asked that we connect with him when we return to Earth."

"Well, we can't do it down here. There's no telling who'll be listening in. If I was the base commander, I'd want to eavesdrop on any NWO interrogators who visited my digs just to try to find out what they're looking for."

"You're right, Danny. Maybe we can figure out a way to go topside for a while."

I dug my cell phone out of my pocket. "Hell, it wasn't on buzz, it was completely turned off."

Mona rolled her eyes. "No wonder you're always unavailable."

I pushed the little button on the top of my cell phone and waited until it went through its long awakening process. "I've got a couple of junk emails from vendors, and I've got phone messages from Mack and Hal. I wonder what she wants. She's called me six times."

"Come on, Danny, let's go see if we can find someone who can help us."

Mona led the way back to the bell that had transported us from Mars. Several technicians in NWO uniforms were working under it. As we approached, two technicians popped to attention. "At ease, gentlemen," Mona told them. "This isn't boot camp anymore." They chuckled and relaxed. "Can you point us to the officer of the watch? We're new to this facility."

"Yes sir," one replied. "If y'all will just go down that corridor a piece, take yer second path to left. When y'all come to a set of double doors, it's a good bet he's tied up in there."

"I didn't know they let good old boys into this chicken outfit," Mona said.

"They's a few of us hereabouts."

"Texas?" I asked.

"Hell yes!"

"What part?"

"McAllen."

"Then I guess you've spent some time in Renosa."

"You can bet he has!" The other one laughed. "We've all been there a few times."

The first one pointed at the second. "He's got a girl he's sweet on down there. She charges him only twenty dollars. The rest of us pay twenty-five." An oily rag found its way to his face.

"Gentlemen, this conversation is going places that aren't appropriate with a female officer present," Mona said.

"Yes, sir. Like I said, y'all is gonna find the officer of the watch behind them double doors."

"Thank you," Mona replied, turning and strutting away.

I quickly followed. When we were out of earshot, I said, "They seem like nice guys. I wouldn't expect them to be in the NWO, especially because they're Texans. I wonder who recruited them?"

"I don't know, and I don't care, Danny. But I guess it was good form to joke with them and keep them on good terms with us. Just don't get carried away like you usually do. Remember that we're interrogators."

"Yeah, I know, baby. I'll keep that right here," I replied, tapping on my temple with my middle finger.

I followed Mona down the corridor to the second left and tailed behind her until she stopped at the double doors. "Here goes nothing," she said, squeezing my hand in hers.

We pushed open the door and walked up to a desk sergeant. If it hadn't been the NWO, you'd have thought it was just any other military organization.

Certainly, its layout, color scheme, and protocols were just like the army. And, you had to get through the desk sergeant to get to the duty officer. When the sergeant looked up, he popped to attention and saluted.

"At ease, soldier," Mona told him. "Is the Officer of the Watch in?"

"Yes, sir. I'll tell him that you're here." He hurried into the next room. When he reappeared, he said, "The captain will see you now."

I followed Mona into the office. The NWO flag was tacked to one wall. On the opposite wall was posted a map of the world with no borders. Major cities were highlighted, and I noticed that the capital of the NWO was the city of Astana, Kazakhstan. Around the map were several pictures of buildings which had already been constructed. One was a huge pyramid beneath which were printed the words "Unification of World Religions." Another was clearly a governmental building with a dome somewhat like the US Capitol and the words *One World Congress* printed beneath. I wanted to keep looking, but, as an NWO interrogator, I was supposed to know this stuff already.

"Welcome to Dulce," the captain said, shaking Mona's hand first and then mine. He never gave us his last name. "I'd like to thank you for returning the bell and the three captives. Why did you drug them?"

"Your message of welcome was brought to us upon landing," Mona replied. "Nonetheless, thank you. It was a long trip in that bell. I much prefer the newer tureens."

"Captain," I interjected, "we exchanged an Ummite corpse for that bell and those greys. They arrived to us like that."

"Those bastard Ummites erased their memories," the captain told us.

"That would explain why we weren't able to interrogate them," Mona said.

"While we were on Mars, we witnessed cold war hostilities between our Draconian brothers and the Ummites," I said. "I think that if the greys' memories were erased, it was to create an annoyance for the Draconians."

"If not to erase something that the Ummites don't want us to learn," the captain replied. "I am afraid that we'll have to scour every inch of the bell to see if they've installed any eavesdropping or tracking equipment. Ever since those Ummites tried to send His Excellency into the sun, I've joined those who doubt the sincerity of their pledge to sit at the NWO's Galactic table."

"I heard that two of them were possibly also involved in the Livermore incident," Mona probed.

"We aren't sure, but our suspicions lean in that direction. Certainly, Commissar Nargas believed that, or he never would have given the order to seize that Ummite tureen for fear of causing a Galactic incident."

"We've been away too long and have missed much. Did the mission launch from here?" I asked, now knowing that Nargas was the lizard whom Waam was seeking.

"Here Earth, or here Dulce?"

"Dulce."

"No, it launched from Kongka La, China." The captain tugged at his belt then awkwardly asked, "Are you here on official business? Are you investigating something in my facility?"

"No," Mona replied, "no official business other than returning the bell and the captives. We would have taken them to Livermore, but it's still a mess. The bell is a piece of shit, and Dulce was closest to our entry point." She smiled, "We haven't been to Dulce before. We were hoping to go topside for some R and R. Is that possible, or are travel restrictions in place?"

"No restrictions here. Livermore has them, for obvious reasons. Denver, too. Some assholes drove a laser mole from below ground through the runway at Denver. It's still under repair."

I wanted to smile. In fact, I had a difficult time holding back a snicker.

"I'll have my driver take you to the surface," the captain continued. "The exit is inside a warehouse."

"Similar to Denver?" I asked.

"Yeah, but a bit bigger. You'll find some lockers there for your uniforms, and a dressing room with a couple of racks of civvies. Ma'am, there won't be much of anything for females."

"Do I look like I care?" Mona asked.

"No, sir, but if you did, I just didn't want you to get your expectations too high."

"I'm fine wearing anything that fits. I just want to get a decent meal and maybe some time in the sun."

"Yes, sir, I understand. You'll find three loaner vehicles there, too. The keys are in the ignition. Take the one you want. We just ask that you bring it back in good condition. When you exit the warehouse, you'll be on the Archuleta Plateau. Take it slow going downhill into town."

We thanked the captain and left his office. A buzzer rang as we did. The desk sergeant said, "Yes, sir, I will," and hung up the phone. He looked at Mona. "Sir, the captain's driver will meet you back by the bell that you arrived in. He will escort you to the surface."

"Thank you, Sergeant," Mona replied.

We retraced our steps to the bell. As we approached it, a door at the opposite end of the large hangar opened and a military grade H-1 Hummer made its way toward us. When it stopped, a tall young man in an NWO uniform emerged from behind the steering wheel. He saluted and then opened the rear door for us. "Lieutenant Driscoll reporting as directed."

Mona and I returned his salute and entered the Hummer. He closed the door behind us. I noted that the space between the front and rear seats was filled with plexiglass. "Bullet proofing?" I asked Mona.

A cracking sound came from the two speakers mounted behind us. "Yes, sir. This baby is fully armored. You're in a bullet-proof cabin. The floors, doors, and roof are four inch steel. The glass will withstand a tank round."

"Nice," I replied. "How often have you needed the protection offered by this vehicle?"

"Never, sir. There has never been a threat down here, not like Livermore."

I wanted to smile again, but I held it back.

Driscoll put the Hummer into drive and exited the hangar, entering a two-lane highway that served as the main thoroughfare between the surface and the below ground facilities. I learned that we were at level five when we came to a large door, guarded by two sentries, who opened it and saluted as we drove through. Painted on the walls on our side were large number fives, and as we passed through the doorway, number fours were painted on the walls with arrows pointing that-away. It was simplistic yet functional.

The doorway, by the way, was the same eighteen inch thick slab of steel that Nelson and I had encountered at level two a few months ago when we climbed down the air shaft on the Indian reservation to see what was down here. I recalled seeing Zeta greys for the first time, and Draconian guards shooting balls of liquid light at us. We narrowly escaped with our lives.

I wondered why I would ever come back here, except to nuke the place. But, then, those doors were built to withstand the blast of a small nuclear device, so in order to nuke this entire facility, a guy would have to set off a device in the middle of each level. That would be nearly impossible to do.

The highway that we were traveling climbed upward at what I estimated to be a twenty degree angle, maybe a little less. As we traveled upward, we could see pedestrian pathways painted onto the floor, and the vehicular lanes divided by a standard yellow line. It was solid, so I figured that no passing was allowed. When we finally reached level four, we were on a level stretch, bordered on each side by doorways and an occasional garage-type door. I assumed that these led to work and recreational areas, perhaps living quarters, storage facilities, and medical areas. I thought I'd ask. "Lieutenant, can you tell me what each level houses?"

There was static again, and then the lieutenant's voice, "Level one houses intake and a small security force. Level two is where we warehouse supplies and some vehicles, and it also has a few training rooms for individuals with low security clearance. Level three is our barracks and recreational area. Level four is medical and above-top-secret educational. Level five is hangars, computer systems, executive offices, and the transportation hub. Level six houses Galactic visitors, including their food storage and dining.

Levels seven and eight are beyond my security clearance, so I'm not one hundred percent sure. You'll have to ask the captain, although he may not know, either. There are rumors of additional levels, but if they exist, they are above above-top-secret and probably only the Draconians know what they're for."

"All the conveniences of home," Mona said. "Do they let you out much?"

"Yes, sir. We get one day per two weeks. I usually save mine and take a two-day weekend once a month."

"Don't you miss the sun?"

"No, sir. With the sun lamps in the exercise room, we get all the vitamin D we need. More than anything, I miss the girls, if you'll pardon my saying that."

Mona squeezed my hand. "No offense taken, Lieutenant. I understand the need to spend time with the opposite sex. The Draconians have that one over us, don't they?"

"Sir?"

"The Draconians don't enjoy the opposite sex the way we do. They raise their young in test tubes full of liquid."

"Only the hybrids, sir."

"I guess that's what I meant, Lieutenant."

Mona may have made a mistake. From the lieutenant's comment, it was clear that the Draconians have some sort of sexual relations within the confines of their species, but they raise experimental hybrids in tanks. In Mona's case, reproduction of the hybrid was conducted by DNA manipulation and in vitro fertilization, with her as the host until such time as the fetus could survive in one of their growing tanks.

I changed the subject. "Where is a good place to eat in Dulce?"

"The best places are outside of town. There is a good Mexican place about eight miles east. One block from it is a small motel with a swimming pool. Most of the officers stay there when on the surface."

Mona and I had been to both places before, and it looked like we were going to revisit our first trip to Dulce.

"If you want to catch some local color, I suggest the Wildhorse Casino. It's full of rednecks and Indians. They sometimes have a local country band."

"Thank you, Lieutenant. I haven't had good Mexican food since San Diego." I was lying, but I wanted to distract him from thinking about what Mona had said about the Draconians. "Would you care to join us? We could use a guide, and it would be on the house."

"Thanks, but I have a pile of paperwork to complete today. And I was on R and R last weekend."

We passed through the gates at levels two and three with the standard salute from the sentries and an open door. "When we come back later, should we anticipate any difficulties with the sentries?" Mona asked.

"The Captain has alerted the guard that you will be returning this evening. I have passes for you, anyway."

"We will be communicating with Kazakhstan while we are topside," I told him. "We are anticipating some news about His Excellency." I hoped that would keep his wheels turning.

"We already know that his migration into a new container has taken place," Driscoll said. "It was done without the fanfare of the Livermore event. Given how that became such a fiasco, it was probably better that he did it this way the second time."

This information caught both of us by surprise. Mona looked at me with concern. I wondered if Waam was aware of it.

I lied some more. "The news we are hoping for is that the date has been set for the release of the viral pandemic. It's time for us to take over."

"No news of that yet. Don't you think it's a little premature for that date to be announced?"

"Those on Mars are already betting on the date. Anticipation is high. That's why we'll be communicating with Kazakhstan this afternoon."

"Why wouldn't you use our communications center? All communications are encrypted."

"Spies!" Mona interjected. "We are aware of spies within the NWO guard, spies who would sabotage any effort to release the virus. His Excellency is depending upon us to root out the would-be saboteurs."

We had reached level one. The last large steel door was operated by a remote control device, mounted on the sun visor over the H-1's steering wheel. Once it had opened, the lieutenant sped forward and up the ramp to the surface. As we neared the top of the ramp, I could see the steel ceiling and interior walls of a warehouse. Other than the ramp to Hell, there was nothing else that would cause a guy to think that this building was anything special. In fact, on a hot day, you wouldn't want to be inside, where the heat of the sun would send the interior temperature high enough to bake a cake.

Driscoll pointed us to the locker room. Inside we found three racks of clothes and lockers where we could store our uniforms while outside on R and R. I went for khaki Dockers and a dark green golf shirt. Mona chose blue jeans and a Grateful Dead tee shirt. We looked like your average middle class civilians. By wearing our shirts outside of our trousers, nobody could see that our pieces were stuffed into our waistbands.

When we came out of the locker room, Lieutenant Driscoll showed us three loaner vehicles. "The captain suggests that you take the CJ-Seven because it offers the most ground clearance," he told us.

That was fine with me. Besides, there was no way I was going to ride around town in a yellow Sorrento or a tan Outback. Especially the Outback.

"Be sure to fill the tank before you come back," Driscoll told us, "and watch the hill going down into town. It's a little steep and twisty."

"We should be back before midnight," Mona said.

"The outside door to the warehouse goes into lockdown at eleven sharp. Be sure to be inside by then."

"Thanks, Lieutenant," I said. "We'll see you for a nightcap at eleven."

"Wait a minute!" he said sharply. "I forgot to give you these." He removed two plasticized VISITOR cards from his breast pocket and handed them to Mona. She passed them over to me.

"Yeah, thanks," Mona said. "Are you sure you don't want to join us? We have the authority to tell your commander that we need you for special purposes."

"Thanks, but no. Maybe next time."

Chapter 10

Jeezus, Danny, can't you steer this thing?!"

"I'm trying to, baby, but the front end is really loose. I have to turn the steering wheel *waaay* farther than I should have to in order to get it to respond. This thing is a death trap, especially on this hill. Wait until I get my hands on Driscoll!"

"Do you think they intended to do us in?"

"No. I just think they don't spend any money on this civilian stuff. Besides, all the NWO types have to be trained to expect the unexpected. Maybe this is part of training."

"How are the brakes?"

"They seem okay."

"Then maybe you ought to try using them every now and then. You're scaring the shit out of me."

"You'll be fine, Mona. You just gotta quit trying to be in control all the time."

"Fuck you, you asshole. This is my life you're risking."

"Tell you what: once we get down the hill, I'll turn this buggy over to you and you can have fun trying to steer it. Ever been in a bumper car? This is one that has grown up, but it still steers like the little guys."

I did like Mona said and rode the brake down the hill. I have to admit that it was easier to control the CJ when we were going slower. When we intersected Narrow Gauge Street, I stopped and let Mona take over. She couldn't drive it any better than I could, but at least I didn't have to hear her complaining about my driving. Now all that came from her mouth was a barrage of four letter words about how badly the CJ handled. But I already knew that.

Mona drove us through town and then headed north two blocks to the Apache House of Liquor. "I know it's only lunchtime, but I could use a drink," she told me. I couldn't disagree. I was thirsty but less from the heat than from stress.

Before we went inside, I called Hal to see what was so important that she called me six times while I was on Mars. Her phone rang three times before she picked up. "It's about time, you stupid prick!" she said. Not even a hello.

"Hal, it's—"

"My cell phone has caller ID."

"Yeah, ugh, right," I stammered. "You called. This is the first time I've been able to retrieve voice mails."

"So what do you intend to do about it?"

"Do about what? Start from the beginning."

"You said that you listened to my voice mails."

"No, I said that I saw that you left me voice mails, but I haven't listened to them. I thought I'd call you to see what's up."

Hal sent a puff of frustration through the phone. "Listen, Danny, I couldn't sell that bar of gold that you gave me. I took it to a gold dealer. He took it into the back of his shop, supposedly to ensure that it was real, but instead, he called the FBI. Did you know that it is il-legal to own Chinese gold in the United States?"

I could see where this was going. "No, I didn't even think about that, Hal."

"The agents poured into his store and arrested me, Danny. They charged me with possession of contraband. I was questioned for eight hours in the basement of some building near the Capitol."

"Aw, geez, Hal, I'm really sorry about that."

"I got my Aunt Vera to go the bail. She had to mort-gage her home to do that. I got myself a court-appointed attorney, but he's worthless. He doesn't believe that the gold ingot came from a space alien named Juan."

"Waam," I said, correcting her.

"Yeah, whatever. Listen, Danny, if my lawyer doesn't believe in me, I don't stand a chance in the court-room."

"When is your court date?"

"It's four days away. My lawyer wants me to claim mental incapacity, especially with my explanation of how I came into possession of the gold ingot."

"I'll see what I can do to help you."

"I'll give you my lawyer's phone number. You can call him and tell him that the gold ingot is yours."

"I can't do that, Hal."

"What's the matter? Are you afraid of being arrest-ed?"

"No, not that. I just can't be in DC in four days. Like I told you when I left, I'm going to be away for several weeks."

"So what are you gonna do, Danny? My aunt is out fifty grand, and I'm gonna be in the booby hatch. On top of that, everything in your office is gonna be thrown out on the curb for the garbage collectors when your rent comes due next week."

"Let me call a friend at the FBI and see if he can help."

"He'd better be quick. And you'd better call me to let me know what's happening."

"I'll try," I said. Hell, I couldn't promise any more than that.

I got Mona to give me Mack's phone number, and I called him. All I reached was his voice mail, so I left a message, hoping that he'd get back to me before ten that night. I didn't call Hal again because I had nothing positive to tell her.

"Are you going to call your ma?" I asked Mona.

"Maybe later tonight. She just wants to talk, maybe to hear my voice, and to tell me about things that are going on within the family. She's sort of into everybody's business and, of course, she wants to find out what I'm doing so she can tell the others about it. She must spend four hours a day on the phone."

"Gotcha." I pointed at the Apache House. "Do you still want that drink?"

Mona pulled into the parking lot, opened the door, and climbed out of the CJ. I did the same. As we walked in, she reached out and took me by the hand. "Who's my boyfriend, Danny?" she asked,

"I'm more than that, Mona. I want to marry you."

"Maybe after we finish this assignment, Danny. I think I'm almost ready to settle down."

I pulled her to me and planted a kiss on her lips. She kissed me back, exploring with her tongue.

We were interrupted by a woman's voice. "Take it to a motel, you two!" It was a redhead in a convertible Volkswagen, wanting to back out of her parking place, and we were in her way. She put the heel of her hand on the horn. I flipped her off and then led Mona into the bar. I heard rubber peeling and gravel hitting metal outside as the door closed behind us. I wondered who pissed off the redhead.

It was self-seating, so Mona and I found a booth with green and silver speckled vinyl seats and slid in. It was nice to be back in something that wasn't constructed of molded alien composite material. Or the uncomfortable steel of the Nazi bell.

A waitress approached us, notebook in hand. She looked Apache, well, I assumed Apache because the local Jicarilla Reservation is Apache. She could have been Navajo or Eskimo, as far as I knew. "Beer?" she asked.

"Scotch," Mona replied. "Make it a double with ice."

"Lone Star?" I asked.

"We don't carry it 'cause this ain't Texas. There's a list of beers right there by the ketchup bottle."

The beer list was printed on the back of the dessert menu. I decided to try Santa Fe State Pen Imperial Porter because I liked the name. I shouldn't have done that because when she brought it to the booth, it was some dark shit sissy concoction that beer snobs like. I asked her to take it back and bring me a Pearl. "Should have guessed by looking at you," she replied with a look of distain. For a moment, I felt a little like Rodney Dangerfield, but then Mona distracted me.

When my beer arrived, Mona said, "Here's to our first day as interrogators," holding her glass in the air so I could tap it with the tip of my bottle.

"I guess it hasn't gone too badly," I replied. "We aren't dead."

Mona's face took on a serious expression. "We need to check on Nelson, Danny. If this was after work, I would expect him to stop in for a few beers. I wonder how he's doing?"

"You're right, baby. Maybe we should drive by his home this evening."

Mona pulled out her cell phone, found Nelson's name in her list of contacts, and hit speed dial. The phone rang three times and then went to an automated message: "The person you wish to reach is no longer at this number. No forwarding information is available at this time."

Mona called information and discovered that Nelson no longer had a phone number. "That's odd," she remarked. "Maybe we should go by his house sooner than later."

I agreed. After we finished our drinks, we hopped back into the CJ and headed west toward downtown Dulce. On the way, Mona said, "Pull over into that lot, Danny." Instinctively, I did as directed without really seeing where I was going. Once I had pulled to a complete stop, I looked up and saw that we were at a small car rental agency. "We're getting rid of this thing, Danny. I don't want to end up as a New Mexico State highway statistic." She was right. We would be much better off in a rental car, and we could give Driscoll directions to come find this piece of shit that he had given us.

I followed Mona into the small trailer that served as the rental office. The guy behind the desk was sweating profusely, as he should have been, given the midday heat. "Can we rent a car for the remainder of the day?" Mona asked.

"Where will ya be going with it?" he asked.

"Just around town, but we'll have to pick you or somebody else up at nine this evening so you can drop us off where we need to be by ten o'clock."

"And where would that be?"

"At a large warehouse northwest of town on Narrow Gauge Street."

"You ain't the first to do that. I thought I recognized that CJ. It'll cost you an extra fifty bucks."

"That's fine," Mona told him.

Ten minutes later we were back on the highway in a white Ford Explorer with more than eighty thousand miles on it. But, the steering was tight, and the air conditioning worked great.

Mona drove three more blocks west and then turned north. Two turns later, we came to Nelson's house. It was situated in a clean middle class neighborhood, but three county sheriff's cars and a hearse were parked in front of it. The driveway and front lawn were bordered with bright yellow crime scene tape. "Shit," Mona muttered. "We may be too late."

We exited the Explorer. Mona approached the first deputy we encountered, flashed her photo ID and said, "Agent Mona Casola, FBI. What's going on here?"

"Suicide."

"Strangulation?"

"Yes."

"Surgical tubing?"

"Yes. How did you know?"

"We've been on the trail of a serial killer. Same MO. Can we go inside?"

The deputy lifted the yellow tape and let us pass. "Be sure to identify yourselves to the head investigator, and be careful not to fuck up any evidence."

Mona waved her hand in the air as we entered the front door. We had never been in Nelson's home before, although we had dropped him off in his driveway a few months ago. There was nothing notable about the hunter green carpet and basic drapes that hid the vinyl venetian blinds that Nelson used to block the bright morning sun. A thirty-inch-by-twenty-inch print of Clint Eastwood as Blondie the Buffalo Bonker was hung on the wall above a pale green sofa. The coffee table was pine, with circular stains in the finish.

Mona walked down the hallway saying, "FBI. FBI. Who is the lead investigator?"

A short woman with greying hair stepped out of a room to our left. She was sporting a .357 magnum on her hip. It looked especially heavy against her thin frame.

"I thought I was done with you guys," she said as she approached us. "The Taos office was here about an hour ago."

"Special Agent Casola," Mona said. "I'm here from the DC office. We're on the trail of a serial killer with a signature MO. Surgical tubing, I assume."

"That would be right, Agent Casola. But you're too late to see the body. It's already at the morgue."

"Any idea who did it? Any witnesses?"

"None. His neighbor knocked on the door, and when the victim didn't answer, the neighbor looked in the window and saw him lying on the floor. He called for the ambulance. The EMTs alerted us. The guys from your Taos office were here fifteen minutes after we arrived. They designated this as a suicide. We think they're right."

"You should double check the body," I told her. "Have your medical examiner see if he was dead before the surgical tubing was placed around his neck. Also, look for any puncture marks or odd markings."

"Do you mean like needles?"

"Exactly: Needles. And ask him to look in unusual places, like between toes, under the tongue, in the scalp. This is all very important. Just because the Taos guys gave it the suicide designation, don't assume that it is. We may be dealing with a serial killer here."

She looked at Mona and asked, "Who is this eagle scout?"

"This is Dan Arrow, a private detective who is on assignment with the DC office. He's the person who first discovered that a similar suicide was, in fact, a murder."

"Private eye, huh? Glad to meet you, Mr. Arrow. I'll call the examiner and order a special examination. Who should I call with the results?"

Mona gave her Mack's cell phone number. "Don't bother the Taos office because they've already written this case off."

When we got back into the Explorer, Mona burst into tears. I put my arm around her and held her until her sobbing diminished. "I feel partly responsible for this," she told me. "If we hadn't gotten him involved in this conspiracy, he would still be alive."

"I'm sorry, baby, but Nelson didn't have to do what he did for us. This stuff is kind of intriguing, and just about any guy would have done what Nelson did."

Mona nodded her head and blew her nose into a tissue. "Do you think Arthur and Granger are okay?" she asked. We decided to call and find out.

Arthur McGarvey was one of a small group of guys who went with me into the subterranean facilities which are under the Denver Airport. The lizards cut them all down, except for McGarvey. While I was underground, I met Granger Taylor, who twice saved my life and helped me escape.

I brought him topside after the Livermore incident because his knowledge about the extent of the underground network and about how several governments and several races of aliens are working with the NWO to take over would shake the world.

Arthur McGarvey's cell phone rang a couple of times before he picked up. "Hello? Is this really you, Miss Mona?"

"Yes, Arthur. How are you? Danny and I are in Dulce. We came here to see Nelson, and we thought we'd check on you, too."

"I guess I'm okay. I still miss the Dweeb Squad. They were my best friends."

"Yes, I know. It's good to hear your voice. Is Granger still living with you?"

"He's disappeared. I went to visit my grandmother in a nursing home in Fort Collins. I was late getting back. I think it was about two in the morning. Granger's stuff is here, but he's gone. It's been two days now. I tried to call in a missing person's report, but the police told me that I'd have to wait seventy-two hours before I was able to do that. They said he's likely to just walk in the door."

"Let's hope he does," Mona replied. "How about you? Have you been followed or harassed by the men-in-black or the military?"

"I'm okay. I don't think anybody is following me, and I haven't been harassed. How about you folks?"

"We're okay, but Nelson is dead. He was strangled with surgical tubing. Does that sound familiar?

"Unfortunately, it does. Do you think I'm next?"

"We're worried that you might be. You need to take some precautions, maybe go visit somebody."

"What about Granger?"

"It already may be too late for him. I wonder if he's been abducted?"

"Maybe worse, Miss Mona. Maybe his body has been distributed across the desert in very small pieces."

"Let's hope not. I'll ask a friend at the FBI if he can put someone on finding out where Granger might be. In the meanwhile, maybe you should make yourself scarce."

"Roger, Miss Mona. Give my best to Mr. Arrow." He hung up.

I turned the key in the ignition switch to start the Explorer and get some air conditioning running. At the exact same moment, a mushroom-shaped fireball filled the sky in front of us. A second later, we were rocked by the wave of concussion from the explosion. Litter and small fragments of wood and metal rained down on us.

"Jeezus H. Christ, what was that!?" Mona exclaimed. "Maybe an oil tanker exploded?"

The sheriff's SUV pulled out of Nelson's driveway with its lights flashing and siren blaring. I followed him, but I stayed about a block behind. After a couple of turns, the sheriff pulled to a stop on the street beside the small car rental lot where we had just picked up the Explorer. Every car on the lot showed evidence of damage from an explosion, and the windows in the rental trailer had been blown out. A small crater sat in the spot where we had left our CJ. A few pieces of metal and rubber lay smoking around the crater.

"It was our CJ, Danny!" Mona exclaimed. "Some-body doesn't want us in Dulce."

"Somebody doesn't want us anywhere," I corrected. "We're going to have a chat with the captain when we get back to the facility."

Rather than bother the sheriff while he conducted an investigation that would tie us up for hours of question-ing, Mona and I drove into the desert, stopping at the last chance gas station for a six-pack of Budweiser, some pre-wrapped ham and cheese sandwiches, a bag of potato chips, and a vinyl tablecloth. Mona also bought two quart bottles of cold water, in case we got lost and needed to walk back. About thirty miles south of Dulce, we found a dirt road heading off to the right, so we turned on it just to see where it went. We raised dust for five or six miles, until we came to a dead end with a fence blocking the entire width of the road. A friendly sign read, *KEEP OUT. US GOV'T PROPERTY*. I think the government owns more of New Mexico than the New Mexicans do. It's probably the same in Arizona, Nevada, and Colorado. Nothing like the desert, you know. You can hide all sorts of stuff out there, from experimental aircraft to dead bodies. And for the most part, John Q. Public doesn't give a flying shit.

The fence that designated the federal property ran perpendicular to the dirt road in both directions. I noticed a house-sized rock to the right, so I suggested to Mona that we hike over to it. "It looks like a peaceful and purdy place to eat our vittles, ma'am," I drawled, trying to lighten the mood. It was a pretty poor imitation of John Wayne.

"You'd have never made it as a cowboy hero, Danny. Have you ever seen a cowboy hero with a shaved head and beard?"

I guess she had a point.

We found our way along the fence to the large rock. The back side of it rose to the surface at a thirty degree angle, so climbing up wasn't difficult for either of us. When we reached the top, I looked around, but nothing in the way of structure could be seen in any direction, other than the fence the led to the horizon in both directions. But, I realized that it was just too damn hot to sit on the top of that rock and eat. Below, however, a shadow on the desert floor told me that a good place was just beneath us. So, we climbed back down and made our way to the shady spot. I checked it out for snakes and scorpions but didn't find any. That was good, because they both give me the willies. I spread the tablecloth on the sand, and we sat down.

Mona popped a beer and handed the can to me. Warm Budweiser isn't too bad, actually. I tore open a sandwich and gave her half. We ate silently until we started in on the second sandwich, and then Mona started to relate her thoughts. "So Danny," she started, "Given our exploding CJ, I'm thinking that we can't go back into the NWO facility tonight without a strategy. What do you suggest?"

Immediately I knew that she had a plan, but that I had a chance to chime in on it before it was set in stone. "I want to get close to Nargas," I told her, "so I can figure out a way to take him back to Waam. And I want to find out who it was who just tried to snuff us out."

"And I want to see the hybrid baby that that bastard implanted in me," Mona said. "And, where are we most likely to find two of the three individuals in question? I'll tell you, Danny: it's the moon."

I nodded. "Yeah, we've got to go to the moon." *Shit, I thought, the moon is full of scaly reptilians. How are we going to survive in a den of snakes?*

"I think we have to catch a ride to the moon on a shuttle that leaves from Dulce," Mona continued. "So, what's going to get us a ticket?"

"Same as Livermore, baby. We have to go as interrogators who are looking for a bomb."

"Better yet, I think we have to tell the facility commander that we have received word from our superiors that one or more dissidents have already infiltrated NWO forces on the moon and that they are suspected of planning to assassinate Hitler and Queen Igua."

So that was Mona's plan. It was something that I might have come up with, but for me, it would have been in the spur of the moment. Mona liked to think things out. Nonetheless, her plan seemed like a good one. Finding one or more people who were conspiring to commit a heinous plan required much greater training than simply finding a bomb. Interrogators would certainly be needed for Mona's plan, but for mine, all the lizards would have to do is sweep their moon facility with dogs and Geiger counters, looking for anything that was out of the ordinary. Interrogators would not be needed at all.

"Great idea, baby," I said. "So we would have heard this from Kazakhstan?"

"Yes, if you think the central offices are there."

"Maybe we should just tell Driscoll that we received a communique from our superiors and that we have been ordered to the moon to apprehend would-be assassins."

"Agreed."

"One last thing, Danny. If one of us is captured or killed, the other has to complete this mission. Agreed?"

I didn't like the possibility that Mona was painting for me, but she was right about it. If I was killed, she would have to continue on. Worse than that, if something happened to her, I would have to complete the mission and then think about mourning her. It was something that all soldiers faced.

"Agreed?" she asked again.

"Yeah."

Mona opened another beer and handed it to me. "Enjoy this, Danny. It may be your last beer ever." Then she popped one for herself. Before she took a sip, she held her can in the air and said, "To Nelson. God bless the poor bastard."

"To Nelson."

જ芥જ

On the way back to Dulce, Mona stopped at the edge of town for burgers and fries to go, and then she drove aimlessly through town while we ate. The burgers were nothing to write home about, but they filled us up. When we were finished, I threw the wrappers onto the floor in the back seat.

A kid was waiting for us when we returned the rental car at eight o'clock. Plastic wrap had been duct-taped across the trailer windows that had been blown out by the explosion earlier in the day.

"What happened here?" I asked.

"That jeep of yourn blew up about half an hour after you picked up this here Explorer," he told me. "The boss called the military and they done hauled the remains away."

"How about the sheriff? Does he need to see us?"

"Naw, the military took care of it."

"Good," Mona said.

"Been in the desert, ain't ya?" he asked.

"How did you know?" I asked.

He pointed at the Explorer. "The layer of dust on it. Now I gotta wash it, too."

"Are you our driver?"

"No, you're driving. I just have to bring it back when you get there."

"Oh, okay."

He piled into the back seat. As Mona drove us to the warehouse on the top of the mesa, the kid cleaned up our mess by throwing the paper bag and wrappers out the window.

"Hey, kid, didn't anybody ever talk to you about littering?" I asked.

"Don't matter. This here is Indian land."

When we reached the warehouse, a single lightbulb in a wire cage was lit over an entry door beside the large overhead garage door. Mona put the car in park, and we got out. Junior hopped into the front seat. I gave him five dollars and thanked him for the assistance. "Be careful going back down the hill," I said. "The road can be treacherous."

"Yeah, I know. I make this trip at least once a week." So, it was clear that we weren't the only ones to have decided against driving the civilian loaner cars back uphill.

As the kid left, an NWO guard opened the door for us. "Decided to leave the loaner for us to pick up?" he asked.

"Wouldn't you?" Mona asked. "I understand that it was in pretty bad shape when it got back here."

"Yes, sir. It was just a box of burned pieces of metal and plastic. We looked for teeth and bone fragments, thinking that you two bit the dust, but we didn't find any."

"If we had been in that CJ when it blew, you'd have had to scour the ground for a hundred miles if you hoped to find any remains," I replied.

He had us show our visitor passes and sign in. Then he made a call to someone named Brett. "Have a seat," he said, motioning toward a short row of folding chairs against the corrugated steel wall. "Your ride will be here shortly."

We walked across the facility to the dressing room and changed back into our interrogator's uniforms. Then we came back to the sentry's station where we waited in silence for ten minutes, before we heard a motor coming up the ramp. Soon a military grade jeep appeared. Brett was the driver, and he was in dressed in fatigues. "Did we wake you up?" Mona asked.

"No, sir. Lieutenant Driscoll told me that you might be back this evening, but he wasn't really sure of your status. Besides, I'm not really on duty at this time of night."

"Where are we bunking?" I asked.

"The lieutenant told me to put you in the dignitary guest rooms on level five, if you came back tonight. That way you'll be near the transportation hub." Brett shifted into first gear and asked, "Are you all battened down? Here we go." The jeep lurched forward. He steered it toward the ramp, and soon we were descending into the tunnels that had become so familiar over the last few months.

We passed through large, thick, steel vehicle doors guarded by NWO sentries at each level, and finally arrived at level five, where our bell was still resting six feet above the ground on three spindly steel legs. Brett pointed down the same hallway that led to the captain's office. "We're going down there, past the executive offices and the officer's mess. There are four guest rooms, and all are empty, so you can take your pick. Will that be one or two rooms?"

"Two, soldier!" Mona snapped. "We may be working together on this assignment, but don't get the wrong idea about us. If my associate even thought about it, he'd wind up in the greys' feeding tanks. And that goes for you, too!"

"Yes, sir!" Brett replied.

Brett turned and led the way to the guest rooms. "There are no locks on the outside, only on the inside, so you can lock the door and not worry about anyone entering unannounced." He opened the first door and held it while Mona walked in.

The room was fifteen by twenty, with a bathroom, somewhat like a three-star motel. Its floors were carpeted in white Berber, and its walls were painted in a basic tan, with video screen windows, permitting occupants to change the view digitally. Brett flipped through several scenes, including places on Earth, as well as several scenes from remote planets I had never heard of. Mona settled on the view of Astana, Kazakhstan. "I love it there," she said to Brett.

"Do you have luggage?" he asked.

"We hadn't planned on staying, but it looks as though we may be here awhile longer. Do you have a PX?" I asked.

"We have a small quartermaster unit where staff can assist you with additional clothes and toiletries in the morning."

"Excellent," Mona replied. "What time does the captain report for duty?"

"He is usually at his desk at oh-six-hundred hours."

"Good. It is important that we speak with him first thing in the morning. Would you see that I am awakened at oh-five-hundred hours."

"Yes, sir."

Brett and I wished Mona a good night and left her room. Mine was next door. The color and layout were essentially the same, except that the bathroom was juxtaposed to Mona's on the same wall. Engineering efficiency, I thought.

Brett wished me a good night's sleep.

"Before you leave," I asked, "can you tell me the captain's last name? I didn't catch it this morning."

"Nobody knows his last name, sir. He's never told anyone, and his signature is illegible. It just says 'captain' with a line after it."

"What's he hiding, Brett?"

Brett shrugged his shoulders, turned, and walked away.

I locked the door after he left and inspected the room carefully. Buried in the upper left corner of the mirror above the room's small vanity I found a camera lens. Somebody was watching. The bathroom, however, appeared to be free from voyeurs.

I opened my door and knocked on Mona's door.

"Who is it?" she asked.

"Sir, it's me, Interrogator Arreaux."

The door opened slightly. "What could you possibly want, Arreaux?" Mona asked.

"I thought you should know that somebody's watching us. There is a small camera lens in the mirror over the vanity."

"And a microphone is built into the base of the overhead light."

"So you already knew?"

"I wasn't born yesterday, Interrogator Arreaux. Go get some sleep. Oh-five-hundred hours comes early."

"Yes, sir."

I went back to my room and locked myself in. I turned out the light, stripped to my skivvies, and climbed into bed. The bed was firm, maybe too firm, but I had slept on worse. I lay awake for a few minutes and then reached for the window clicker. Somehow I managed to hit the right buttons, and the video window came on. The scene appeared to be some place in the Rockies, maybe west of Denver. I hit the clicker again, and the scene changed to Mars, probably outside of the Draconian facilities. I hit the clicker again, and the scene changed to outer space. It reminded me of the trip to Mars in Waam's tureen, so I left it on that image. Before I knew it, though, I was awakened by knocking on the door. "Oh-five-hundred hours," a voice said from the other side.

"Fuck."

಄಄಄

Mona and I sat for a few minutes sucking down black coffee in the officers' mess. Nobody else was there except the cook and his staff. "No thank you, we aren't interested in your goop of the day," I muttered to Mona after she waved away a skinny man with an NWO tattoo on his forearm who asked if we wanted some SOS. His hair was greasy, and his hands were covered with blisters, so we weren't sure how sick the food might make us if we ate any of it.

When the clock on the wall hit zero-six-ten hours, we walked down to the captain's office and made our way inside. Like Brett had told us, the captain was sitting at his desk inhaling some orange stuff from a glass hookah. He looked up and stood up to greet us.

"Hey, you made it back! We weren't sure if we'd see you again," he said. "Hell of a bang that CJ made when it went!"

"We expect you to conduct an investigation to determine who tried to assassinate us," Mona told him.

"The investigation has already been completed. It was a leaking gas line that dripped onto a hot muffler. Nobody's to blame. It was just an unfortunate accident."

"How can you make such a determination when you are left with only a small box of burned parts?" Mona asked.

"Chemical analysis," he replied, sucking on the end of a tube that came from his hookah. "The chemists found gas residue on everything. It was no conspiracy, and there was no foul play."

I nudged Mona with my thigh. "Interesting breakfast," she said to him, moving her eyes to the hookah.

"Got it from the lizards. It's some kind of weed that has medicinal properties. It's supposed to help cure some weird mold that I inhaled while down here. I've had respiratory trouble ever since I moved in."

"Maybe you need to go sit in the sun and dry your lungs out," I suggested.

Mona touched my arm, signaling that she didn't want to digress any further. "Captain, yesterday we received a communique from our superiors about a coded message that they intercepted and translated. It's important that you arrange for us to travel to the moon as soon as possible. It appears that several dissidents have infiltrated the NWO and have made their way to the lunar facility to assassinate Commissar Nargas and Queen Igua. We need clearances to travel immediately."

"Who'd give a rat's ass if either of those two were terminated, especially Nargas? He has a nasty disposition and an ego the size of a Mack truck."

"Many of us feel the way you do, Captain, but Astana wants us to find and terminate the assassins before they succeed in their mission. I agree with your sentiments about Nargas, but if we fail, the murder of Queen Igua could have ramifications of intergalactic proportions."

"As much as I'd like to see Nargas get what he deserves, if Astana has ordered you to keep him alive, I'll have to follow their directive. A shuttle leaves for the lunar artifact at noon every day. I will ensure that you have ticketing priority on today's flight. Be at the Transport Center by eleven-hundred-thirty hours."

"What time does your quartermaster open?" I asked.

"Oh-nine-hundred hours."

"Thank you," Mona said. "You run a tight ship. Astana will be pleased when I file my report about your assistance during our visit."

We shook hands with the captain and went back to the officer's mess for another cup of coffee. People were stirring now, and the mess was beginning to fill with junior officers. Mona found a table that was off by itself, and we sat down. "Danny, he called the moon 'the lunar artifact.' What does that mean?"

"I heard that, too, baby. Isn't an artifact something that you find, like maybe something that's left over or left behind? You know, like going to a museum and seeing Indian artifacts, maybe pieces of pottery and arrowheads that have been dug up."

"Doesn't it sound like something that Dr. McCloud might have said, that the moon was brought to the Earth by Man fifty thousand years ago? If you can believe the theory that Man is a superior race that seeded the Earth and that the moon is a piece of space junk that they brought to Earth to serve as a space station, then it's not too far of a leap to call the moon an artifact."

"I have to leave that kind of speculation to you, Mona. When I try to think about stuff like that, it makes my head get all crazy. It's all too intellectual, too weird."

"Not any weirder than discovering that the Earth's crust is full of tunnels that are inhabited by aliens of all sorts and that a large intergovernmental organization has been formed to take over the planet. If you had told me that six months ago, I would have asked you what you were smoking. But here we, at least a mile underground, having coffee in a cavern with NWO officers and several aliens, and these bastards are planning to kill off ninety percent of mankind sometime soon."

I nodded, wanting to look around to size up who was seated around us, but I caught myself before I did. "Just a reminder, Mona: I know it's tempting, but be sure you don't look any of the lizards or the greys in the eyes, or they will know what you're thinking."

"Yeah, that's the hardest part about this assignment. I want to stare, but I don't dare."

"Come on, let's go find the quartermaster's hole."

We got up and walked out. As we did, many eyes followed us. I wasn't sure if their interest in us was because we were strangers or because we were interrogators, but either way, it gave me an uncomfortable feeling.

As we passed my room, Brett was coming out of it with an armful of dirty linens. "You catch all the good assignments, don't you, Brett?"

He laughed. "The captain said you wouldn't be sleeping here tonight. Where are you going?"

"On a special assignment. It's top secret." Mona told him.

"Well, I wish you good luck on whatever it is."

"Where's the quartermaster's shop?" I asked.

"Follow me. I am going right by it."

Brett wound around several corners in poorly marked corridors until he came to a door marked with some alien symbol and the word *QUARTERMASTER*. As we followed him, I tried to make mental notes about where to turn to get back to the transportation hub. It didn't work, however, and I was completely lost by the time we reached our destination. "Do you ever get lost?" I asked him.

"Only when we have a power failure. Groping in the dark can be frightening. It's only happened to me once, but because of that experience I always carry a pocket flashlight whenever I leave my bunk area."

"It sounds like you were a Boy Scout."

"I did a couple of years back in Utah, but I didn't really commit to scouting."

Brett pushed open the door and marched in ahead of us. "Sergeant Greely, these folks are from headquarters and are in need of basic toiletries and undergarments. If you happen to have any uniforms with interrogator insignias, they could use them, as well."

Greely studied us. "Nope, no uniforms. Not even insignias that you could sew onto new uniforms. But I do have underwear, socks, soap, deodorant, and stuff like that." He looked at my beard and said, "I guess you don't have much use for razors."

"On the contrary, I need them for my head," I replied.

"Oh yes, I can see that your cranial whiskers are starting to show. Isn't that five o'clock shadow itchy?"

"I'm used to it," I lied. "I've worn my hair like this for ten years."

"What hair?" he asked, chuckling.

Mona was picking through stuff on the shelves, taking deodorant, razors, antibacterial soap, and feminine products, and piling them on the counter. Greely began writing down each item and its value. "What division gets the requisition?" he asked.

"Send it to the Interrogator Division at Astana."

"Are you stationed there? I've heard that it's beautiful."

I remembered the picture in Driscoll's office. "Yeah, lots of new buildings have already been erected and are occupied. We're already launching stuff from the Galactic center. Maybe someday you'll get to visit." I sounded like I knew what I was talking about. Well, I guess I did know a little about it because last week I heard a news report about a botched launching to the space shuttle from Kazakhstan.

Hell, I didn't even know where Kazakhstan was until I saw a map of it in Driscoll's office. Actually, I couldn't find it on a globe if my life depended upon it.

I swallowed hard because my life actually might depend on knowing more than the bullshit I was flinging at Greely.

I made a mental note to go learn more about Kazakhstan as soon as I was in a library or near the internet.

When Mona was finished, I gathered a few things. Most important was toothpaste and a brush, because I hadn't brushed my teeth since Mars, and clean underwear and socks, especially the socks, because my feet get smelly when I sweat, and the anxiety of playing the interrogator role was definitely causing me to sweat. I also found a small bag, just large enough to hold my stuff, so I took a second one and gave it to Mona. They would make great souvenirs because they bore the NWO logo in full color.

We signed the necessary chits and headed out the door with our goodies, as my grandmother would have called them. When we passed a latrine, I made Mona wait in the hallway while I emptied some coffee and brushed my teeth. When I was finished, I guarded the door so Mona could have some privacy. There were no women's rooms down below.

We interrogated enough NWO soldiers along the way to find our way back to the transportation center by eleven-hundred-twenty hours. Mona went to the ticket office and spoke to the person who was behind the counter. Then she turned and waved for me to come join her. "Two priority tickets to the lunar artifact," the agent said, "compliments of Captain Driscoll." He looked at the bands on our arms and asked, "What would two interrogators be doing on the artifact?"

I noticed from the side that his eyes were solid black with gold colored vertical slits for irises. He was definitely a hybrid of some sort, probably half lizard. Without making eye contact, Mona said, "It's above above-top-secret. I can only discuss it with Commissar Nargas and Queen Igua."

"You seem familiar," he said. ""Have we met before, perhaps worked together?"

Mona looked at him briefly and then turned away. "This is my first visit to Dulce. Have you been to Kazakhstan?"

He handed her one ticket. "I must be mistaken, but I feel as though I have seen you before. I can't seem to put my finger on it."

"I have been on many assignments, so perhaps our paths have crossed."

"Thank you for your help," I said, tugging on Mona's arm to coax her away from the window and to a seat.

The hybrid pointed at a set of double doors. "When the light above those doors turns blue, you will find your shuttle on the other side. Be sure to hang onto your ticket for the return flight."

"Thank you," Mona replied.

"Next," the hybrid announced. I stepped forward. "You are traveling with the other interrogator?"

"Yes."

"Under approval by Captain Driscoll?"

"Of course."

"And where are you going?"

"To the lunar artifact."

"And what is your relationship with your traveling companion?"

His questions indicated that he was fishing for something. I answered tentatively. "We have worked on one other assignment together. She is my superior officer on this assignment."

"There is something all too familiar about that woman with whom you are traveling."

"I'm sure she's okay. We worked together at the facility on Mars and brought back a Nazi bell and three captive greys. That could not have been accomplished without her leadership."

"It is probably nothing but keep an eye on her."

"I'm sure there's nothing to worry about. She's loyal to the NWO and to the grand plan."

Mona stepped back up to the window. "Is there something wrong with his ticket?" she asked.

"No," the hybrid replied. "I just wanted to ensure that your traveling companion offered the same answers that you did about where and why you are traveling." He handed me my ticket. "Your companion knows where to go to catch the shuttle."

As we turned to find a seat in the waiting area, the hybrid picked up a communications device and began speaking to someone in a language that I could not understand.

Chapter 11

T he light just turned blue, Danny. Let's go. If we're first on, we can pick our seats and keep our eyes off of the others who come aboard." I rose quickly and followed Mona to the double doors that led to the shuttle's hangar.

The shuttle was a standard tureen like Waam's, but unlike his, it was gray in color and bore the NWO logo on the upper portion of its composite surface. It hovered about three feet off the floor, and its ramp was open and awaiting our arrival. At the foot of the ramp, a Reticulan grey in an orange jumpsuit took our tickets, tore them along the perforation, and handed half back to us. I assumed this was our return ticket. I hoped that we might actually get to use it some time.

There was motion behind us, but I didn't turn around for fear of looking some alien in the eyes. Mona moved forward quickly and took a seat at the central core behind the pilots. After we sat, we stuffed our bags under our seats and kept our eyes focused on the floor. We were not alone on the flight. The black boots of NWO soldiers passed by, as well as the three-toed boots of Draconians, all trying to find seats, especially seats that were not next to ours. The NWO interrogator uniforms were continuing to work like a charm. However, I wished that I had brought a book to pretend to read, but I hadn't, so staring at the floor was all that I had left to do.

Mona gave me a gentle nudge with her elbow. I looked toward her lap. She handed me a pair of mirrored aviator sunglasses. "Where did you get these?" I whispered.

"From the quartermaster, while you were fumbling through the underwear."

"Thanks. These should help a lot."

I put them on, but I was still unsure about looking an alien in the eye, so I looked no higher than chin level at the other passengers seated in our vicinity. On our side of the tureen, I counted three reptilians, two greys, and two humans. The humans wore NWO uniforms. I assumed that an equal number of passengers were seated behind us, on the half of the tureen that I could not see.

I heard the ramp shut, and then a tone filled the tureen. On the interior walls all around us, the same message was projected in several languages: *Fasten your seatbelts. Launch will commence in thirty seconds.*

Around us, passengers all did as instructed, so we followed suit. A few moments after all the clicking of seat belts had ceased, a slight sensation of motion passed through my belly, letting me know that our ascent had begun. Within less than a minute, the interior walls of the tureen projected bright light as we exited the ground and entered the atmosphere.

Then, the walls turned white for perhaps only a second, as we passed through a layer of cloud cover, and then they returned to the brightness of the clear sky. I looked down at the floor and watched Dulce fall away from us. The Archuletta Mesa and surrounding mountains soon appeared flat from the perspective of their distance below us. It was clear that we were climbing away from the Earth and escaping its gravitational hold on our vessel. The pilot then flipped the tureen on its side and shot in an easterly direction across the country, out over the Atlantic and, near the coast of Africa, launched us into space. Total time elapsed was about fifteen minutes.

"Why did he do that, Danny?" Mona whispered.

"Don't they call that 'sling-shotting'? I think our astronauts did that when they left the moon to return to Earth back in the 'sixties. The pilot uses the planet's gravity to whip up speed." I really didn't have a clue what they were doing, but Mona was looking for an answer, and I didn't want to disappoint her.

"Maybe the moon is on the other side of the Earth right now, and they had to get a visual on it," she replied.

Mona always seemed to have a better answer than I did. Well, most of the time, anyway. She was right. It was mid-morning in Dulce, and the moon was definitely on the other side of Mother Earth.

∽∾∽

The trip to the moon took less than three hours, which meant that we were traveling about 200,000 miles per hour. I was surprised that it took us that long, given that Waam shot by the moon in less than half an hour. But we weren't riding in a military vehicle, and we weren't going into deep space. If I could make an analogy, we could have taken a speed boat, but we were riding in a tourist-class tureen that was operating more like an amusement park shuttle.

As we approached the moon, we entered into the shadows on the dark side. It was busy on this side. I saw several vehicles of odd shapes hovering motionless above the surface. One was triangular in shape, another was a long cylinder, like a cigar. Small balls of light were entering and exiting the ends of the cylindrical vehicle. Signals from my physical motion detector, my stomach, let me know that we were slowing down. As we did, we were joined by two smaller tureens, which flew on either side of us as we descended toward the surface. Without warning, they broke away, flying upward rapidly. A moment afterward, the walls of the shuttle went black. We had entered an underground tunnel or facility of some type. However, within a moment, the walls grew light again. We were actually inside the moon! Thousands of spotlights connected to its structural beams illuminated the interior.

At the center was a tower which extended from its uppermost to its lowermost poles. It reminded me a bit of a golf tee with two heads. Only this golf tee was hundreds of miles long and probably ten miles in diameter. It was dotted with lights and doors of all sorts and sizes, some of which had to be military while others were for maintenance functions. It was incredible.

"Are you looking at this?" Mona whispered.

"I'm speechless."

"That's a first!"

"This is amazing. It's kind of like that movie with Darth Vader."

"*Star Wars*?"

"Yeah."

Our shuttle approached the upper quadrant of the tower, very near the top on the interior of the moon. *No wonder they call it "the hollow moon,"* I thought. This had to be where Mona's baby was being kept. I took her hand. She squeezed mine and shook it. I could sense the excitement that was oozing from every pore in her body. I hoped that she wasn't going to be disappointed when she found out that her baby was a lizard with dark hair and three claw-like fingers. Anticipation of good things can crush you when they wind up being not so good.

Our pilot guided the tureen into a shelf-like landing zone, where the ceiling was only two hundred feet high. The tower must have had hundreds of similar landing zones, and I wondered how many lizards and NWO troops could be occupying this place in space. Possibly tens of thousands. Well, whatever the number, it was more than we would want to deal with if they decided to invade the Earth at seven-forty-eight a.m. on a Sunday.

The co-pilot opened the ramp, and the passengers beside us stood up to disembark. Mona and I held back to be last getting off. This way we could watch what the others were doing and not stick out like the newcomers that we were.

Although there were fewer than sixteen of us total, we were forced to go through a questioning line, much like going through customs. The signs behind the uniformed personnel who questioned us said it all, and again, in several languages: no firearms permitted—with the exception of those worn by Draconian soldiers—no drugs, no alcohol, no anti-NWO literature. I guess they saw us coming. As we walked through some sort of an X-ray device, Mona and I were pulled aside abruptly and frisked. They removed our pieces, extra clips, and identification papers. Then they separated us and moved us into interrogation rooms.

"Why did you bring a firearm to the lunar artifact?" I was asked by a middle-aged female with a German accent.

She was wearing an NWO uniform, so I countered, "I am the interrogator. Why am I being detained from my mission? Astana will not be pleased."

"You know that no firearms are permitted here!"

"Except for those of our Draconian friends," I reminded her. "I am less than comfortable putting my life on the line for His Excellency, when any subversive reptilian could terminate me in less than a second for no other reason than he's having a bad day."

"Who is the woman with whom you are traveling?"

"She is my superior officer. Her last name is Casola."

"How long have you known her?"

The hairs on the back of my neck stood up in anxiety. Maybe the NWO suspected something about Mona. Remembering my promise to her about the mission, I lied. "I was assigned to her at the facility on the red planet earlier this week. I don't necessarily like working with females, present company excluded. My superiors gave me no other choice than to report to Interrogator Casola while on this mission."

"And what is your mission?"

"It is classified as above above-top-secret, and if we fail this mission, His Excellency will be very displeased, as will Queen Igua,"

"We have reviewed your papers. You may go. However, we must detain your superior officer a little longer. We have more questions for Interrogator Casola."

"Watch out for yourself. She can be bitchy, and she has friends in high places in Astana."

"Thank you for the warning, Interrogator Arreaux." She returned my identification papers.

"What about my piece?" I asked.

"No firearms are permitted here, not even for interrogators."

"Will it be returned upon my departure?"

"No. Headquarters will have to issue you a new one when you return to Astana."

I was escorted back into the customs area by an

NWO guard. "When you exit those doors, you must report to the concierge for quartering assignment. Follow the yellow arrows on the wall. If you get lost, ask anyone with a purple name tag for assistance."

I opened the door and walked down the corridor. It was good that I had to follow a yellow line like some kindergarten kid, because my mind was working overtime with concern for Mona. Why was she being detained longer? What had she done that caused her to be suspected? Would they hurt her? How could I negotiate her release? How could I rescue her?

Chapter 12

Commissar Nargas was preparing for his afternoon snack of a live kangaroo rat when he was interrupted by a messenger from the lunar artifact security force. "Can't it wait?" he hissed, dangling the rat by its tail.

The security officer was visibly nervous. Nargas had a reputation for being unpredictable when he received trivial messages, especially if he was being interrupted from something he would rather be doing. "Sir, Intake Processing has identified a possible spy."

Nargas threw the rat back into its cage and slammed the cover down. The rat jumped twice against the top of the cage but was unable to escape, so it quickly buried itself in the wood chips that covered the cage floor.

"Where is this supposed spy?"

"Sir, she is being held in an interrogation room in Intake Processing."

"A female? That is unusual. Why don't you just squeeze the truth out of her and then terminate her?"

"Sir, the processing inquisitor asked me to invite you

to the interrogation room. He thinks that you may have some interest in this female."

"And why would that be?"

"She spoke of you by name in a derogatory manner."

"What did she say?"

"Sir, I would rather you spoke with the inquisitor about that."

Nargas grabbed by security officer by the throat with his left hand and squeezed. "What did she say?"

Gasping, the young officer said, "Fuck that bastard Nargas!"

The commissar's eyes gleamed, and he released the young man from his grip. "That is better, son. Never withhold information from your superiors."

"Yes, sir!" the young officer said, rubbing his throat.

"Take me to this supposed spy."

ℰↄℰↄ

When the door to the interrogation room opened again, Mona didn't even look up to see who was coming inside to ply her with more questions. Then a familiar hiss sent a shudder through her body.

"You haven't captured a spy, Inquisitor," Nargas said, sniffing at Mona's neck with his protruding, scaly nostrils. "You've brought me the female whose container carried my seed until we relocated it to a growth chamber. Has she been a handful?"

"She has a mouth like a human male, Commissar."

"Yes, her word selection can be colorful. However, her container did its job extraordinarily well, and I am most pleased with the product."

Nargas ran his claws through Mona's hair then took her chin and turned her head until her eyes met his. '*You have changed your hair color, missy,*' he hissed into her mind.

"I heard that blondes have more fun," Mona replied.

'*Did they hurt you?*'

"Only when they took away my gun. It had a bullet in it with your name on it."

'*They think that you are a spy. Are you a spy?*'

"I came here to see my baby, you bastard! You had no right to take it away without my permission, but you did. I saw you during the procedure. You told me that I was a good girl."

'*You remember?*'

"Yeah, and if I could have clawed your eyes out then, I would have. I was angry that you put that monster inside me but even angrier that you didn't give me the opportunity to get rid of it myself. You violated me twice. You took my baby, you son of a bitch, and you didn't even ask!"

Nargas turned to the inquisitor. "She continues to have the high spirit of a survivor. I would order you to terminate her, but I have been told by the nursery staff that the hybrid offspring needs a mother's touch. So, I will see if she is willing to assist with the further development of her own child."

"I understand, Commissar. We will release her to your custody."

Nargas returned his gaze to Mona's eyes. '*That which you sought to destroy is not a monster. She and those like her are the future of your planet. They will accelerate the evolution of humankind by ten thousand years in a single generation.*'

"So it's a girl?" Mona asked.

'*Yes, you have a female offspring.*'

"Have you named her?"

'*She has an identification number.*'

"She needs a name, you asshole. She needs a name that gives identity and meaning to her existence."

'Would you like to meet her?'

Mona didn't blink an eye before she said, "I came here to see her, didn't I?"

'We will discuss how you came here at a later moment, missy, but for now, we will go see your female offspring.'

The inquisitor unlocked Mona's wrists from shackles on the table where she was seated. When Mona rose, he turned her toward him and put handcuffs on her wrists. Then he put a collar around her neck, attached a cable to it, and handed the cable to the commissar.

'When I last saw you at the Livermore facility, you wore such a collar, Nargas said into Mona's eyes. *I am sorry to return you to this state of confinement, but I must ensure the safety of our offspring.'*

"The last time I wore this collar, you left me to die in that arena like a throwaway toy. You didn't give a rat's ass about my life then, and you don't give a rat's ass about it now. So why are you taking me to see this child?"

'Our hybrids appear to have a difficult time adjusting to human culture, especially those who have been raised in our culture. Many take their own lives after a few days among humans. Our psychologists theorize that they may need a human mother's touch from the moment of birth, that enculturation begins at that time. If you will agree to raise our offspring as you would a human, you will be permitted to live.'

"If she looks like you, you may as well kill me now."

The commissar gave Mona a look of distain and then gave a light tug on her leash. *It's time to go see little lizardella,* Mona thought.

Nargas led Mona down several corridors and then into an elevator, which quickly climbed ten floors before coming to a stop. Mona couldn't decipher the four symbols which designated the floor number. When the elevator doors opened, Nargas led her into in a large room which contained dozens of rows of growth tubes. Through their clear glass exteriors, she could see hundreds of babies at various stages of growth, but none more than seven or eight months in development in her estimation. Some were odd in color, exhibiting bluish or yellowish tones, while others were clearly dark brown and others white.

They walked along a wide pathway between the growth tubes until they came to a set of double doors. The commissar pulled on Mona's leash, stopping her forward progress. A reptilian pushed a gurney past her and through the doors. On it laid a small child, tubes connecting it to a machine of some sort.

The commissar looked into Mona's eyes and told her, '*That one has just emerged from the growth chamber and will soon join ours in the nursery.*'

Mona nodded. Anger was beginning to leave her body. In its place was a sense of awe at the magnitude of the hybridization project and the technology that was brought into play to enable it to occur.

The commissar led Mona into the nursery, where the air was hot and moist, reminding her somewhat of the air in the indoor swimming pool area at her Y back in DC. At least four nurses were visible, moving in and among dozens of small rectangular boxes that held hybrid babies. The babies were unclothed and rested on perforated hard plastic.

Mona tugged on the commissar's arm. When he turned to look at her, she asked, "Why aren't these babies wrapped in blankets? Why aren't they lying on soft cloths or mattresses?"

The commissar smiled at the change in Mona's attitude. *'Our experts control the babies' body temperatures by managing external heat and humidity. The perforations on the floor of each unit permit bodily fluids and excretions to move to a centralized waste containment chamber.'*

"Your experts have it all wrong. Human babies need a close-fitting blanket, which gives them both warmth and a sense of security. It holds them, as a mother would. And their bodily wastes should be wiped from them by human hands. Feeling someone's touch lets them know that they're not alone and that they're being cared for. No wonder that your hybrids kill themselves when they're older. You've set the stage to create lonely, insecure adults."

'I will convey your concerns and advice to the medical staff.'

Nargas tugged lightly on the leash again, and Mona followed him to a unit with a star taped to its side. A tall nurse rushed to his side and said something to the Commissar in the guttural and hissing language of Reptilians. Nargas then turned to Mona and told her, *'Nurse Tongu assures me that our offspring is receiving the best of care. Her every need is being attended to.'*

"Is this her?"

'Yes, this is the baby that you came a long way to see.'

Mona stepped closer to the unit and looked in. Her baby looked familiar, with facial features reminiscent of Mona's own baby pictures that hung in the hallway at her parents' home. *Her clear skin and dark hair are definitely Italiano,* Mona thought. Resting on her side with her forefinger in her mouth, she was making gentle sucking sounds. A rush of love gushed from Mona's heart and engulfed her body. "She's beautiful."

The commissar gently touched Mona's chin. When Mona turned to look at him, Nargas looked deep within her and sensed her emotions. '*You may touch her if you wish,*' he said.

Using the back of her finger, Mona lightly brushed the baby's cheek. The baby reached with her left hand and grasped Mona's finger. Mother and daughter had connected, and Mona's face now wore a loving smile.

Mona did not notice when Nargas signaled to the nurse, who quickly came to his side. He said something unintelligible and the nurse departed.

"Her skin isn't quite the same as mine. It actually seems cooler," Mona said. "How much does she weigh?"

Nargas signaled to another nurse, who came to his side. He asked her something, and the nurse responded. He turned to Mona and said, '*According to our doctors, her body density is slightly less than that of a human. She is now at the four-month stage of post-natal growth. A human might weigh as much as eighteen pounds by this stage, but your female weighs ten. She eats well and eliminates regularly. Her heartbeat and respiration are normal.*'

"How can she be four months old? If I were still carrying her, she would not yet have been born."

'*Growth in the chambers is accelerated, and that acceleration continues for several years after leaving the chamber. She should reach full physical maturity at age ten and should be ready for reproduction and adult occupational assignment at age twelve.*'

"That is so abnormal for a human."

'*I remind you that she is not fully human. She is a hybrid, approximately eighty percent human. Her cooler body temperature, rapid maturation, and superior intelli-*

*gence and mental functioning are reflective of the Reptil-
ian components of her DNA.'*

The inquisitor entered the nursery. "Commissar Nargas, you sent for me?"

"Yes. I would like you to remove the handcuffs from
my prisoner."

"But that is highly irregular—"

"Remove them!" Nargas spat at the inquisitor.

The inquisitor touched the six buttons on the side of
Mona's handcuffs in an exact sequence, and the cuffs
opened. Mona rubbed her wrists.

"Thank you," she said to Nargas. "How about this
collar?"

'Not yet, missy,' he hissed.

"May I hold her?" Mona asked, looking again at her
baby.

Nargas sent the nurse away again. When she returned, she brought with her another reptilian. Nargas
again spoke in reptilian tones to the new arrival. They
conversed for a few moments, and then the commissar
turned to Mona and said, *'Security guards will join us in
a few minutes. When they are here, you may slowly and
carefully pick her up and hold her. Any effort to harm this
hybrid will cause your immediate termination.'*

Mona nodded.

*'This is Doctor Gila. You would call his function a
psychologist. He will observe your interactions with our
offspring and look for measureable improvements in the
neophyte's enculturation. He is here to learn from you.'*

Mona looked at Dr. Gila with curiosity. He was taller
than the commissar but much leaner. His scales moved
from dark brown around his back to medium purple as
they approached his face. His snout and throat were light
tan. His eyes were deep orange, except for the black vertical slits common to some snakes. He wore a lab coat

and a belt with an array of small electrical devices, each with one or more blinking lights, meaning either that the device was simply on or that it was monitoring some sort of activity. She wanted to learn more but felt it best to wait until she and the doctor had achieved a basic working relationship.

Three reptilian soldiers arrived, each in full uniform. Mona noted the plates on their chests, with the telltale buttons that could send a burst of liquid light from their headgear if they were provoked. They stared at her, and she stared back. "Don't piss me off, and we'll all get along," she said to them.

They appeared surprised that a human female would be so bold with them. The commissar spoke to them in reptilian, and then he turned to Mona. *'They have been ordered not to touch you or to provoke you but to ensure the safety of the hybrid. If it appears that you intend to harm the hybrid, they will stop you.'*

"And how will these assholes know if I am harming my baby or caring for it the way a human should?"

'You should inform Dr. Gila about your intentions as you move around the hybrid, telling him both the action and the rationale behind it. He wants to understand why you do certain things with which he is unfamiliar. Your instruction may improve future conditions for all hybrids under our care. We want them to grow up able to function comfortably in the human culture.'

"Does he understand that there are many human cultures and that not each culture shares the same practices?

'You will have to instruct him.'

"Jeezus H. Christ! How do you teach a lizard to act like a human? This may be an impossible task!"

Nargas gave Mona a corrective look. He pointed one claw at her and said, *'You have it wrong, missy. The hybrid is our child, and you are its mother. Teach our child to assimilate into your own culture the way a mother would. Dr. Gila will do the rest.'*

Mona turned to Dr. Gila and said, "I am going to pick the baby up. I will slide my left hand under her head to support it until her neck grows strong enough to support it on its own. I will slide my right hand under her back to support it, as well. Any questions?"

Dr. Gila grunted, and Mona heard a voice within her say, *'None at the moment.'*

As she moved toward her baby, the three reptilian guards tensed. Dr. Gila waved them off. Mona smiled at the doctor, as if to say "thank you." Then she slowly slid her hands under her baby girl and lifted the child to her breast. Her daughter's skin had a strange, but pleasing scent. The warmth of her daughter's body was comforting. She began to sway back and forth and hum. But she caught herself and stopped.

The commissar positioned himself in front of her. *'Go ahead, missy. Go ahead and sing to our offspring. The doctor has never seen that. He will be intrigued.'*

Mona changed the baby's position, moving her slowly in her arms so she could look into her daughter's eyes. The three reptilian guards stepped forward quickly, surprising Mona. She looked at Dr. Gila and apologized. "I forgot that I had to tell you what I am doing. I wanted to look into my baby's eyes and sing to her. That's why I moved her. In this position, we can both look at each other and connect our souls."

Dr. Gila waved the guards off again. Commissar Nargas nodded at the soldiers. Their demeanor switched back into a more passive stance.

Mona stared at her daughter. Her skin was smooth but of a more porous texture than that of a pure human. She was thankful that her baby did not have scales. Her eyes, though, were striking. They were just a little larger than a human's, with coal black irises, and sky blue where the whites should have been. Her daughter blinked once, and then again, and then a second set of eyelids blinked from the outside toward her nose and back.

Mona looked at Dr. Gila in surprise. "What was that?" she asked.

'*Many hybrids have a second set of eyelids. They are reptilian in nature and offer a second layer of protection from harsh solar radiation, water, and dust. You will soon get used to them, and ultimately you will wish that your species had them, which it eventually will.*'

"I am now going to touch my baby's nose and chin with my finger. Then I will sing. Is that okay?"

Dr. Gila nodded and said something in reptilian into a small recording device.

Mona began swaying and humming a tune that she remembered from her childhood. It was an old Italian song that her mother had taught her. The words came back to her, and she began to sing:

> "'Cheecha, cheecha la dee, dee la
> Quanto bella a mama
> Quanto brute u papa
> Cheecha, cheecha la dee, dee la'"

"I'm going to kiss my baby," Mona said.

Commissar Nargas moved in front of Mona again. '*I remember telling you that it is contrary to human nature for mothers to harm their babies. Instead, they nurture them. Do you remember?*'

Mona continued humming her tune and nodded at the Commissar. She smiled.

'*You will also recall that you have been warned that any attempt to harm our hybrid will result in your imme-*

diate termination. Any attempt to escape will end in the same result.'

Mona continued humming and nodded.

'Then you agree to stay on the lunar artifact and raise our offspring.'

Mona continued humming and nodded one last time.

'Excellent!' the commissar hissed. He turned to the doctor and said something in reptilian. Then he spoke briefly with the three reptilian soldiers.

'I must leave, missy. You take good care of our hybrid issue.'

"She will be fine," Mona replied.

The commissar turned and walked out of the nursery. As he did, Mona began singing again. As the words tripped off of her tongue, she thought of the translation of the working class Italian lyrics: *How beautiful your mother is...How ugly your father is...Cheecha, cheecha la dee, dee la!*

Chapter 13

Yes, your Imminence, Queen Igua will be informed of your concerns. Thank you for bringing this issue to my attention, and please assure the Galactic Command that the Draconian Sector will continue to comply with all treaties. Yes, I will ensure that such hostilities cease immediately."

When the transmission ended, Commissar Nargas roared and threw a chair at the monitor, shattering its screen and sending sparks in all directions. "Someday the Galactic Command will cower at the feet of Draconian children! Damn the Command!"

The commissar burst through the door of his private office and into the space occupied by his executive officers. "I want all executive officers here in ten clicks. Anyone not present will answer directly to me!" Nargas then returned to his private office.

Every officer in the room picked up a communication device and contacted those on his team to report to the executive offices immediately. Within a few moments, officers began pouring into the office area, and all were present before eight clicks had elapsed.

When all were assembled, Nargas strode from his of-fice, clearly upset and under stress from an unknown source. "Where is Lieutenant Maug?" he demanded, nos-trils flaring.

A young reptilian stepped forward. "Here, sir."

"How long has the monitor in my office been dam-aged, Maug?"

"Sir, I was not aware…"

Nargas touched his breastplate and sliced Maug in half with a bolt of liquid light. Blood splattered onto those nearest to the body.

"Who is next in line to replace Maug?"

"I am, sir," replied another young reptilian.

"My monitor will be in working order by morning!"

"At your command, sir!"

"Resume your place."

The commissar stared intently at those in the room. "I was the recipient this afternoon of an official inquiry by the Galactic Command due to reports that Draconian forces on the red planet have been harassing peaceful Ummite shuttles and cargo vessels. I insisted that the re-ports are unfounded. Tell me that the reports are false!"

"Sir," replied a mid-career officer, "such exercises are excellent training for our junior officers who have not yet experienced combat. They are harmless!"

Nargas cut him down with a bolt of liquid light. "I will have no combat training exercises going on without my prior knowledge. Is that understood?"

The officers in the room stood silent.

"Does anyone dispute my orders or question my command?"

Silence ensued.

"I am now required to travel to the red planet to en-sure that these hostilities cease, at least for now. I will be forced to offer my humblest apologies to the Ummites for the stupid actions of my junior officers. They will desire some form of reparation. Do I have suggestions of some token that I might offer?"

The officers remained in silence for fear of invoking the Commissar's anger.

"I want the heads of the two whom I just dispatched. They will suffice as evidence of my sincerity. Box them and have them loaded onto my tureen prior to my departure at twenty-two-hundred hours."

Chapter 14

I put both of my palms on the countertop and leaned forward. I felt a slight electrical tingling in my fingers. *There's a short in their wiring*, I thought. "Tell him that Interrogator Arreaux has traveled from Astana to see him on an urgent matter."

"Yes, sir!" snapped a young enlisted soldier. He left the stainless steel counter and disappeared down a narrow hallway into the recesses where the unit commander's office was located.

I had made my way to the commander's office by winding through the maze of corridors and elevators that were everywhere in the central tower. And, I was going to need a tour guide or a GPS in order to find my way back to the tureen docking station, especially since I was not schooled in the symbols or the Reptilian language on the directional signs.

This was a total immersion experience into the NWO sector of Lizard Land, and I wished that Waam had given me a quick seminar on signage. I made a mental note to tell him to do that for the next sucker he sends on a mission into uncharted space.

When the enlisted man reappeared, he escorted me to the commander's office, a space about the size of small camping trailer which was poorly decorated with six or seven stacks of papers that should have been stored in filing cabinets. "Sir, this is Interrogator Arreaux."

The commander saluted, but I waved it off. "No formalities, please, Commander. The name is Arreaux."

"Coffee, Interrogator?"

"Black, unless it is ugly dark."

The commander laughed. "Sergeant, would you please get Interrogator Arreaux a cup of our finest mud."

"Sir, yes, sir!" The enlisted man disappeared down the hallway.

I got up and closed the door.

"This looks serious," the commander said.

"Astana received word from undisclosed but credible sources identified by Project Stellar Wind that your unit has been infiltrated by one or perhaps two subversives who intend to disrupt our plans, perhaps even assassinate His Excellency."

"Impossible! I run a tight ship here."

"This is no reflection on you. Headquarters believes that the subversives may be co-conspirators with those who infiltrated Livermore and abducted His Excellency."

"Damn! What details can you give me?"

"Few. That's why I am here. They may be male or female. At least one may have joined your unit in the past sixty days. The other may have been a sleeper, planted here up to a year ago and waiting for instructions to carry out the assassination."

"Bastards!"

"Yes, and cowards, as well! I'll need a list of all soldiers who have joined the unit in the past sixty days."

"I can have that for you by morning."

"My purpose for being here must be totally confidential. If word gets out that suspected subversives are in this unit, we'll never be able to find them."

"I fully understand. How can I help you?"

"You should assign me to bunk with the members of the guard."

"But you are an officer. That would be improper protocol."

"Let the word get out that I am here to investigate your unit as the first step in a promotional process. You must suspect some in your command of having loose lips. Tell your gossip tree that you are being considered for promotion to a higher command, and that the purpose of my mission is to inspect unit processes from the non-com perspective. That should do the trick."

"Intriguing. It's disappointing that I am not really being considered for promotion."

"Who said that you aren't? You know how Central Command does its business: you never know what my real objective might be. In fact, considering you for promotion might be my real agenda."

There was a knock on the door. "Come in, Sergeant," the commander said.

"Here is your coffee, Interrogator. I hope you'll find it satisfactory."

"Thank you, sergeant," I replied.

"Sergeant, Interrogator Arreaux is here on an investigative mission as part of my annual performance review. He has asked to bunk with the troops. I recognize that some may find this to be out of protocol, but Astana has made this request. Can you make it happen?"

"Yes, sir. There are several empty bunks in Pod Four."

"Good. When the interrogator has finished his coffee, will you see that he gets settled and oriented?"

"Yes, sir. I'll see to it now." The sergeant saluted and left the office.

I took a slug of coffee. "Commander, this is the best joe I've had in several weeks. It sure beats the crap on Mars."

"You were on Mars?"

"Yeah. I negotiated the return of a Nazi bell and three doped greys for the body of a dead Ummite. They gave me the farm for a cold piece of meat."

"Impressive. You'll have to tell me how you managed that."

"I can't really do that. I probably shouldn't have told you as much as I already have."

"I haven't been to Mars, yet. Our facility there is very small."

I realized that I had painted myself into a corner. I hadn't been to the NWO facility on Mars, either. Maybe the NWO didn't have a Martian facility, and he was testing me. Maybe he meant the Draconian facility. I wasn't sure. "The negotiations were held in a tureen at the entrance to the Ummite facility. We were protected by two Draconian tureens which hovered nearby. I didn't go inside. The Ummites brought coffee and some kind of strange meat sandwiches to the tureen. That shit was awful."

The commander laughed, but I wasn't sure if he was really laughing or just pretending. If Mona had been there, she would have had him sized up in less than thirty seconds.

"So where's my tour guide?" I asked.

"He's calling ahead to be sure your bunk is made up." The commander looked up. "Oh, here he is now!"

"Are you ready to inspect Pod Four, sir?" the sergeant asked.

"If you'll excuse me, Commander, I'll be about my business. I'll keep you apprised."

"Just watch your back, Arreaux. Interrogators tend to heighten everyone's anxiety."

Chapter 15

Sergeant Ramey told me his name as he led me down to Pod Four. The excursion involved a ride on a moving walkway and a two floor climb in an elevator to level 346 in what he called the "habitation zone," an area that he later described as "a vertical city in the sky."

"This is my first visit to the lunar artifact," I told him.

"You'll find that it has everything that you might need," he replied, "all the conveniences of any city. We have parks and recreational areas, educational facilities, barber shops, delicatessens, a library, hospitals, entertainment venues, and even a small brig."

"What you describe sounds like an entire block of New York City."

"Well, I think that the concept of the skyscraper was borrowed by George Fuller, who visited this tower before the turn of the nineteenth century."

"George Fuller? Should I know his name?"

"Probably not. He's credited with being the developer of what we know as the modern skyscraper. Back in his day, there were tall buildings, but none as tall as his and none which contained all of the modern conveniences. If you lived in one of his buildings, you never had to leave it because everything you would ever need was right there."

"And you think he came to the lunar artifact in the early 1900s?"

"Sure do. It's inscribed on a plaque that's hanging on the wall in our mess. You know, a hall of heroes sort of thing."

"How would he have gotten here?"

"Draconians or Reticulans."

"Yeah, I guess that makes sense. They've been interacting with us humans for thousands of years."

Sergeant Ramey pushed open the door to Pod Four, and we walked in. Three non-coms popped to attention.

"At ease, gentlemen," I said. "While I'm bunking here, all military protocol is suspended inside this pod. My name is Dan, but outside of this room it's Interrogator Arreaux."

They seemed to like what I had to say. Two came forward and introduced themselves, Spivey and Merkel.

"There's an empty bunk next to mine," Spivey told me. "It's in the best part of the pod because it's away from the door and the pipes."

"Pipes?"

"Yeah, the drain pipes. Sometimes the noise of liquids draining down the pipes can wake you up at night."

"And sometimes they clang," added Merkel.

"Well, show me the bunk. You've already sold me on its location."

Ramey took his leave of us and returned to the commander's office, so Spivey and Merkel led me to the far left corner of the rectangular room. I estimated that it held about twenty beds total, which made it about half the size of a military barracks.

On the way, we passed by the latrine and showers, and I figured that I could make good use of both of them later. Well, maybe sooner.

"We made this bunk up, thinking that you'd prefer this location," Spivey said.

"You didn't short sheet it, did you?" I asked.

Merkel laughed. "No, but he done thought about it!"

Spivey hit him in the shoulder with the back of his hand. I figured these guys were going to be okay as bunk mates.

"Where's your bunk?" I asked Merkel.

"Just on the other side of Spivey. If you sleep in this bunk, we'll be the two roses with the thorn in the middle."

"Then it's settled," I said. I plopped my small bag on the foot of my bunk and excused myself to go to the latrine.

ဢၣဢ

When I finished my business, I returned to my bunk. Merkel was gone, and Spivey was sitting on his bunk, reading a letter.

"Girlfriend?" I asked.

"Naw, you know we wouldn't be assigned here if we had any family. This is a letter from a recruit who is in basic training in Astana. They've started this program where we're supposed to mentor the new recruits. We sort of become their family, like their big brother."

Spivey's remark reminded me of a training program that I once took on why kids join gangs. There are lots of reasons, but high on the list of reasons is being part of a loving family, where people watch out for you and take care of you.

"So what does your little brother have to say?" I asked.

"Little sister," Spivey replied. "She's from Switzerland, but her English is pretty good."

"Does she know that you're on the lunar artifact?"

"Yeah, I told her that in my last letter. She don't believe that I'm actually here. She thinks I'm pulling her leg."

"Maybe you should send her a piece of Swiss cheese to prove that you're here," I said with a smile.

"That would be funny, wouldn't it? I like the way you think, sir!"

"Call me Dan, Spivey."

"Yes, sir, but it'll be hard for me to do that."

"Just pretend that I'm your big brother, except when we meet outside of this pod. You know the drill."

"Thanks, Dan. Can I tell her about you, Dan? That my big brother is an interrogator?"

"Sure. You can tell her that I came here after completing a mission on Mars. I'm here with you, looking for a couple of renegades who are trying to disrupt the plans of the NWO."

"Is that really true?"

"Yeah, it's true. I may need your help to figure out who they are. One has been here for a long time, but the other has joined this force in the last sixty days. How long have you been here, Spivey?"

"This is the end of my fourth month."

"Then you aren't one of the renegades, are you?"

"If I was, I wouldn't tell you. But I ain't no renegade."

"I know that. Your commander wouldn't have bunked me here if he thought you were one of the renegades. Besides, you don't fit neatly into their profile or the timeline I've been given for their arrival."

Spivey folded the letter and put it under the pillow on his bunk.

I changed the subject, "So tell me, Spivey, this is my first visit to the lunar artifact. We're on floor three-forty-six, right?" How many floors are there above this one?"

"Exactly one hundred fifty-four. There are one thousand floors, five hundred on each side of the core." He thought for a second and then added, "Didn't they put you through the normal seminar before they let you come here?"

"No," I said truthfully. "I did the Mars orientation, and then I was sent there to recover a Nazi bell. When I returned with it, I was briefed about the two dissident renegades. Because of the emergency nature of this mission, they put me on the next shuttle to the lunar artifact. I didn't even have time to shower before the shuttle departed."

"Well, Dan, do you want the long version or the short version?"

"Have they figured out who built it? How's it constructed and what was it made from?"

"No, they've never figured out who built it. They think it drifted into our galaxy from a neighboring one, and that it had been drifting for a million Earth years before Man found it on the outer edges of our galaxy. The original technology wasn't familiar to the scientists who tried to back engineer things to find out how it worked. Eventually, they retrofitted it with fiberoptics and pneumatics, but there are still mechanisms working on this thing that ain't nobody knows for sure how they work."

"Can you give me some examples?" I asked.

"Yeah, the central core provides both the energy and the lunar gravity, but nobody knows exactly how both can come from a single source. If you're standing on this side of the core, the people on the other side of the core are upside down from you, but they think that you're upside down."

"That's just like being on Earth," I replied. "A guy on the North Pole and a guy on the South Pole would both be standing erect, but each one would think that the other is upside down."

"Yeah, but look at the size comparisons. The core of the moon is considerably smaller than the Earth. It has something to do with its mass. The core is basically a ball that's ten miles in diameter, but its mass is only a little less than the Earth's. According to science textbooks back on Earth, we should be a whole bunch lighter here on the artifact, but we're actually three percent heavier on the lunar core than we are on Earth."

"I thought our astronauts were lighter topside. They looked that way on the films they shot"

"Yeah, they tried to make it look that way because our scientists didn't want to rewrite the textbooks. I think NASA used slow motion technology to make it appear like the astronauts were floating for a moment whenever they jumped."

"Maybe…"

"And the core produces limitless power. It is actually a solar energy storage unit, collecting both solar light energy and cosmic energy produced by millions of stars from everywhere in space, and it stores that energy somewhere inside. No matter how much we use for all the electrical needs inside, the storage unit is always full and it ain't never depleted, not even one percent!"

"That's really incredible! And nobody has replicated it on a smaller scale for use on Earth?"

"They still can't figure out what kind of alloy it is made from. It's a combination of metals, including aluminum and copper and zinc, but there are at least three metals that don't exist in our galaxy, and they hold the key properties that make it all happen."

Men started coming back into the pod—a few singletons and then spurts of two or three at a time. Merkel reappeared among them. "We'd better hurry up and get ready," he said.

"God, I almost forgot," Spivey replied, jumping to his feet. "How long until the assembly?"

"About fifteen minutes."

"What's the rush?" I asked.

"His Excellency is addressing the guard this afternoon!" Spivey answered.

"Really? I wasn't aware that he was here."

"Yes. And this is his first public appearance since his migration."

"I thought he might still be in hiding after being abducted by those renegades at Livermore," I said.

"Commissar Nargas and the Draconians rescued him," Merkel said.

"Yeah, I am aware that they took out those Ummite rebels like a thing of beauty. They exterminated everyone on board and sent the tureen into the sun."

"If you see an Ummite, don't trust him. Dan," Spivey said, tucking in his shirt. "You'll notice that there ain't no Ummites here among us in the lunar artifact. Nobody trusts them anymore."

"There's good cause," Merkel added. "That disaster at Livermore almost cost His Excellency his life, not to mention the dozens of dignitaries who couldn't get out in time and were killed in the explosion."

"It'll be interesting to see His Excellency," I said. "The last time I saw him, he was an old woman."

"They say he's in a young man's container now, and that he has a full life ahead of him before he has to be migrated again," Merkel said.

"This will definitely be interesting," I said. "Can I march in with you guys?"

"No, they won't permit that. I think you'll have to see the commander for permission to observe, because it's for NWO guard members only. We're supposed to receive special orders from His Excellency about the new timetable and our responsibility during the event."

I assumed that Merkel was referring to the release of the pandemic, but I didn't say anything about it, just in case there were new plans. But no matter what it was, it had to be stopped, and this time I was alone.

Chapter 16

Sergeant Ramey looked up when I entered the outer office. "Interrogator Arreaux, we didn't expect to see again you so soon. Are your accommodations satisfactory?"

"I'm glad that you bunked me in Pod Four. The men I've met thus far are highly professional and appear to be dedicated to our cause."

"How can I help you, then?"

"I assume that the commander briefed you on my mission?"

"Yes, sir. He shares most vital information with me."

"As he should," I affirmed. "My purpose in coming to see the commander is related to my mission. I wasn't aware that His Excellency would be here today to address the guard. I'm concerned that the two dissidents could strike during his address. If possible, I would like to observe the meeting, specifically to see if I can identify any attendees whose behaviors might give away their true feelings."

"I'll have to check with the commander. This request is coming very late. His Excellency is supposed to begin speaking in five minutes, and the commander is already on the dais."

"Please do what you can. If anything happens to His Excellency, I'll have failed in my mission, and both your commander and I will probably be terminated."

The commander's voice interrupted Sergeant Ramey just as he was about to speak. "Ramey, please escort the interrogator to my box on the second level of the amphitheater."

"Yes, sir," Ramsey replied, looking at me with a 'we've-been-caught' expression.

He knew that I now knew that the commander eavesdropped on discussions that occurred in the office when he was out. It was shades of Richard Nixon, and I smiled at the thought of it.

"Follow me, sir," Ramey said.

We left the office and found an elevator about fifty yards down the corridor. Ramey pushed the button, and we climbed three floors When we exited the elevator, we were in a wide hallway with floor-to-ceiling glass windows which overlooked what must have been the amphitheater because its ceiling was bowed glass, somewhat like a greenhouse or sunroom, only it was large enough to hold maybe ten thousand people. It would have been a great place for Hank Williams Junior or Jefferson Starship to hold a concert, depending upon your taste in music. I stood for a moment, looking down at the crowd of NWO guardsmen who had gathered on the floor below to hear Hitler. "Beautiful facility," I told Ramey.

"Yes, sir, it is. Your observation deck is through that door. I think we shouldn't linger."

I nodded and followed him to a secure door that stood perpendicular to the atrium windows. Ramey positioned his eye on a clear glass plate, and the door popped open. We then walked down a narrow corridor past several observation rooms emblazoned with alien symbols before entering one that was identified with the term *NWO Officials*. "Whose boxes are those?" I asked, pointing to the small observation rooms that we had passed.

"They're reserved for visiting dignitaries from the Galactic Federation. Sometimes Queen Igua uses one. Most often the commissar."

"Nargas?" I asked. "I thought he might be on the dais today."

"He's away at the moment, but unfortunately he's due back sometimes soon."

"I take it that you don't care for him either."

"He's a nasty, unpredictable bastard. I don't understand why he's still in power, except that everyone is afraid of him."

"I've seen him cut a man in half without blinking an eye," I told him.

"I think we all have." Ramey pointed toward the windows and changed the subject. "His Excellency will be speaking in a few moments. You should have a clear view of all the troops from here. Good luck in spotting the dissidents."

"Thanks, Sergeant."

Ramey looked toward the dais and waved briefly at the commander, who nodded from his seat and then turned his attention toward the podium at the front. There, a young dark-skinned man raised his hand in a Nazi salute. The NWO guard erupted into cheers and applause. Hitler definitely looked different than I had imagined, because in my mind I still saw him in the body of an old woman. Ramey stood motionless, staring at the spectacle.

"I hadn't expected His Excellency's container to be so young," I said.

"I hadn't expected it to reflect a minority race," Ramey replied. "He always preached that they are inferior, and he was so very opposed to their existence."

"It's a new world, Ramey. Whites are soon going to be a minority race."

"Not after the pandemic."

"Yeah, I forgot about that."

Ramey turned and headed back to his office. On his way out the door, he said, "The commissar is going to want to see you upon his return. He likes to interview all NWO officials."

"Set it up and let me know when. I have a lot to discuss with him, as well." I was lying, but I was deeply into my role as an interrogator. Besides, I wanted to meet Nargas and see if he remembered me.

As the door closed behind Ramey, the cheers and applause from the amphitheater began to subside. I turned to watch, while Hitler stilled the noise by raising both palms, and then he began to speak.

"Comrades, it is indeed an honor to stand before you in this new body, now capable of fifty or more years of service to the goals of the New World Order." The crowd erupted into cheers again. Hitler smiled and moved his hands from the top of his head to his waist, like Vanna White displaying a new washing machine to an audience of frenzied women.

Hitler returned to a more serious posture. "But I am here less to display my new appearance than to encourage your resolve to see our plans through to fruition." The crowd became quiet, anticipating news of the final emergence of the NWO as the dominant force on Earth.

"As you are aware, our forces have been working diligently with the Draconians, Reticulans, and multinational NWO representatives to complete the subterranean facilities where our troops and valued civilian supporters will live in hermetic security while the augmented Australian Antigen virus completes its mission on the surface. It is anticipated that the time to our emergence from the caverns after the release of the virus will be less than four months, and when we emerge, we all will be protected by the immunization series that we have already begun receiving.

"As we emerge, your mission will be control of the populace. This will be accomplished through the provision of food, water, and medical supplies to survivors. In support of the United Nations' sustainability goals, the populace will be relocated to urban areas where food and medical supplies will be readily available, and where individual safety protocols can be maximized. Those who resist relocation will be shipped via train to re-education centers where they will learn to comply. Renegades, dissidents, and brigands will be terminated. Though this may seem harsh, survival of humankind is the penultimate goal. To this end, the needs of the individual must become subordinate to the needs of the greater community.

"As leaders of the New World Order, you will each be appointed to positions of honor and authority in the designated population centers. It will be all of our responsibilities to ensure that human conditions do not exceed the ten living principles which have been engraved on the granite guidestones in Georgia.

"When the desert areas are free from human habitat, our Draconian friends will emerge from their subterranean facilities to occupy those areas, as they are most like the living conditions on their home planets. There, the Draconians will assist us to develop engineering and medical solutions to human problems, easing the suffering of those of us who become infirm due to disease. It will clearly become a new world!"

The amphitheater erupted into applause again.

"Our friends in governments around the globe have already taken steps to ease the transition to the New World government. Britain, France, Germany, Greece, and other countries are moving toward cashless societies, opting in favor of electronic economies. This will eliminate the power of the rich to hoard funds and will enable us to monitor the distribution of wealth such that all members of the global society will have equal access to wealth and prosperity."

Applause and general enthusiasm followed that remark.

"I ask that you all hold true to the goals of the NWO and that you adhere closely to the directives that emanate from Astana over the next few months. As governmental representatives, you will have power and authority beyond those of the average members of society. But it is what you *should* have, because you have sacrificed for so long to bring about this new world. Join me in applauding those around you for their efforts to ensure the best possible world!"

Cheers erupted, and applause rang out.

Hitler permitted the applause to carry on for half a minute, and then he raised both hands again. "I must leave you now, for the time is quickly approaching for you to assume the power and responsibility that has been promised. I urge you to make preparations and be ready to move with only a few hours' notice. The time is at hand! The time is now!"

The NWO erupted into applause. From the rear of the amphitheater the chant "Heil Hitler" began. Slowly it moved toward the front of the assembled guard, and soon all members raised their right arms in unison in the Nazi salute. "Heil Hitler! Heil Hitler! Heil Hitler!"

It was all I could stand. I felt like I was watching some kind of B-rated movie, yet here it was post-Iraq, post-Afghanistan, and post-Livermore, and the Nazi socialist movement was alive and well on the moon. Hell, it was alive and well all over the planet, not just underground, but among the leaders of every governmental agency on Earth.

Only this time, it had a new name and came as a well-orchestrated set of supposedly unrelated political and social movements. How could we as a species forget the lessons that were etched into our history books? In the past, whenever the Communists and socialists took over any country, common people shared wealth equally, and, in no time, nobody had anything. Isn't that what the NWO was about—all humans sharing everything equally, with a single political party, a single monetary system, a single health system, equal housing opportunity, and equal access to products and services? It has never worked!

But in this case, the beneficiaries of the eventual collapse of such a system would probably be the lizards, especially after we killed each other off! How could the New World Order be stopped? Jeezus H. Christmas, I had to do something—and soon!

I pushed my way out of the reserved seating box and marched down the hallway, still muttering to myself about what I had heard and seen in the amphitheater. I guess I marched right past the elevator that I was supposed to take back down to the bunking level. After a few semiconscious turns, I soon discovered my error and tried to figure out where I was.

The corridors were empty. I turned around in an attempt to collect my bearings. As I walked back from where I had come, I passed by a series of small windows on my left that opened into what appeared to be a nursery—at least I saw rows of clear plastic bins that held babies. I paused and looked at them for a few moments.

They all appeared human, except that their eyes were a little larger. Then I realized that their eyes were a single color and they had no whites!

Movement in the rear of the nursery caught my attention. It was probably a female nurse, given the white frock that she wore. From the rear, she appeared to be holding a baby in her arms and swaying back and forth as a mother would.

Then she turned sideways and brushed a cluster of blonde hair from her face. It was Mona!

I smacked the glass with my hand, but it was thick, triple pane plastic of some sort, and it didn't convey sound. There was no door to the nursery from the corridor, so the entrance was somewhere else, perhaps in a smaller hallway on the side or in the rear of the room. I had to find a way to get to Mona, to let her know that I was alive and that I was grateful that she, too, wasn't swimming in the Reticulan feeding tubs.

"May I help you?" asked a young woman with jet black hair and the eyes of a snake. Her voice surprised me, causing me to jump. Seeing Mona had turned my attention away from my surroundings, and I reminded myself that I needed to keep my wits about me at all times.

"I think I've lost my way," I told the female hybrid. "Can you help me find the elevators? I have an appointment with the commander."

"Sure," she replied. "I'm headed that way myself. What is an interrogator doing on the lunar artifact?"

"If I told you, I'd have to kill you," I replied.

She stepped backward in horror.

"I'm sorry," I said. "That's an old expression from my youth. It means that my business on the artifact is top secret, and I'm not at liberty to say."

"You frightened me, sir," she replied. "They haven't taught us that expression yet."

"So consider it a new one to tell your friends. I gather that you're preparing for assignment to the garden planet?"

"Yes, sir. I'll be relocated later this week, probably to Luzern."

"Switzerland?"

"Yes. They say it is really beautiful there."

"Yes, it is, unless they keep you in some kind of underground facility all day. Hopefully, they'll let you mingle with the humans."

"At first, we'll be able to take short guided walks to shop for clothing and to learn how to eat in dining halls."

"Restaurants and bistros."

"Yes, restaurants," she replied. "After we have passed a rigorous internship, we will be permitted to mingle with selected humans."

"Who is teaching you about the customs and languages on the garden planet?"

"We have several teachers of languages, and we learn customs by mentored experiences in simulation laboratories."

"It sounds all too contrived. You'll do better if you experience total immersion. Tell your teachers that I said so."

"Yes, sir." She began walking, and I walked beside her.

"Where do visitors go if they wish to visit the nursery," I asked.

"There is a special elevator which opens directly into the nursery. It's found on level three-forty-six near the workout room."

Super, I thought, that's the same level as Pod Four. I'll nosey around until I find it.

"And where do the Star Children live?" I asked.

"Do you mean the human hybrids like me?"

"Yes," I replied. "Did you grow up here? Have you traveled elsewhere?"

"No. I mean, yes, I was born here and grew up here, but no, I haven't traveled elsewhere. My class has taken field trips around the lunar artifact. We've explored the simplistic technology used by early humans who landed on the lunar surface, and we've seen the crystal city constructed by Man on the dark side."

"But you haven't traveled to the red planet or to the planets of your fathers?"

"No, we've been prepared for the special purpose of colonizing the garden planet, raising its consciousness, if you would."

"Raising its consciousness?"

"Yes, we all have been pre-programmed with knowledge that will advance medicine, language, and religion among the humans on Earth. Over time, humans will disappear and their children—the ones like me and the others—we will assume guardianship of the garden planet."

"Will the reptilians permit that to happen?"

"That's the grand plan. But, surely you know that."

Somebody had better tell that to the Draconians, I thought. I suspected that they plan to inhabit the Earth and eliminate all human life forms.

We reached the elevator that would take us to level 346. She passed her hand over a plate on the wall, and the door opened.

"After you," I said.

"Superiors first," she replied.

"Ladies first," I told her. "You have much to learn about customs on the garden planet."

She walked in, and I followed. She hit a button which bore a reptilian symbol that looked like a trident. I made a mental note of that. We dropped several floors quickly.

When the elevator door opened, Spivey was in the hallway chatting with two other members of the guard. "Interrogator Arreaux!" he said exclaimed when he saw me. "Were you able to hear His Excellency?"

I said goodbye to the young hybrid who had helped me find my way back to the bunking area, and then replied, "There has never been anyone quite like him!" I wasn't lying, either. Hitler was always one of the most unforgettable individuals in human history.

Spivey broke away from his two companions and walked with me toward Pod Four. Along the way, he did nothing but chatter on about Hitler's address and the promises that Hitler had made about giving NWO Guard members positions of authority in the New World government. Eventually, when he realized that I wasn't as enthusiastic, he asked, "What's eating at you, Dan?"

"I was afraid that the two dissidents might have assassinated His Excellency during that speech. I'm glad that they didn't. What worries me now is who, when, and how they will strike."

"Do you figure they're suicidal types?" Spivey asked. "If anyone had assassinated His Excellency, he would have been beaten to death by those of us who were close enough to take him down."

"Good question about their mental make-up. I'm not really sure if they're the suicide type. Maybe they plan to use a bomb, like they did at Livermore. The question is where they would plant a bomb, if they had one."

"It depends on the type and its purpose. If they used conventional weaponry, like plastique, they would have to put it very close to their target, but if they used something like a nuke, they could set it off a mile or more away from their target and get the job done."

"You sound like an expert, Spivey."

"Explosive ordinance is my military specialty, Dan. My primary job here is to clean the nuclear devices that are stored in the artifact, so they're in proper working order if needed."

"I always wondered who polished the warheads," I replied with a chuckle.

"You aren't far off," he told me. "Conventional warheads need to be disassembled, dusted, and their components tested on a regular basis. That's part of my job. The other part is cleaning the tactical nukes."

"Tactical?"

"Yeah, they're different from strategic nukes. Strategic nukes take out entire cities. Tactical nukes are like the neutron bomb that takes out life but leaves the buildings and infrastructure intact. Other tactical weapons include small suitcase nukes that only destroy a few blocks and even smaller ones that will level a single building."

"Sometime, you'll have to show me where you do your work, Spivey."

"It can be arranged, Dan. I'll see about it tomorrow."

"Cool." I didn't know what else to say.

☙❧

Spivey worked in the afternoon. When he came back to the pod, he told me that he had gotten clearance to show me his work station in the morning. I was looking forward to seeing some of the smaller nukes. I couldn't imagine that they actually stored them inside the moon, where, if one went off, the explosion and radiation could kill everyone inside. I thought it would be smarter to store them in a bunker topside, but I was no technical expert on such things. I just knew that if you held a fire-cracker in your open palm, it left a small burn when it went off. But, if you held it in your fist when it went off, it took a couple of fingers with it.

While Spivey had been working, I had strolled around the corridors on level 346, hoping to find the elevator to the nursery. It would have been helpful to have had a map or a GPS because I was still pretty turned around when it came to figuring out the corridor system. I was just about to give up, when a technician came out of an elevator near the enlisted dining hall pushing a cart with a small blanket covering an infant's shape. "Deceased?" I asked.

"Yeah, this one didn't make it. Sometimes shit happens."

"So are you taking it to autopsy?"

"No, there was a failure in the electronics of his crib. It wasn't a disease or organ failure. It was purely mechanical. This one goes to the Reticulans for their feeding baths."

Jeez, I thought, no funeral or kind words said over the body. No mourning parents or grandparents. That poor little fuck was just a piece of meat to feed to a humanoid like he was a sausage. I hoped that it wasn't Mona's baby because she'd be a wreck right now if it was.

But on the brighter side, I now knew where the elevator was, and when I had time, I planned to slip upstairs to see Mona. She had to know that I was okay and that I was working on developing a plan to take Commissar Nargas back to Waam for a little payback.

⁊ↄ⁊ↄ

When I walked back into Pod Four, Merkel jumped up, excited to see me. "Dan," he said urgently, "the commander has asked you to come to his office. An important official is arriving shortly from Earth and has asked to meet you!"

I didn't like the sound of that. I wondered who the hell from the Earth even knew that I was here. This couldn't be good.

"Thanks, Merkel," I replied. "Did the messenger give an appointment time?"

"He expected to escort you to the commander's office. I told him that as soon as you returned from your business, I would send you right down."

I went to the head and relieved myself, splashed some cold water on my face, and headed to the commander's office to meet an unknown person who probably would see through my disguise.

Chapter 17

Mack Smith stepped out onto the ramp of the tureen and looked around at the hanger in which it was hovering. The floor was smooth concrete. The walls were some kind of metal, maybe an aluminum alloy, but he wasn't sure. This was Mack's first visit to the moon, a lunar artifact which was presently controlled by the Draconians and in which approximately twenty percent was sublet to the New World Order to house a thousand troops.

An NWO corporal snapped to attention and saluted. Mack returned the salute and asked, "Where will I find your commander?"

"He and other representatives have been awaiting your arrival in the conference room on level three-eighty-seven. I will escort you there."

Mack picked up his single piece of soft-sided luggage and walked down the ramp. The corporal took the luggage from him and led the way to a small elevator.

He pressed his palm against the flat plate on the wall beside the elevator, and its doors opened.

Mack entered first. "This is my first visit to the lunar

artifact," he told the corporal. "Do you find it claustro-phobic?"

The corporal pushed a button and the elevator doors closed. "No, sir. I just miss the fishing hole back home and the changing seasons. There's no plant life here, ex-cept for a few small gardens in specially equipped nurse-ries and park areas. It's not the same as the wide open spaces on Earth."

He sounded British. "Where's home?" Mack asked.

"Australia. My family runs a sheep station in North-ern Tablelands, New South Wales."

"This has to be a big change for you. How long have you been assigned here?"

The door to the elevator opened. "Three years, which is about two years too long. I could use a furlough." The corporal pointed to a set of double doors. "The com-mander and your greeting party are in that room. Have a nice day."

"Thanks, corporal."

Mack crossed the corridor and opened the right side of the double doors. As he walked in and set down his luggage, the commander looked up and announced, "Here he is now! Agent Smith, welcome to the lunar fa-cility!"

"Commander Grauber?"

"Yes, Agent Smith. Please call me Johann."

"Call me Mack."

"Thank you, Mack. Permit me to introduce you to those in attendance. Commissar Nargas is away at the moment but should return in a day or two. On my left is Assistant Commissar Anole, his second in command of the lunar artifact."

Mack looked into the reptilian's eyes. "It is a pleas-ure, Assistant Commissar," Mack said, nodding his head.

Grauber continued. "Next to the Assistant Commissar is Bellatrax, leader of the four hundred Reticulan greys who are quartered here below the core."

Again, Mack looked into the grey's eyes. "I am pleased to meet you Bellatrax. Thank you for being here today." Bellatrax blinked and nodded at Mack.

"And finally it is my pleasure to introduce you to Interrogator Arreaux, here on special assignment for a few days from Astana."

"I have heard of your exploits, Interrogator. I am indeed honored to be in your presence." Mack turned to Commander Grauber. "Interrogator Arreaux has single-handedly foiled three separate plots against NWO Council members in the last eighteen months. His specialty is identification and extermination of dissidents."

"Thank you for your comments, Agent Smith," I replied, "but no interrogator can be successful on a mission without the full cooperation and assistance of the unit commander. Commander Grauber has been especially helpful to me already." Finally, I had learned Grauber's last name. Everyone simply called him "the commander," and he had not told me his last name when I met him on my arrival.

Mack took a seat near the end of the table, directly across from me. I thought maybe he planned to pass me a note under the table. "I am sorry that I missed His Excellency's address. Was it received well?"

Commander Grauber pointed to a translator unit on the table. "This is so our spoken languages can be understood by all. Please place a bud into your ears. Appropriate buds are identified by symbols in your own languages."

We did as directed, and then Grauber replied to Mack's question. "My troops were generally pleased with His Excellency's comments. They are becoming bored with daily duties and training regimens, and are anxious to return to Earth to begin their individual missions toward the success of the NWO plan."

"They will be pleased to learn that, barring any further disruptions like the tragedy at Livermore, they'll see the unfolding of the first stages of the New World within a few short months. In fact, I am here to meet with Commissar Nargas to discuss FBI cooperation in the next phase of the implementation of Agenda Twenty-One."

"Are you at liberty to share any of the details with us, Agent Smith?" Grauber asked.

"Please call me Mack, Johann." Grauber nodded. "Yes," Mack said, "although I must discuss the details with the commissar, I am free to tell you that our discussion will involve the implementation of commandment number one."

Bellatrax and Anole looked at each other and nodded in anticipation. Grauber nodded as well, but with less eagerness, as though he knew that many people whom he once called friends, school mates, and neighbors would soon be facing gruesome death sentences. I tried to show no emotion and kept my eyes on Mack so that the lizard and the grey could not read my thoughts.

I remembered that the first commandment on the Georgia Guidestones said something about reducing the human population on Earth to 500 million people. If that was money, it would be a lot, but when we are talking about people, it meant a major reduction.

The population of the USA alone was already more than 320 million, and the population of the Earth was approaching eight billion. To reduce it to 500 million meant that the NWO planned to unleash some aggressive pandemic upon the surface, and it was about to happen.

This was not good.

"Are our Draconian and Reticulan allies ready for

their emergence from the subterranean facilities?" Mack asked.

"That is a question for the commissar, Agent Smith," replied the Assistant Commissar. "However, our five thousand tureens are fully armed, and our four divisions of regulars are eager to board them for the cause."

"How many men does that total, Assistant Commissar?"

"Approximately two hundred and fifty thousand, less those who might be ill or in the brig at the time we depart."

"Excellent." Mack turned to the grey. "And the Reticulans, Bellatrax?"

"We are a modest one thousand infantry and another twenty-five hundred general support, but we are ready to assist the Draconians and the NWO as needed and instructed."

"Your support is always appreciated, and you will be rewarded handsomely."

"All we seek is continued support of our efforts to hybridize our species to ensure our survival into the future. Thus far, with the use of bovine and human tissues, we have made progress toward improving our own reproductive capabilities. We think that within the next few years our medical research teams will achieve the success we have hoped for."

"Excellent," Mack replied. "And what is your business on the lunar artifact, Interrogator?"

"I am here to ferret out two dissidents whom Astana believes are here to assassinate His Excellency."

"Are they related to the group who interrupted His Excellency's migration at Livermore?" the assistant commissar asked.

"We believe so. When we look at history, it's not difficult to see that every great movement included those who hoped to see it fail. His Excellency survived several attempts against his life back in the 1940s. He's used to such distractions. But it's a new world, and technology exists to make such a goal easier to accomplish."

"Spoken like a scholar, Interrogator," Mack Smith said.

"I look forward to terminating the dissidents with my own hands."

Mack turned to the others. "Gentlemen, I have other matters, in addition, to discuss with Commissar Nargas. However, the purpose of my discussions must remain confidential. Officially, I am here to inspect the FBI office and to conduct performance evaluations of our ambassadors who are stationed here."

The group nodded. Mack made appointments to speak with each representative on a one-to-one basis, beginning with the assistant commissar, first thing in the morning. He would then speak with Commander Grauber. He would meet with Bellatrax after noon mess, and then with me following that meeting. He had a busy day tomorrow, but it was all talk.

When the meeting broke up, I took the elevator to level 346 and walked back to Pod Four. Mack and Grauber headed down the corridor talking about golf, a sport that has never made sense to me, and the lizard and the grey headed the opposite direction, walking together but silently. I figured that they were talking as well, but telepathically, which was their preferred method.

When I walked into the pod, Merkel and Spivey were sitting on their bunks facing each other. They were in deep discussion. "What's so serious?" I asked.

"We received word that one of our best friends, a guy named Maug, was terminated by Commissar Nargas before he left," Merkel answered. "He was a Draconian, but he was still a good friend."

"Why did the commissar do that?"

"Maug was in charge of the communications hardware in the commissar's office. Somebody damaged one of the monitors, and Nargas took his anger out on Maug by cutting him down."

"Too bad. Nargas is like that, isn't he?"

"Maug had just installed that monitor," Spivey said. "It was brand new and had never even been used. Some of Maug's reptilian friends think that Nargas damaged the monitor himself and then blamed Maug for it."

"Someday somebody is going to kill Nargas," Merkel said, "and cheers will go up from the Draconians."

"And from the NWO," I added.

"Nobody likes that bastard," Spivey said. Merkel nodded his head in agreement.

We sat silently for about a minute and then I changed the subject. "Listen, maybe you guys could give me a hand sometime tomorrow."

"Yeah, we're both off tomorrow," Spivey replied. "But remember that I'm going to show you my work area in the morning."

"Yeah, I am looking forward to that. Maybe you could help me afterward. I need to inspect the upper structure of the central tower. I'm afraid that it might be an excellent place for the dissidents to plant a bomb that could damage the entire lunar artifact. Can you take me there?"

"As long as you aren't afraid of heights!" Merkel said. "When you're on the catwalk, if you fall, you'll have time to write your autobiography before you hit bottom. It's about twenty-one hundred miles down."

"Yeah," Spivey added, "and the weird thing is that there isn't any breeze up there. It's as still as the inside of a coffin."

"Then maybe you can show me your work area, then we can go see the upper infrastructure, and then I can buy you two lunch."

"Now that's definitely a good deal!" Spivey said.

Chapter 18

I felt somebody shaking my shoulder. I hoped that it was Mona and that we were back in her apartment in DC. This hollow moon thing had to be a dream.

"It's time to get up, Dan."

I recognized the voice as Spivey's, so this was no dream.

"What the hell time is it, Spivey?"

"This is the lunar artifact, Dan. We have our own time. Right now it's time to get up if you want to see my work station."

I rolled out of bed. "Do I have time to get a shower?"

"Yeah, but make it a short one."

I grabbed my shaving kit and headed to the shower. The top of my head was feeling prickly, so I knew that I needed to shave it in order to keep my identity intact. I did a three-minute shower and then spent five minutes shaving my top knot before dripping my way back to Spivey with a towel around my waist. I dressed quickly and checked myself in the full length mirror on the wall by the head.

Water spots had bled through my shirt and pants. I

hadn't dried myself very well. What the hell, I thought, they'd dry in a few minutes, anyway.

☙☙☙

Spivey showed me that my hand would now operate the elevator. "Because you're an interrogator," he told me, "you have all the same privileges as staff, except you can't enter certain offices or the brig. They took your hand print when you placed your hands on the metal counter in the commander's office."

"Yeah, I remember the slight electrical tingling. I thought it was static, or maybe a short somewhere in the wiring."

"They were also checking to see if you are who you say you are. I guess you passed."

I took a deep breath. Waam must have figured out a way to have my name and identification data uploaded into the NWO computer database. *Someday, if they ever arrest NWO officials on conspiracy charges, I'll be right there among them in the paddy wagon.*

We took the elevator to the level 443, only fifty-seven levels from the top of the habitation zone. When the door opened, Spivey said, "Follow me. It's just down this corridor."

We came to a large door, somewhat like the ones that guard the entrance to the alien habitation levels back in the subterranean facilities on Earth. "Put your hand here, Dan, and the door might open." I did, and it did.

"Just as I figured," Spivey told me. "You've got above top secret clearance, maybe level Q."

"You mean I can go anywhere?"

"Yeah, like I said, except into certain offices and the brig. And who knows, maybe they've even given you brig access."

Spivey led the way into his work area. Two middle aged men and a woman were working at separate tables. In front of them were numerous metallic parts and odd shaped pieces. "They're cleaning live nukes, Dan." Spivey corrected himself, "Well, they aren't live, but they could be, once they are reassembled and if we received the directive to arm them."

"What does the cleaning entail?"

"They have to remove the detonator and the connecting wires. Sometimes on the newer models, it's a small motherboard with a couple of memory chips."

"These aren't the same as the nukes that you put into a warhead, are they?"

"Warhead days are over, Dan. With the help of the Draconians and Reticulans, if anybody launches an ICBM, we can simply destroy it in the air, or we can fly alongside it and catch it before it finds its target."

"Interesting—"

"Besides, modern alien weaponry is eons ahead of the stuff used by regular ground forces on Earth. They're still shooting bullets, while we shoot condensed light that has four times the range and melts right through body armor. The nukes that we've stockpiled presuppose that a ground war will be over in a matter of a few hours. They're for eliminating clusters of enemy troops or dissidents in an area no larger than a city block."

"Like suitcase nukes?"

"Yeah, that would be a larger variety. Some that we maintain are as small as a grapefruit, and weigh about the same."

"I've never seen a nuke that small."

Spivey pointed to a door at the end of the room. "That's the storage area. Come on, and you'll see more than you've imagined."

The door was not secured, which was a chink in the armor that I thought might play to my advantage sometime soon. Spivey entered first and flicked on the lights. The room was about forty feet deep and thirty feet wide, which was much smaller than I had anticipated. However, it was floor to ceiling shelves and cabinets, and all were full of nuclear devices, none of which was larger than a briefcase. Spivey showed me traditional suitcase nukes, nukes in odd shapes, and the grapefruit nukes that he had mentioned. He told me that the odd-shaped nukes are malleable, which permits them to be hidden in unique places where they blend in with the environment.

"You know," I told him, "seeing these makes me worry that the two dissidents could have access to similar devices, and they could have planted them in the support beams that hold the central tower in place. When we go up there this morning, we should inspect places where you think a nuke might cause the most damage to the lunar artifact. A thorough inspection would be a good thing to do."

"I hadn't thought of that, Dan. I'll get Merkel to help us out. There are dozens of places where a nuke could weaken the structure. I hope you're wrong about those bastards."

"Me, too. A couple of strategically planted nukes could do a lot of damage."

"If they used a couple of suitcase nukes, they could collapse the whole thing, Dan."

"Do you trust the staff you work with, Spivey?"

"Do you mean do I think any of them might be dissidents and might want to set off a nuke?"

"Well," I replied, "they all have access to the nukes and the skills to set them off."

"It would be suicide, Dan."

"Well, suicide bombers have become very common phenomenon in recent years."

"I don't think any members of the nuke staff are that type."

"Are any of them new?"

"No, and they have to go through a year of training before they can clean a nuke without someone looking over their shoulders."

"Is it possible that a dissident could set one of these nukes off from a remote location?"

"Most of them can be detonated from as far away as a thousand miles. You have to add a quarter of a second for the signal to get there."

"So it would be possible for a dissident to hide a nuke and then detonate it from a tureen that has already departed from the lunar artifact?"

"I think so. I'm not sure what effect the crust of the lunar artifact would have on the signal. It might block it or deflect it. It's an interesting question, Dan. I'll have to ask my supervisor about that."

"Yeah, it would be good to know. But be careful about asking that question, though, because your supervisor will know that you've been thinking about remote detonation. He might think that you're a dissident for even asking the question."

"Good point."

"Can you show me a remote detonator?"

"Sure. They're in a cabinet in the back of the storage room."

I walked behind Spivey. A cream-colored plastic cabinet stood at the end of the aisle. Spivey opened it. Inside were small boxes, each about the size of a pack of cigarettes. He removed one, opened it, and handed me a device that looked like a television remote control.

"That's it? It's so small!"

"Yeah, but it does the trick. All you do is push that red button two times quickly to turn the detonator on. Then you hold down the red button and the blue button at the same time while you press the detonator against the bomb you want to set off. When the detonator beeps twice, it's set, and the bomb is armed. See the button with the skulls and crossed bones? That's the baby that detonates the bomb. There's a digital timer on the back if you want to set the nuke to go off at a specific time."

"How many bombs can a single detonator set off at once?" I asked.

"The detonator has to be touching the bomb in order to program it, so if you're using small nukes, like the grapefruit nukes and even the suitcase nukes, you can program four on any one detonator."

"So after you've armed a bomb, how do you shut the whole thing down?"

"Look on the back. Below the digital timer is a green reset button. Press that one time and everything that you've programmed into the detonator is erased."

"I'm glad that you guys have that capability. We all could be in big trouble if you forgot what you programmed the detonator to do."

"Yeah, the nuclear engineers who developed this thing made sure that it was simple to operate and even simpler to shut off. They were Draconians."

"Really? I thought nukes were strictly our domain."

"Draconians gave us nuclear technology. They were working early on with His Excellency's scientists, but the project was delayed when the Americans and Russians invaded Germany."

"Is that when all the German scientists found their way to the United States to complete their work?"

"I don't remember my history lessons well enough, but it was something like that. I just know that if the Draconians hadn't given us nuclear technology, we wouldn't have nukes or nuclear power plants or nuclear submarines."

I handed the detonator back to Spivey. "Be sure to lock that away," I told him.

"It's safe in here. Nobody can get in without specific authorization."

Good! That was another chink in the armor, I thought. They didn't secure the nukes because they thought that the facility was entirely secure.

We left the storage room, but before we exited the cleaning facility, Spivey introduced me to the staff members who were hard at work. "This here is Dan Arreaux. He's an interrogator from Astana," he said.

I could tell they were surprised that an interrogator would be here and that I was interested in their work area. "Any problems we ought to know about?" the woman asked in a gruff voice. She was a gnarly example of womanhood, with a nose like Carl Malden's and big pores to complement her lack of beauty.

"Nothing that you should worry about," I replied. "I'm just checking safety protocols in case of an emergency."

She nodded, wiped her nose on her shirt sleeve, and went back to her work.

✸

Spivey called Merkel. "We're on the way."

When the elevator door opened at level 500, Merkel was waiting for us. In his hands were three flashlights and a map of the basic infrastructure above the habitation area. The main column consisted of eight round beams of an unknown alloy that catapulted upward to the ceiling which was, in fact, the underside of the lunar surface.

Halfway between their exit point from the floor at level 500 and the ceiling above, the beams spread outward, similar to the way that aluminum table legs would leave a central bundle and spread outward to hold the top of a round picnic table that a suburbanite would put on a backyard deck. I wondered if the designers of those kinds of tables had been here to see how it was done.

Spivey pointed to a doorway at the bottom of each beam. "Inside of each doorway, Dan, is a narrow stairway that leads to the top."

"Like inside the Statue of Liberty?" I asked.

"I've never been there."

"I have," Merkel said, "and, yeah, it's sort of like that."

"You lead, guys," I told them. "I guess we'll have to do these one at a time."

"That may take several days," Merkel replied.

Merkel went in first, then Spivey, and I followed. As we climbed, I told them what to look for. "We have to inspect any spot where a small nuke could be hidden to escape detection. If we find one, Spivey, you're going to have to disarm it, if you can."

He patted his fanny pack. "I brought the right tools along, just in case."

The beam, however, as was smooth as glass on the inside, and the only way a guy could attach a nuke would be by duct tape to the bottom of a tread. I estimated our climb to be at least half a mile, and it reminded me a little of the air shafts that Nelson and I had climbed back in Dulce, except that as we got higher, the angle of the climb decreased, making the going easier.

At the very top of the stairway, we found another door, more like a doorway on a battle ship or submarine. It was oval in shape, and the latch was operated by turning a wheel. Merkel spun the wheel, and the door opened easily. We stepped outside in turn, and I immediately saw the safety issue that Spivey had warned me about: the walkway was grated metal, giving me a dizzying feeling because I could look straight down into eternity. The handrails were supported by a single guy wire and post every ten feet or so, but if you slipped and lost your grip on the handrail, it would be really easy to freefall for a very long time before hitting bottom.

"You okay?" Spivey asked me.

"Yeah, I guess," I replied. "You warned me about this, but I think I have a problem with the height."

"You'll get used to it. We all got that feeling the first time we came up here," Merkel said. "Keep your eyes looking ahead, and you'll find it easier going. Looking down just prolongs the nausea."

I followed his advice. The walkway connected each of the ten hollow beams, forming a huge circle, maybe two miles in diameter, about one hundred feet from the ceiling. As they reached the ceiling, the beams divided into four legs which appeared to be connected directly to the ceiling. On the underbelly of each of the legs was a ladder which climbed to the ceiling. Merkel, Spivey, and I each chose a leg and began climbing to see what we could find. It took about ten minutes to reach the top, inspect the connector, and return to the walkway.

"See anything unusual?" I asked.

"Clean like a baby's ass," Spivey said.

"Mine, too," Merkel said.

"Same here."

We followed the walkway to the next vertical beam and repeated the process. The results were the same. And we found the same at the third beam. It was beginning to look as though the structure was impervious. But, when I climbed my leg at the fourth vertical beam, I struck pay dirt. Two points at the top of the leg had broken free from the ceiling, apparently due to a stress crack that was about four feet wide and extended in the direction of the fifth beam. I pointed my flashlight into the crack and turned it on. The light just disappeared into the opening. A deep opening like that was exactly what I had hoped to find.

When I met up with Merkel and Spivey again, I told them about the crack. "You'd think that the Draconians would have a crew up here fixing that thing," I told them.

"Maybe they don't know about it," Merkel replied.

"Maybe they don't think they'll be staying here long enough for it to make a difference," Spivey remarked.

"You may be right," I replied. "Will they have any need for the lunar artifact once they've been designated a specific territory on Earth?"

"I still think that maybe they don't know about it," Merkel said. "The moon has been occupied for at least fifty thousand years. I don't think anybody thinks it'll be empty for long if it's abandoned."

Merkel had a point. My high school science teacher once told us that Mother Nature abhors a vacuum. Thus, anything that's empty won't stay empty too long. In this case, some other species from another star system would occupy the hollow moon as soon as they discovered that it was empty, and their presence would create a threat to whatever species was occupying the Earth at that time. I concurred that the lizards probably didn't know about the crack.

We explored the sixth vertical beam. Merkel and I climbed the same leg because we thought that it was the most likely place that the crack was headed. We were right!

The crack from the fifth beam followed the curvature of the ceiling directly to this leg and then headed off in the general direction of the seventh vertical beam. If you were looking for cracks in the ceiling, I guess we had found the motherlode.

"What do you think, Dan?" Merkel asked.

"I think we need to explore the seventh beam. So far, I haven't seen any evidence that the dissidents have been here or that they've planted a bomb of any type. We may be too early, or they may be planning a different type of event."

When we climbed back down to see Spivey, he agreed with our assessment. So, we followed the walkway to the seventh beam. Spivey and Merkel climbed the same leg this time. "Dan! Dan!" Merkel called down to me once they reached the ceiling. "You've got to come up and see this!"

I climbed up the stairs. When I reached the top, Spivey and Merkel weren't there, but I could hear their voices coming from the crack above. As I looked upward, I could see that this leg, too, had broken free from the ceiling, exactly where the crack met the two contact points. Only here, the crack was at least fifteen feet in width. Merkel and Spivey had found a pathway up into the crack. "Is it safe for me to come up?" I shouted.

"Yeah, come on!" Spivey shouted back down at me.

I placed my hand on the top of one loose contact point and pulled myself up so I could stand on the other. It was a small perch, but when I pointed my flashlight into the mouth of the crack, I could see that somebody at some time had driven mountain climber's foot pegs into the ceiling structure, creating a stairway of sorts into its darkness. I aimed my flashlight into the top of the crack, and I could see two feet dangling about thirty feet above me. Spivey and Merkel were sitting on a ledge of some sort. I shut my flashlight and followed the foot pegs up and into the dim light above me.

"We've found somebody's secret hideaway," Merkel

told me when I peered onto the ledge where they were perched. "There is a mattress, some canned food, magazines, and some homemade weapons."

"Do you think maybe it's a deserter's camp?" I asked.

Merkel laughed. "I think it's where Spivey comes to masturbate."

Spivey gave him a shove, and Merkel let out a small scream when he slipped off the ledge. As he grabbed at anything to prevent his fall, I reached out and took his arm with my left hand, while hanging onto the last foot peg with my right. I let out a grunt as his weight suddenly pulled on my arm and shoulder. He dangled in the air for a moment, and then found a foot peg below me, where he quickly planted a foot and took his weight off my arm.

"You shouldn't ought to have done that, Spivey. A guy could get killed up here!" Merkel complained.

"You're lucky that Dan was there to catch you, Merkel. If you had fallen where you were supposed to go, I'd be sleeping in your bunk tonight."

"It would serve you right, you asshole. I pissed in it last night!"

That last comment let me know that there were no hard feelings and everything was good between these two pod mates.

Merkel found his way around me and back to his perch before I climbed onto the ledge next to him and Spivey. I shined my flashlight directly above me and saw that the crack was more like a cavern, stretching deep into the ceiling, far beyond my flashlight's beam.

"How deep do you think this goes?" I asked.

"I'll bet if we kept climbing, we could go a mile into the surface," Spivey replied. "I've already been up a hundred feet, and the width just doesn't get any smaller."

"That's interesting, but a hundred feet doesn't make

a mile," I said. "Come on. Let's see if this crack goes to the final support beam. I have a meeting to make with an FBI representative."

We climbed back down to the walkway and followed the crack to the eighth vertical beam. At least now, the height and open construction of the walkway weren't bothering me anymore, even when the grating below me jiggled unexpectedly. I had hoped that the crack in the ceiling would continue to the eighth beam. However, from the walkway, as we approached number eight, we could see that the crack in the ceiling had reduced in size to only a foot or less in width, and that it zigzagged into solid ceiling about thirty yards before reaching the point where the beam was connected to the ceiling. There was no point in climbing up. Besides, I was probably going to be late for my appointment with Mack Smith, and I was sure that he had important information for me. Another climb would simply eat too much time.

❧❧

When we entered the elevator for the trip back down to Pod Four, I told Merkel and Spivey that I was too late to have lunch with them.

"That's okay," Spivey replied, "we've always got shit to do."

I gave Spivey my mess card and told him to buy whatever they wanted for lunch. "Maybe it will help ease the pain of losing Maug," I told them. "Put both meals on my card. Astana is paying for it."

"Thanks, Dan," Spivey said. "Lunch would be good. It still won't ease my feelings about Nargas. He's a nasty bastard, and maybe someday I'm going to get the opportunity to take him out."

"You know," I reminded him, "making threats against your superiors isn't a good habit to get into, Spivey. If someone overhears you, you might get arrested, and then Nargas will have the opportunity to peel you and put you in a bag of salt."

"Yeah, Spivey," Merkel added, "you know that the walls have ears."

"Well, if it isn't me, somebody else is going to do it. It's just a matter of time."

Chapter 19

Assistant Commissar Anole arrived ten clicks early for his meeting with FBI liaison Mack Smith. His brown scales gave way to purple iridescence as they approached his eyes and snout, complementing his purple uniform with green piping, as though they had been custom made by a New York designer.

"Good morning, Commissar," Mack said. He did not extend his hand because reptilians did not participate in that human custom for fear of germ contamination.

Anole looked into Smith's eyes and replied through thought transference. *'Good Morning, Agent Smith.'*

"Have you heard from Commissar Nargas?"

'Yes. His meeting with the pontiff went well. The Vatican is continuing to promote the viewpoint that the garden planet would be a better and kinder place if countries did not exist and if a single government provided for the well-being of the population.'

"Good. The pontiff's continued support will better enable us to govern after the pandemic has subsided. When will the commissar be returning to the lunar artifact?"

'Possibly as soon as tomorrow. He has to stop at the red planet to conduct some business before he returns.'

"Are both you and the commissar aware that as many as two dissidents may be plotting to harm him?"

'He is aware that some among all species would like to see him removed from power, regardless of the means. He has not yet spoken with the interrogator who was at our meeting yesterday, but he is aware of the interrogator's mission.'

"I have heard rumors that the commissar may be holding an FBI agent here against her will."

'She is not a dissident, Agent Smith, although her unanticipated arrival was cause for alarm.'

"She should be returned. She should be ours to discipline."

'The commissar will not permit that. Although I would have terminated her immediately upon her arrival, the commissar chose to include her in a larger experiment involving the assimilation of hybrids into human culture. She is under his protection.'

"An experiment?"

'Earlier this year one of the human female's eggs was fertilized with a hybridized male spore which contained elements of the commissar's DNA. While she carried the fetus, the Commissar kept her container near him. It was very uncharacteristic of his normal behavior and has raised questions among some in our species about his stability.'

"Has the fetus been removed?"

Yes.

"Then the female should be returned to us for discipline."

'As I said, the commissar will not permit that. There is a growing belief among our scientists that, unlike our species, the human element of hybrids causes them to re-

quire contact with their mothers if they are to develop without psychological impairment. The commissar has selected this human female and her hybrid issue as an experiment to provide data which may prove or disprove the hypothesis.'

"Do you believe this female came to the lunar artifact to terminate the commissar?"

'No. As I already told you, she is not one of the suspected infiltrators. Because of her previous interactions with the commissar, she is now seen as a human mother who possessed knowledge of our security systems and used that knowledge to reunite with her issue. She remains here of her own free will in order not to be separated from her child again. She participates in the experiment of her own free will. She will not return to the garden planet until after the experiment has concluded, perhaps several of your years from now.'

"Do you have any questions or suggestions for me?"

'Are you one of the suspected dissident infiltrators?'

"The answer is 'no,' Commissar Anole, and I believe our discussion has come to an abrupt end."

Anole rose and marched out of the meeting room without the usual cordialities. Mack sat back in his chair and exhaled heavily. 'The reptilians are direct and generally unfriendly toward us humans, he thought. How will we ever live in harmony with them when they emerge from the subterranean facilities?'

Commander Grauber sent a representative to inform Mack Smith that their meeting would have to be postponed due to preparations for Commissar Nargas's anticipated return. Mack sent word to the Reticulan grey, Bellatrax, to ask him to meet sooner than previously scheduled.

Bellatrax arrived ten minutes later and extended his three-fingered hand in greeting.

Like Anole, Bellatrax preferred to converse by thought transference. *'I trust your first visit to the lunar artifact has been pleasant,'* he said to Mack.

"Thank you. Generally, it has been."

'Don't let the Draconians get to you. Their power over humans has always been based upon intimidation. Your mythologies are full of their cunning. The evil one in your own religion was a serpent, wasn't he—the one who tempted the female with the apple?'

Mack smiled. "So you don't think my meeting with the assistant commissar went well?"

'We both know that they want the garden planet for their own. Don't you think they will take steps to acquire it after the pandemic reduces your numbers to so few? As for the assistant commissar, it is common knowledge among my species that he covets Nargas's position. My superiors are surprised that Anole has not yet been cut down by Nargas, or that Anole has not yet had Nargas terminated in some manner. That is their custom.'

"This is perhaps not a healthy discussion for us to have. The walls have ears."

'My species would have terminated Nargas ourselves if we did not fear retribution.' The grey paused and then blinked twice. *'So what is your agenda with me?'*

"My superiors are concerned that your scientists are exceeding the number of cattle and cats that you have been authorized to harvest. They believe that you have multiplied the negotiated number by three fold."

'We may have harvested a few more or less. I am not sure. However, it is imperative that our harvest continue because it is only through bovine and feline tissues that we are now able to reproduce. We believe that we will be able to fully regain reproductive capabilities as a species within the next three generations.'

"That's good news. But perhaps you should consider

breeding cattle and cats on your home planet. You could then produce and harvest as many as you'd like without drawing the attention of our farmers and animal rights activists."

'I will convey your concerns to my superiors. Will there be anything else?'

"Yes," Mack replied. "Do you know anything about the female human that the commissar has been holding captive here?"

'She is his breeder. She carried his seed and then made her way to the lunar artifact to see the child. It is a female, as well.'

"Why didn't Nargas have her terminated?"

'I believe his interest in her lies in three domains. First, as a breeder, she could bear many hybrids through the first quarter, when they then are removed and transferred to the growth tubes. Second, there has been a problem with Draconian/human hybrid suicide at maturity. He is interested to see if human nurturing will result in more psychologically resilient hybrids. And third, although a human female, she is more like a male in language and attitude. Her personality intrigues him. She is the first of any species to speak down to him. Knowing Nargas, however, he soon will tire of her and will terminate her as an annoyance.'

"Thank you, Bellatrax. Your responses bear an air of honesty. However, I would encourage you to be less vocal about your feelings about the commissar and his assistant, or you might find yourself in the feeding tanks."

'There is truth in what you say,' Bellatrax replied with a smile. *'Your advice is appreciated, Agent Smith.'*

❧❧❧

I passed a Reticulan grey in the corridor. He appeared to want to talk, but I brushed him off because I was late for my meeting with Mack Smith. As it was, I arrived two minutes late, which was uncharacteristic of an interrogator, and I was supposed to be one. When I knocked, Mack gave me permission to enter. His demeanor immediately let me know that others probably were eavesdropping on our conversation, and he didn't want the eavesdroppers to suspect that we knew each other.

"Interrogator Arreaux, I understand that you inspected the infrastructure above the central tower this morning," he said to me matter-of-factly. "Did you find any evidence of tampering by the infiltrators?"

I was surprised that he knew that I had been to the ceiling. Hell, I had just come down from there. "I didn't find anything that looked threatening," I replied, "except that if repairs aren't made within the next year or two, the whole thing might come tumbling down. It's gonna take a structural engineer to figure out what's wrong, and also how to fix it."

"Will you be reporting that to the Draconians, or shall I?"

"I will when I meet with Commissar Nargas."

"I understand also that you have interest in the nursery."

I figured that the young hybrid woman must have reported me to the higher ups. "I was traveling with a woman, my superior on this assignment, who was detained by the Draconians when we arrived. I lost my way coming back from hearing His Excellency's address to the NWO troops and, by sheer luck, saw her in the nursery. It's really odd that she hasn't contacted me since we've been here. I thought that she had been arrested or maybe even terminated. And Astana has sent no word about her."

"Then you have seen her?"

"Yes, but she didn't see me. I was in the corridor, and she was inside a soundproof facility."

"I have spoken about her with Assistant Commissar Anole. She is being detained as part of a hybridization experiment. Did she speak with you about that during your travels?"

"No. We only discussed this mission. It was the first time that either of us had been assigned to the lunar artifact, and neither of us was given an orientation prior to our arrival."

"I see."

"Do you suspect her of being one of the dissidents who intend to harm Commissar Nargas?"

"Commissar Anole assures me that she is not a dissident. Instead, she is the mother of a hybrid that is being raised here."

"I would never have expected—" I stammered. "Is Astana aware of this? If not, I am obligated to report it. My superiors will be pissed about her behavior and, worse, with the fact that she's being held here."

Mack raised both palms and shook his head. "No, Astana is outside of my sphere of influence. Remember, I am FBI ambassador to the NWO, but I have no direct authority within the governance structure. I asked that she be turned over to my custody, but the Draconians refused."

"I'll ask to be given the opportunity to interview her in person. Any support that you can give to the Draconians about my request would be appreciated."

"I'll see what I can do, but I can make no promises. The Draconians have been on edge since the incident at Livermore."

"I understand that you were at Livermore for His Excellency's migration."

"What a tragedy that was."

"You and the commissar were lucky to have escaped the bomb. I understand that many did not."

"It was a failure in facility design. Newer facilities under construction now will have many avenues for egress in case of similar emergencies. Newer facilities will also have upgraded security systems requiring all visitors to wear terminal digital chips. No uninvited dissidents will be able to sneak in, and security cameras will ensure that all corridors and meeting areas will be carefully monitored and recorded to rapidly identify and ferret out those who hope to disrupt such events. When discovered, the perpetrators will simply be eliminated by detonating their computer chips."

"Good, then. It sounds as though proper steps have been taken to exterminate the vermin."

Mack nodded. "Do you have any other questions or perhaps some insights to share with me?"

"Right now, my only concerns are the two dissidents who may be here planning to do in the commissar and maybe the queen. And I'd like to interrogate Interrogator Casola as soon as possible."

"I'll see what I can do."

Mack showed me to the door, and I was soon on my way back to Pod Four.

Chapter 20

I felt like it was the middle of the night when rough fingers touched my shoulders and shook me into consciousness. I rolled over to see three Draconian guards standing over my bunk. One caught my eyes and telepathically told me, *'It is time for you to interview the female infiltrator.'*

"What?" I asked groggily.

'The female that bore Commissar Nargas's issue. It is time for you to interrogate her.'

I realized that Mack had fulfilled his promise. As I stood up, the three lizards backed away to give me room. Around me, I noticed that Spivey, Merkel, and the other NWO guard members were still fast asleep. "I need a few minutes to shower and shave," I told the lizards.

'Make it no more than five of your minutes. The nursery is on an exact schedule, and every moment that you waste here is a moment that you will not be able to interrogate the female.'

I got his point and dressed quickly. The shower and shave would have to wait. In less than two minutes, I was being escorted down the corridor to the elevator that would take us up to the nursery. As we walked, the tallest of the lizards led the way, and I was second, followed by the two smaller lizards. When I say smaller, I mean they were only a head taller than I am, while the guy in front was maybe a head taller than they were. I felt intimidated by my place in the parade because it reminded me of a few movies where prisoners are led to firing squads in a similar procession. I guess that intimidation was the intent of their behaviors toward me. Besides, reptilians weren't known for being warm and fuzzy. Certainly, if I tried anything funny, I'd have been cut down in a matter of seconds. I had to play the role.

"When will the commissar be back?" I asked as the elevator door closed and lurched upward. "I need to speak with him."

One of the smaller lizards touched my shoulder. When I turned to look at him, he told me, *'Probably later today. He is looking forward to interrogating you.'*

That didn't sound good, but I didn't flinch. I looked away so my emotions wouldn't be conveyed through my eyes. I tried to tell myself that Nargas wouldn't know who I was, but reptilians had all sorts of senses that we didn't, and I suspected that once he looked at me, he'd have my number.

The elevator opened, and we marched in order to the nursery entrance. The taller lizard placed his palm on the identification plate, and the door popped open. In we went, passing rows and rows of clear plastic bins, each holding an infant hybrid.

All races seemed to be included, as though women from all around the world had donated their babies to the alien agenda. I wondered how many mourned the loss of their unborn children, unaware that they were being raised to maturity by NWO and alien nurses. I wondered, too, if Planned Parenthood and all other government supported abortion clinics weren't simply fronts for the hybridization of our planet.

As we neared the back of the nursery, my heart leapt. Mona was standing beside one of the bins, dressed in a baby blue jumpsuit. She looked beautiful, except that her dark brown roots had grown out, exposing that she wasn't a natural blonde. I wanted to hug and kiss her, but I knew that I couldn't.

At the sound of our approaching footsteps, Mona turned. When she saw me, her eyes lit up for a moment, and then then they turned downward. In her arms was a baby. I had always suspected that she was going be a good mother, and now I knew that she was a natural.

The tallest lizard signaled to a nurse, who quickly came to his side, looked into his eyes, and then told Mona, "Let me have your female. The interrogator is here to question you."

Mona gently passed the sleeping baby into the nurse's arms. As she did, I was able to catch a quick glance. The baby had fair skin, no scales, and dark hair, like Mona's.

"Where can we talk in private?" I asked the tall lizard.

He took Mona forcefully by her arm and pushed her in the direction of a smaller room. Mona pried his claws off of her arm and told him, "When your boss gets back here, I'll have him cut you in half for hurting me!" The draconian hissed at her. I couldn't tell what he might have told her.

The room was small, maybe ten by ten, with a small table where the nursing staff could sit on breaks. There were only four chairs, so one of the smaller lizards stood at the door while the rest of us sat down. The big guy pushed Mona into a chair. I knew that I had to play the interrogator role well, and I was sure that Mona would play along.

"Miss Casola, or whatever your name is, I now know that you are not from Astana. You're an imposter. Who gave you the papers that looked like official orders?"

Mona turned her head and did not respond.

"It would be in your best interest to cooperate," I told her. She looked up at me with angry eyes. Good, I thought, she is playing her role. "Why did you come to the lunar artifact?" I asked firmly.

"I wanted some Swiss cheese," Mona replied, rubbing her arm where the lizard had squeezed it.

"You're being treated well, aren't you?" I asked. "There's no need to be sarcastic. I'm just seeking information to help me do my job."

"Fuck you NWO bastards," Mona replied. "Why should I make it easy for you to do your job?"

"Why did you come here? Is it your intent to harm Queen Igua or His Excellency?"

"Who is Queen Igloo?" she asked.

"Igua."

"Who is Queen Igua?"

"You know who she is. Is it your intent to harm her?"

"Fuck the queen."

The tall lizard grabbed Mona's arm and wrenched it upward. Mona gave out a small cry of pain.

"Watch what you say about the Draconian Queen. Our friends don't like your vocabulary or your attitude, Miss Casola."

I nodded at the lizard, and he released Mona's arm.

"I don't give a rat's ass about their queen. I came here to take back what is mine."

"And what would that be?"

"The baby that I was holding when you interrupted my morning."

"That hybrid that belongs to the Draconians."

"Not according to the laws of the United States. That bastard Nargas took my baby from my body without asking my permission. In the United States, he is a kidnapper, and kidnapping is a punishable offense."

"Then you *are* here to kill the commissar!"

"I didn't say that. I came here to take back what's mine. That's all."

"How did you come here?"

"You already know that. I came in a turneen with you."

"Yes, but I came only because I received orders from Astana to accompany you. Who in Astana issued those orders for you?"

"I don't know."

"They came from somebody, Miss Casola."

"Look, in my real life, I'm an FBI agent. You know that the FBI supports the NWO agenda. I simply sent a request to Astana for orders that would permit me to come to the moon, and they arrived about two hours later."

"How did I become involved?"

"I don't know. Your name was included in my orders. Maybe they thought that I needed a pet gorilla."

"Your attitude is showing itself again, Miss Casola."

Mona rolled her eyes and feigned a sigh. "Are we finished yet? I need to go change my baby's diapers."

"How did you get an interrogator's uniform and credentials?"

"The FBI has all sorts of disguises. I simply opened my closet and there it was."

"Miss Casola—"

"I borrowed it from our wardrobe. It isn't real."

"Who are your accomplices?"

"Accomplices?"

"Yes, accomplices. Did you hope to take the hybrid back to Earth? How could you do that without accomplices?"

"I didn't think that far ahead."

"Nonsense. Who among the Draconians is helping you?"

The lizards stirred and hissed at my question. Obviously, they didn't like it.

"Look, I wasn't even sure that my baby was here," Mona replied. "I took a chance that she might be, and I came to find out."

"The hollow lunar artifact is top secret. You shouldn't have known about it. Why would you have suspected the hybrid was here?"

"The hollow moon is no secret. You guys ought to know that a lot of people know about it. If you think it's any kind of secret, then you don't know shit."

"Who among the NWO guard has plans to help you?"

"I already told you that I have no accomplices."

"Then what are your plans?"

"I have no plans. Nargas discovered who I am, and he brought me to see my baby. He cut a deal with me that he would not kill me if I stayed and raised my baby the way human beings do. I figured that I'd rather do that than go swimming in the feeding tanks."

"I have one last question for you, Miss Casola: Do you plan to have more babies with the commissar?"

"Fuck you, you asshole! I'm not answering any more questions!"

I looked the tall lizard in the eye and said, "We're finished here. Let her go back to the hybrid."

Mona stood and walked toward the door. The guard

at the door wouldn't let her pass until the tall one motioned that it was okay.

I looked at the tall lizard again and said, "I'm convinced that she's not the one we must worry about. She's simply a woman who wants her baby and who had the authority to find her way here. The commissar should never have picked an agent of the FBI for breeding purposes. It complicates things. Abducting her is cause enough for some to doubt the sincerity of the Draconian agreement with our government, but terminating her could possibly bring about hostilities."

"I will apprise Commissar Anole of your conclusions."

As I rose, I said, "I'll have to discuss this situation with Commissar Nargas."

"You will have the opportunity soon enough," he replied, "but let me warn you that the commissar does not deal well with those who question his actions or authority."

"I am well aware of his reputation for volatility. I'm also aware that some among you would like to see him dispatched and replaced."

The lizard blinked and looked at me with suspicion, as though he had been found out.

Chapter 21

Seeing Mona and being unable to hold her made me even more conscious of how much I loved her. She was in a tough spot, constantly under supervision by the nurses who reported indirectly to Commissar Nargas and locked several floors above me in a secure facility. I needed to get her out of there. Seeing her with the hybrid, though, made me realize that she wouldn't leave the moon without her baby. To complicate things, Commissar Nargas was due back at any moment. It was time to launch my plan, but I was going to need help, and there was only one place to turn.

Merkel was walking out of the shower with a towel wrapped around his waist when I entered the pod. Spivey was sitting on his bunk, bent over and tying the laces on his boots.

When Merkel approached our bunks, I told them both, "We need to talk. Something very important is in the air."

"This sounds serious," Spivey replied.

"It is." I looked around and saw that too many guard members could overhear what I wanted to say. "Not here, though. Where can we talk in confidence?"

"Let's go to the mess," Merkel suggested. "Most of the guys have already eaten, and we can get a small table in a corner."

It sounded like an okay idea, so I nodded, "Meet there in ten minutes?"

Spivey asked for fifteen. I agreed and laid down on my bunk to wait for him. When he had taken care of personal hygiene and had dressed, the three of us left the pod for the mess.

It was a short hike, and we didn't speak as we walked. As Spivey had suspected, the mess was almost devoid of guard members when we entered. I bought coffee for the three of us. Spivey asked if I'd spring for a couple of donuts. "Of course," I said. So, Merkel got some, too.

Like Merkel had suggested, we found a small table in a corner, far from anyone's ears—unless, of course, someone was eavesdropping electronically. I took the risk. "I received a communication from Astana early this morning," I told them. "My assignment has been changed. If I tell you what I am supposed to do, I'm trusting that you will keep it to yourselves. If you divulge it, you will be toast." Both of their faces turned serious, but they both nodded. "I'm going to need assistance, and I'm hoping that both of you will help me," I continued.

"You can count on us, Dan," Spivey said.

"This is highly dangerous, and if we fail, the lucky ones will be in the feeding tanks."

"What is it, Dan?" Merkel asked. "It sounds really bad."

"Astana wants me to terminate Commissar Nargas."

"Holy shit!" Merkel exclaimed with a big grin.

Spivey put his hand over Merkel's mouth and forcefully told him, "Shhh!"

I looked around. A couple of Draconians were at a table about thirty feet away, busily chomping on the bones of something ugly, and too busy to notice the commotion at our table.

"Sorry," Merkel whispered. "It's just funny that you are here looking for somebody who's planning to kill that asshole, and it turns out that it's really you!"

"I hadn't expected this," I told them. "I'm an interrogator, not an assassin. I didn't sign on for something like this."

"But you're a soldier, like us," Spivey said. "You gotta follow orders or face the consequences."

I nodded thoughtfully and then told them, "Dispatching Commissar Nargas is part of an agreement between his Draconian superiors and Astana. Nargas is seen as detrimental to the cause. His temper makes him too unpredictable, and his men fear him."

"He's probably killed too many guys from the NWO, not to mention his own men," Merkel said.

"Yeah, and don't forget that he killed our friend Maug," Spivey added.

"His Excellency also wants Nargas terminated because he blames him for the Livermore fiasco," I said. "The assassination cannot be accomplished by Draconians but must be done by greys or humans. It's up to me to figure out a way to carry it out."

"You can count me in," Merkel replied.

"Me, too," added Spivey. "Nobody in the guard likes Nargas. He has a nasty temperament, and his behavior is unpredictable. It would be a pleasure to give him what he deserves."

"Yeah," Merkel said in agreement, "nobody will miss him."

"So how do you think we ought to pull it off?" I asked. "I'm thinking a small bomb that we could blame on a grey or a dissident, or maybe some kind of accident."

"At the first sign of trouble, Nargas disappears," Spivey said.

"Where does he go?" I asked.

"Usually he takes off in his tureen and doesn't come back until whatever happened is long over," Merkel replied.

"Then we ought to plant a bomb in his tureen," I told them.

"We could rig it to detonate by remote control when he's in space, if he's less than three thousand miles away, or we could simply use a timer," Spivey added. "That would be a piece of cake!"

"Planting the bomb could be tough to do," I said. "His tureen is probably closely guarded."

"Then we have to figure out some sort of diversion in the lunar artifact—something to drive him to his tureen," Merkel added. "Maybe a small fire fight or something."

"Good idea, Merkel," I said, "but we don't want to get anybody else killed. Besides, who are we gonna get to shoot at each other, and where are they gonna get weapons?"

"You've got a point," Merkel conceded.

"Spivey," I asked, "do you have any regular ordinance in that explosives storage locker of yours?"

"Do you mean, like non-nukes?"

"Yeah, something small, that would make noise and do minimal damage?"

"That's really old technology, but I'm pretty sure we have a few concussion and smoke devices somewhere."

"If we set off something small, maybe in a vacant room or corridor, it might be just the ticket for getting Nargas to exit the artifact for a couple of hours, especially if he thinks it might have been intended for him. Then, when he leaves, we could detonate a small nuke in his tureen."

"It sounds plausible, Dan," Spivey replied.

"Yeah," Merkel agreed.

"So we have a basic plan," I told them. "Spivey, when you go to work this morning, would you see what you can dig up that can be used to create a diversion? Merkel and I will go check out the security situation at the commissar's hangar."

"Sure," Spivey replied. "We're short staffed today. It shouldn't be a problem."

"Remember, Astana is counting on us to pull this off in complete secrecy. If we're successful, it will mean commendations and promotions. If we fail, it will mean a death sentence at the hands of the Draconians for all of us."

They both nodded.

Motion from my left caught my attention. Merkel and Spivey looked up as well. A middle aged man in an NWO officer's uniform walked up to our table, carrying a cup of coffee. Merkel and Spivey popped to attention.

"At ease," he told them.

They returned to their seats.

He looked at me. "How did you manage to escape the blast at Livermore?"

"Excuse me, Major?" I asked.

"Aren't you the interrogator who warned us all that a bomb had been planted at the Livermore during His Excellency's planned migration?"

"I think you have me confused with somebody else," I said.

"I have a good memory for eyes," he replied. "I can easily forget a face, but I never forget eyes. It was you, wasn't it?"

"I think you have me confused with somebody else, Major," I repeated. "Would you mind excusing us? These gentlemen and I are conducting some business that I'd like to complete."

The major apologized and then walked away. I watched as he went up to a reptilian, pointed to our table, and said something. The reptilian nodded. I hoped we weren't fucked.

We didn't finish our coffee. We agreed to meet again at the mess for a late lunch to share what we had learned. At Merkel's place, one donut remained uneaten. I hoped that he had an appetite for what we were going to do to Nargas. Actually, I hoped we were going to have the opportunity to carry out our plans before the major brought a load of shit down onto our heads.

I was still too new to the lunar facility to know my way around very well. I could get from Pod Four to the mess, the command offices, the nursery, Spivey's nuke maintenance center, and the top of the central core, but I had never been to the military hangars. So, Merkel led the way. As we walked, I tried to get to know Merkel a little better.

"What's your MOS?" I asked.

"MOS?" he replied quizzically.

"Military Occupational Specialty."

"Oh, where did you hear that term?"

"It's from the Marines. I was a Gyreen before I joined the NWO." I was lying, but he wouldn't know. Just about everybody in the NWO had gotten there in some strange way, usually by word of mouth. Hell, to my knowledge, the NWO didn't have any formal recruitment offices.

"It must be different for you interrogators," Spivey said, "but in the guard, we use the term UTS, which stands for Unit Task Specialization."

"Yeah, I knew that," I lied.

"My UTS is maneuver logistics."

"Sounds interesting…"

"We plan vehicular movements during training maneuvers, evacuations, relocations, and assaults."

"It must require a lot of math."

"Maybe in the old days, but today so much of it is done by computer algorithms that we are often assigned to other stuff."

"So you're more of a computer programmer than a mathematician?"

"I'm more like a computer operator. I just plug in the numbers, and the computer does the rest. The computer even communicates movements directly to each tureen. The pilots don't have to do that much, except to take over once the UTS system releases control of the vehicle."

We took the main elevators down to the bottom floor on the elevator control panel. Merkel told me that it was level 225. When we exited the elevator, we crossed the corridor to a series of three elevators with red doors. They were express elevators that descended more than one hundred floors before reaching the twenty-five levels of tureen hangars. Nargas's tureen was garaged at level 100. That was going to be easier to remember than level 344, which was where our shuttle docked when we arrived from Earth, two floors below Pod Four at level 346 and the nursery at level 348. I reminded myself to keep these numbers straight in my head, or when it was time to leave I was going to wind up in the wrong place at the wrong time.

When the elevator door opened at level 100, we took a right down a short corridor that ended at a door with a glass window. Through the window I could see two rows of tureens lined against the walls on both sides, leaving a space the width of a runway down the middle. The runway must have been a quarter of a mile long. At its end was a wall that, I assumed, must have been a hangar door. The ceiling appeared to stretch about three hundred yards above us. Around the tureens, which hovered six feet above the floor, I could see a half dozen technicians or mechanics moving on the inside, performing service and maintenance functions.

"Nice facility," I said to Merkel.

"It holds forty tureens, Dan, twenty on each side."

"So, which one is the commissar's?"

"His is through a special doorway, to our left once we enter the hangar."

Merkel opened the door using the palm of his hand on the identification plate. I assumed that his UTS designation gave him the authority to enter hangars. We hugged the wall, walking between it and the first tureens in line. As Merkel had told me, a door greeted us at the intersection of the wall and another that met it at a perpendicular angle. Merkel pressed his hand on a plate beside the door, and it popped open. We walked through it and into a smaller, narrower hangar that held two silver tureens which were emblazoned with both the NWO insignia and the green dragon Draconian Empire flag.

"Oh," I said, "I guess the commissar is back!"

"No, he ain't," Merkel replied. "This hangar houses three tureens. These two are his escort tureens. His looks a little like these, but it's green in color and smaller and don't display the NWO seal."

I remembered seeing Nargas's tureen when Mona and I escaped from the Livermore facility with Waam, and I remembered that it bore a green hue. Nargas also had seen us at the same time, but we escaped in a random direction before he could shoot us down. I was still worried that Nargas might recognize me from that incident, especially since my face was telecast throughout the facility when I announced to the thousands in attendance that dissidents had planted a bomb which was going to explode. It caused a panic, and many dignitaries were killed in the ensuing chaos. As I thought about it, I didn't give a shit that anyone died there. As far as I was concerned then and now, they were all planning to wipe out ninety percent of the human population and take control of the planet. I wish the nuke had gone off in time to kill all of them. However, Nargas had escaped and, as a supposed interrogator, I was scheduled to interview him about possible dissidents who planned to kill him and the queen. If he recognized me, I was gonna be fried in an instant…well, if I was lucky.

Suddenly a command rang out, "Halt!" It was a lone NWO guard.

"It's me, Smitty. It's Howie Merkel!"

"Who's with you, Howie?"

"This is Interrogator Arreaux. He's here to inspect the hangar."

"You should have gotten clearance first."

"He's an NWO interrogator. He don't need clearance!"

I saw the barrel of an AR-15 move toward the ceiling from behind a stack of plastic drums. Then Smitty, the guard, stood erect and motioned for us to come forward. "How do I know you're an interrogator?" he asked me.

I pointed at the stripes on my sleeve and asked, "Why am I being asked such stupid questions? Merkel here already told you who I am and what I do."

Smitty's eyes looked toward the floor.

"Interrogator Arreaux has some questions for you, Smitty," Merkel told him.

"How can I help you?" he asked me.

"There are at least two renegades in the lunar artifact who plan to assassinate Commissar Nargas and Queen Igua," I said. "I'm here to check the security of the commissar's tureen."

"It ain't here. The commissar's got it. He went to Mars."

"When the commissar comes back, will you take me on board so I can inspect it?"

"When the commissar is back, this hangar is manned by reptilians. You'll have to ask them."

"How many reptilians guard the tureen?"

"When it first returns, the Draconian maintenance crew refuels it and checks it out for incidental damage. There's four of them. When they done finished their work, they leave one guard at the ramp. They change guards four times a day."

"Is he armed?"

"Of course he's armed. He's in full armor with a liquid light helmet."

"Why do they have only one guard?"

"All vehicles are scanned by the reptilians for viruses, bacteria, weapons, and radiation as they enter the lunar artifact. Vehicles with biological and radioactivity issues are cleaned before being permitted to enter the interior."

That explains how they knew that Mona and I were carrying pieces when we arrived on the shuttle. "Have you seen anything suspicious over the past few days?" I asked.

"Just you guys. Nobody else ever comes down here."

"When is the commissar due back?"

"Actually, any time now. I'll know when he's entered the interior of the artifact because the reptilians will come to relieve me. A buzzer goes off about two minutes before they walk out of that elevator." He pointed to a flat panel of stone on the wall. "It's Draconian. I don't know how it works. The wall just sort of gets fuzzy, and they walk out of it."

"I guess I'll have to come back to speak with the reptilian guard," I said.

"You'd better clear it first. They ain't as nice as I am. They'll cut you down and ask who you are later."

"He's right," Merkel told me.

"How many ways can people get into this hangar?" I asked Smitty.

"Just the door that you came in and the other one, same side but fifty yards down the wall."

"Is it always kept locked?"

"Yeah, except that it just requires a minimum security clearance."

"What does that mean?" I asked Merkel.

"It means that Spivey and you and I are cleared to open it."

"Is that right?" I asked Smitty.

"Probably." He was full of good information, I thought.

We said our goodbyes to Smitty and walked back through the main hangar to the elevators. "At least we know that there's only a single guard," I said.

"Yeah," Merkel replied. "But it's gonna be hard to get by him and get into the tureen."

"Maybe…"

✌✺✌

Spivey met Merkel and me at the mess about an hour

after the lunchtime rush. He was carrying a small box made of standard corrugated cardboard. I bought coffees and sandwiches for all three of us, and then we sat down at the same table where we had met in the morning.

Spivey handed me the box and told me to open it on my lap. I pulled the lid flaps apart and peered inside at a green cylinder with a black stripe around its middle. The yellow letters printed directly on the surface of the cylinder read *GRENADE HAND ~ OFFENSIVE MK4A3 ~ TNT*. It was a post WWII concussion grenade, but it had been modified because it didn't have the standard five second fuse.

"It's an MK-Four-A-Three concussion grenade, Dan," Spivey said. "It's got an eight ounce TNT charge."

"Yeah, it's maybe Viet Nam era?" I asked.

"Yeah, but I modified it. I replaced the standard five second fuse with a digital timer. We can set it to go off at any time we want."

"This may do the trick," I replied.

"Yeah. The cool thing about it is that it won't do much damage. It's mostly intended to be anti-personnel. The concussion does them in. It won't damage the structure too much."

"Awesome, Spivey," Merkel said.

"I agree, Spivey," I said. "It's exactly what we need. What about the nuke?"

"I'll get one just before we need to plant it. I can take it right from the storage unit to the tureen."

"Don't you think it might be better to have it close by so we can plant it on a moment's notice?"

"When we do this, we'll need to be sure that we don't leave too much time between the time we take it and the time we use it. Otherwise, somebody might notice that it's gone and set off an alarm and security search."

"I hadn't thought of that, Spivey."

"Besides," he continued, "NWO officials have already been to the facility twice to identify nukes to use on the western fault line. They could show up again at any time, so our inventory needs to be pretty much intact at all times."

"What's the western fault line?"

"I'm sure that you know about that, Dan. It's the San Andreas. In about three months, Astana plans to set off a series of nukes that will send California plunging into the Pacific Ocean."

"Oh, yeah," I lied. "I forgot about that. Lots of people will die, huh?"

"Yeah. It'll get rid of a lot of Mexicans, and because of the population density of California coast, it'll eliminate a huge number of people who would otherwise have to be fed after the disaster."

"But it's a necessary step toward the ultimate reduction of the Earth's population to five hundred million," I said. "It will also cause the general population to look for a government to save them during the aftermath. That, in itself, will have them welcome the NWO."

It was good that the Dweeb Squad had educated me on this stuff a few months ago. Otherwise, I wouldn't have had a clue about what Spivey was talking about. It was also good that Spivey had found the concussion grenade because it was step one. We just had to wait for the commissar to come back and then set the time to launch our plan.

Chapter 22

Mona rolled over onto her left side, hoping to relieve the kink in her lower back. She had been sleeping on the cot beside her daughter's clear plastic bassinet for too many nights now. Had it been a week? She couldn't remember; however, when Commissar Nargas returned, she planned to ask him for a private room with a bathroom that didn't require her to ask permission of a nurse in order to use it.

She hadn't been able to sleep well last night because her mind was racing with thoughts about Danny, interspersed with thoughts about her baby, and whether Danny would object to her desire to keep Stella. Yes, Mona had decided to name her daughter Stella, after the stars from where her father's DNA had originated and the moon where she and Stella had been reunited. Mother Nature was doing her thing, creating a strong connection between Mona and her hybrid daughter. Stella resembled Wendy, Mona's younger sister who had gotten married in Florida a few months ago, except that her eyes were a little larger and almond shaped. Then, of course, were the baby blues where the whites should have been. In human time, Stella still should have been in the womb, but because of the Reptilian DNA and the effects of the growth chamber, she was already approaching eleven pounds in weight and seemed much more alert than a purely human baby could be at this time in its development.

At the same time, Mona's arms ached for Danny. He had surprised her when he had come into the nursery facility yesterday. She would have hugged and kissed him, except for the presence of the three reptilian guards who had accompanied him. Anything that she had wanted to do to show him her love would have aroused instant suspicion and would have caused him harm. She wished that this game of role playing could be over and that she, Danny, and Stella could be together back home on Earth. But she doubted that Nargas or the NWO would ever let that happen.

The sound of Stella cooing brought Mona back to reality. She rose to a sitting position, and then stood so she could look down upon Stella as she lay in the bassinet. Stella smiled again at the sight of her mother, and she cooed when Mona's fingertips brushed lightly across her cheek.

Mona reached down and lifted Stella to her breast, cradling her and swaying back and forth as she sang an old Italian lullaby that her own mother used to sing to Mona and her sisters:

> "*Dormi, dormi bel Bambin,*
> *Re Divin, Re Divin*
> *Fa la nanna bel Bambino,*
> *Re Divin, Re Divin*
> *Fa la nanna bel Bambino.*
>
> "*Fa la ninna, fa la nanna*
> *Fa la ninna nanna a Gesù.*

> *Gli angioletti su nel Cielo*
> *Veglieran su te Gesù.*

> "'La, la, la, la, la, la, la, la, la, la, la, la
> La, la, la, la, la, la, la, la, la, la.'"

A Draconian hybrid maid in an NWO custodial uniform was mopping the floor in the nursery and stopped to listen to Mona's song. Using her three fingers, she set her mop handle against one of the bassinets, but it slipped sideways onto the floor, causing a loud sound. Several of the babies began to cry. Mona turned to look at who had disturbed the peace of the morning.

"That song you're singing," the maid said, "is it Italian?"

"Yes," Mona replied.

"The Gesu you sing about in that song—he was a man from the Galactic Federation."

"Excuse me?" Mona asked.

"Your song mentions the angels in the sky and a man named Gesu. He was sent to the Garden Planet from the Galactic Federation. The angels were Draconians."

"Jesus was the son of God," Mona replied. "He came to Earth to preach peace and love for our fellow man."

"He was sent to teach you humans not to become violent when abducted or put to work in Man's gold mining operations."

Mona looked at her with a puzzled expression.

The maid continued, "The experiment was relatively unsuccessful at first, especially when you humans tried to put him to death. However, over time, the message of peace toward your oppressors was carried forward by certain humans in return for special favors."

"I don't care what they taught you on your planet," Mona replied, "but on Earth, we believe in God."

"Mankind is the God that you humans pray to. Mankind gave you food and medicine when you were created to be laborers under their occupation of the Garden Planet. You have been left alone now for five thousand years and what have you done but fight each other and destroy your planet. Soon, your kind will be and should be terminated so that your hybrid children can try to make habitable what little of the garden remains. Your generation will be the last of your kind. Your daughter and these others soon will be given the keys."

Mona gave the Draconian hybrid a dirty look and returned to swaying and humming to Stella. The maid picked up her bucket and mop and left the nursery.

Chapter 23

"Welcome back, Commissar," said one of the two Draconian guards.

"Yes," said another, "we hope that your trip yielded positive results."

"What do you know of my mission?" the commissar hissed in anger, suddenly clutching the guard's throat in his clawed hand.

"Nothing, sir!" the guard replied in fear. "I just hope that your trip was uneventful and fruitful, whatever you were doing!"

The commissar released his grip and pushed the guard backward and to the ground. "I am in a good mood today, or your mother would be crying for you tonight."

The door to the hangar's Draconian elevator became fuzzy and then opened.

A large Draconian dressed in green and scarlet royal garb stepped out and hailed the commissar, "Graam-bissss, Commissar. On behalf of Queen Igua and the Council, we welcome you, and we celebrate the success of your mission!" They clasped forearms and turned to walk into the elevator.

"Tell me, Ambassador Chula, how goes our agreement with the Chinese?" the commissar asked.

The two entered the elevator. As its door turned fuzzy and regained its granite appearance, the Ambassador replied, "Very well, Commissar. They delivered another shipment of gold yesterday. They have achieved ninety-two percent of their goal."

"When do they anticipate the final deliveries?"

"Within the next three months."

"They will expect us to relinquish this decaying orb to their ownership soon after the final payment. We must ready our forces to relocate to the Garden Planet."

"The queen wishes to speak with you about that, Commissar. Her Majesty has negotiated an additional month or two, if we should need it, but the price is high."

"And what do the Chinese want for a month's rent?" the commissar hissed.

"Our migration technology."

"That is too high a price!" the commissar hissed.

"But the queen has agreed to their request."

"Then we must vacate the lunar artifact before the three month period elapses."

"Yes. Her Majesty expects you to launch our total occupation of the Garden Planet in less than two months. When the lunar artifact is empty, we can turn it over to the Chinese."

"Screw the Chinese!" the commissar hissed. "We have their gold. We have no further need of their kind!"

"The Galactic Federation would disapprove of your sentiment, Commissar."

"And screw the Galactic Federation as well!"

The door to the elevator opened. Commissar Nargas stepped into his living quarters. He turned and said to Ambassador Chula, "I have a meeting with the Chinese delegation tomorrow. I will ensure them that we will acquiesce to their price, if need be, but that we hope to turn this facility over to them within sixty of their days."

"I will inform the queen of your support of her agreement, and that you plan to complete the relocation before the ninety day deadline."

The elevator door became fuzzy again and then returned to granite.

Commissar Nargas removed his communicator from his belt and quickly looked at his appointments. In a few clicks he was scheduled to meet with the NWO interrogator, and he hoped that there would be something more than rumors about the possible assassins. A dinner meeting with the Draconian leaders had been scheduled for this evening, and the breakfast meeting with the Chinese delegation was scheduled for tomorrow. "Good," he muttered, "I have time to strategize a way around this mess the queen has created."

Chapter 24

When I entered Commissar Nargas's command center, I was stopped immediately by an eight-foot-tall lizard in full combat garb. He looked into my eyes, and I heard him ask, '*What is your business, human?*'

I pointed at the stripes on my sleeve and replied, "I am NWO Interrogator Arreaux. Commissar Nargas is expecting me."

The lizard held his communicator beside my face and looked at its screen. '*You appear to be who you say you are. The commissar is expecting you. Follow me.*'

As he turned to lead me to Commissar Nargas, I saw that my photograph had appeared on the screen of his communicator. I guess that all humans look the same to lizards.

If I had had the balls, I'd have told him the same thing about lizards, except that subtle differences in the colors of their scales give them some form of differentiation, at least to the human eye. I was glad that I had taken the time to shave my head and re-point the barbs on my beard again this morning.

Nargas' command center was a large, semicircular space, with three tiers descending toward a wall that contained one huge video monitor which was surrounded by a dozen or more smaller monitors. On the large monitor was a video projection of a facility on some planet somewhere. It looked desert-like, similar to what I had seen on Mars. Wherever it was, it was smoking and reminded me of the videos of Bagdad after United States forces had bombed it for three days.

'This is the commissar's office, Interrogator,' the lizard told me. *'He is expecting you.'*

I entered the office and approached Nargas's desk. "I am pleased to meet you, Commissar," I said. "I have heard much about you." I didn't extend my hand because I knew that lizards don't shake hands with humans. Nargas didn't look up at me, but I noticed his nostrils flare twice. I thought his behavior might have been some form of intimidation technique. It was working.

When Nargas finally looked up at me, our eyes met, and I heard him say, *'I have heard much about you, too. What have you learned?'*

"Astana believes that someone in the lunar artifact is here to assassinate His Excellency and possibly you. I am here to find the assassin."

'This is old news. What have you learned?'

"I observed His Excellency's speech to the NWO guard, but saw nothing suspicious. I have inspected the superstructure for possible bombs and have found nothing out of the ordinary. I also have queried the woman who came on the tureen with me, impersonating a superior in my unit. I am convinced that she is not the assassin."

'I could have told you that. She is my guest.'

"I now suspect that one or more greys have conspired against you. Whatever you do, you must keep His

Excellency out of harm's way until his return to the Garden Planet. And you, Commissar, should make a hasty retreat at the first sign of anything out of the ordinary."

'*Are you accusing me of not protecting His Excellency?*' the commissar hissed.

"No. Don't misinterpret my words. You did an excellent job of rescuing His Excellency and of protecting him thus far. However, with the possibility of as many as two assassins, I'm encouraging your forces to remain on high alert."

'*Thank you for your advice, Interrogator. My forces are always on high alert.*' The commissar stood and then asked, '*Where have we met before, Interrogator? There is something familiar about your scent.*'

"We've never met before, Commissar. Perhaps my deodorant is worn by others."

The commissar's eyes gave me a stern look.

"Perhaps we have passed in the corridors," I continued. "I've seen your image, but I've never met you before today."

The commissar continued to study me with his eyes.

What the fuck, I thought. So I continued, "I've learned that you were at Livermore at the time of the abduction of His Excellency. You were fortunate to have escaped the explosion."

'*Yes, I was,*' he hissed. He nodded toward the door. '*We are done for now, Interrogator.*'

I figured that it was time to leave, so I turned and walked out. The same tall goon who escorted me to the commissar's office escorted me to the door. We didn't talk.

When the door shut behind me, I breathed a sigh of relief. The commissar was the kind of guy who could make anybody sweat. As I walked back to Pod Four, I hoped that I hadn't said too much or made the connection for the commissar. I never should have said anything about Livermore.

☙ ❧

Back at the pod, Spivey and Merkel were awaiting my arrival. With them was another member of the NWO guard, a skinny guy that I had never seen before.

"This here is Washington. He's from the combat unit," Spivey told me. "He's gonna help us."

"What?" I asked in surprise. "You were supposed to keep this between us!"

"We did, but Washington saw me put the concussion grenade back in its box and asked me what was going down. I had to tell him that it was top secret NWO stuff."

"Don't worry," Washington told me, "I won't let anybody else know. Besides, I want in on this operation. Nargas has kept us from getting access to the higher tech weapons that the reptilians use. I think he doesn't want us to be capable of defending ourselves against them. I figure the reptilians plan to turn on us once the Earth is secure, like we were supposed to do against the Russians at the end of World War II."

"I can't believe that you guys have already told somebody else about my mission," I told Spivey and Merkel. "Who else knows?"

"Nobody, I promise," Merkel replied.

"Yeah," Spivey added, "only Washington, and it turns out that the three of us done already figured out how to plant a nuke in Nargas's tureen."

I wasn't happy that somebody else knew what I was up to, but I had to hear them out. "So how do you figure we can get by the lizard guard?" I asked.

"We stage a scuffle in the corridor, like you're arresting one or two of us," Merkel explained. "You call out for assistance. When the guard comes to help, Spivey will go plant the nuke."

"Somebody might get hurt," I replied.

"Have you figured out anything better, Dan?" Spivey asked.

"No, not yet."

"We gotta do something soon," Washington said. "The commander has ordered us to be combat ready. Our unit is leaving the lunar artifact in four weeks. If you don't get Nargas in the next couple of days, you'll never get him because we'll all be engaged in readiness preparations."

"Do you have the nuke, yet?" I asked Spivey.

"I can get it as soon as we need it."

"How about by this afternoon?"

"Yeah, sure."

"I guess there's no time like the present," I said. "If we can plant the nuke his afternoon, then maybe we can do the deed tonight." The three nodded their heads. "If we get caught," I reminded them, "any one or all of us could be killed. If we're successful, Astana will grant us promotions and ribbons." I was lying again.

Spivey took a standard issue NWO back pack from his locker and put it on. "I'll be back in about forty minutes," he said.

Meanwhile, Merkel, Washington, and I strategized how we would conduct the scuffle. When we were finished, I felt better about Washington, but I was still annoyed that Merkel and Spivey had let him in on the plan. The more people who knew about it, the greater the risk of being found out!

As we finished our planning, a Draconian grey entered Pod Four and asked for me. He was carrying a shoebox under his left arm.

"Over here," Merkel said, waving him in our direction.

"Are you the interrogator?" he asked in a squeaky voice.

"You can speak?" I asked.

"Yes, some of us are bred with that capability. Not all of us are telepathic, but I have both capabilities."

"How can I help you?" I asked.

"This package is for you."

He handed me the shoe box. I opened it and saw that it contained a bottle of wine with a label that read *Chateau Luna 2016*. A plain white card contained the message, *From Your Friends in Livermore*, typed neatly, probably by a computer printer.

"Chateau Luna." I laughed. "This wine must be outta this world!" I held the bottle out to him, bottom end first. "Please take this back and thank the person who sent it, but an interrogator cannot accept gifts and, besides, I don't drink this wimpy shit."

As the grey attempted to grasp the end of the bottle, it slipped from his three fingers and struck the hard edge of my steel bunk, shattering the glass. Wine splattered onto his legs. Instantly he began squealing in pain, and I could see smoke rising from the flesh on his spindly calves.

"Fuck, Dan, it's acid!" Merkel cried.

Washington threw my blanket over the bottle and remaining acid that had puddled on the floor.

I grabbed the grey by his shoulders and threw him onto my bed. "Who sent you here with this gift?" I demanded. The grey continued crying out in pain. "If you want to go to the infirmary, you'd better tell me who sent you here with this bottle of acid! If you don't tell me, I'm going to pour the rest of it onto your face!"

"Please!" he squealed. "Don't hurt me. I'm just a

courier. I was sent to pick it up at the commissar's office and was told by a guard to bring it to you. That's all I know."

I told Merkel to take the poor slob into the shower and hose him off with cold water. While Merkel and the grey were in the shower, Washington called the clinic for emergency care. A few minutes later, the grey was carted off on a gurney by two medical technicians.

❧❦❧

After Spivey returned, we briefed him about the wine incident.

"Somebody's trying to kill you," he said.

"That's a no-brainer, Spivey," I replied. "Nobody really likes an interrogator, and I suspect that there's at least one NWO officer who would like to see me pushing up daisies. I think he's carrying a grudge."

"Who is it, Dan?"

"It's that major who interrupted us in the mess. I don't know his name, but when I see him again, my fists are going to ask him a few questions."

We told Spivey our plan, and then the four of us headed out of Pod Four to the elevators that would carry us down to the hangars on floor 100. Before we left the pod, Spivey turned and reminded us, "Don't nobody look any lizards in the eye. They can read what we're thinking, and all I'm thinking about is blowing that bastard Nargas to Hell."

We all nodded. It was a good thing that he had thought about that.

It was now mid-afternoon, and the hallways weren't too busy. We passed an occasional lizard and a few NWO staff, but nobody asked us any questions.

We simply nodded as we passed, and I was careful to

avoid looking any of the lizards in the eyes, thank you, Spivey.

When we reached the level 100 hangar, Merkel pressed his hand on the metal plate, popping the door open. We entered and stood for a moment as a group. Nothing seemed out of the ordinary, so Merkel led us to the door that led to the Commissar's hangar. Washington and I waited beside the door while Merkel went with Spivey to be sure he could open the door that Smitty the guard had told us was about fifty yards down the wall.

Two very long minutes later, Merkel returned. "Spivey is waiting behind the door that links this hangar to Nargas' hangar. The door is slightly open. When the guard moves to help with the commotion, Spivey is going in."

I felt a lump in my throat, and I could see anxiety in Washington's eyes. "Then we're moving forward," I said. "No going back, right, guys?"

"Right!" Merkel replied.

"Yeah," Washington said. "Let's do it!"

I placed my palm on the door plate to the commissar's hangar. The door popped free from its lock, but I didn't open it. "I guess that my security clearance is still valid," I whispered.

Before we walked in, Merkel took an open-ended wrench from a mechanic's stand and handed it to Washington. "This is your noisemaker," he said. He took a rubber mallet for himself and banged it on the door several times.

"Hey, what are you doing?" Washington shouted, and then he grabbed Merkel by the collar and slammed him against the door. It opened violently, and the two tumbled inside the hangar and onto the floor. They began wrestling, the wrench and mallet looking like weapons and making noise as they hit the concrete floor. From my vantage point, I could see the Reptilian guard's eyes look quickly in the direction of the two men who were rolling on the floor. The guard turned and reached for his breast plate.

I stepped into the hangar, held my palms toward the guard, and shouted, "Don't shoot! Commissar Nargas wants him alive! Don't shoot!"

Washington and Merkel continued to roll about on the floor, yelling obscenities at each other. I reached down to try to separate them, but to no avail. "Don't shoot!" I shouted again. "Come help me! Commissar Nargas wants this one interrogated."

The guard just stood looking at the spectacle, unsure what to do. Behind him, I saw Spivey quietly slipping close to the ramp. "Come help me!" I shouted to the lizard. He took a step toward us and then stopped. As he did, Spivey slipped past him and up the ramp into the Commissar's tureen. As though he may have heard something, the lizard turned to his right, opposite of the direction Spivey had gone, but Spivey was safely inside. "Hey, come help me!" I shouted again to the lizard. "Commissar Nargas will reward you. He wants this human interrogated! I need your strength to subdue him!"

The lizard walked over to me. I could feel his presence above me, but he couldn't communicate with me because I wouldn't look him in the eyes. Washington and Merkel continued to writhe on the ground, as though really struggling with each other. "Help me separate these two! The thin one is the one I need to detain, but I think I'd better interrogate both." Without warning, a ball of liquid light burst against the wall, sending sparks flying in all directions and surprising all three of us humans. Washington and Merkel quickly separated and huddled in fear. I fell backward, looked the lizard in the eyes, and demanded, "Please don't shoot! I need these men alive!"

'They are separated, Interrogator. Isn't that what you wanted?' the lizard asked me through my eyes.

"Do you know me?" I asked. "How do you know that I am an interrogator?"

'Your rank is on your shirt sleeves,' the lizard replied.

"Can you stand here to keep these men quiet until I have them handcuffed?

The lizard nodded. I pulled handcuffs from my belt and cuffed Washington while he was still sitting on the floor of the hangar. Then I quickly handcuffed Merkel. As I was helping Merkel to his feet, I heard Washington cry out in pain. When I turned to look, I saw that the lizard was holding him six feet in the air, lifted from behind by the small chain that held the cuffs together. "Drop him!" I demanded. "He's no good to us if you rip his arms out of their shoulder sockets!" The lizard released him, and Washington crumpled to the floor in pain.

'He will not try to escape from you now, Interrogator! If you break a dragon's leg, he cannot run!'

"Thanks, but I didn't want to put him in the infirmary."

The lizard turned and walked back to his guard post at the base of the ramp to Commissar Nargas's tureen. *Fuck*, I thought, *I hope Spivey had enough time*.

Just then, Spivey appeared at the door. "I'm here to help you, Interrogator," he said. "I'm sorry that I was delayed."

I breathed a sigh of relief at seeing him. He took Merkel by the arm and escorted him out of the hangar. I helped Washington to his feet, trying not to apply too much pressure to his arms, as he was visibly in pain. We exited the hangar and entered the elevator. When the door closed, I removed the handcuffs from Washington and then gave the keys to Spivey so he could release Merkel.

"Are you okay?" I asked Washington.

"I'll know in a little while," he replied, rubbing his shoulders. "That bastard tried to break my arms!"

"Can you move them?"

Washington slowly spun his arms in circles and then bent his elbows. "They seem to work okay, but they still hurt."

"Maybe you should get them checked out by a doctor in the infirmary," Spivey said.

"And how do you suggest I tell him that I hurt them?"

"Yeah, I guess you should wait a day. I've got some prescription anti-inflammatory drugs left over from when I hurt my knee. I'll give you some." I turned to the others. "Phase One of our operation is over," I told them. Next, we move on to Phase Two."

"Where did you plant the nuke?" Merkel asked.

"Right under the pilot's control panel," Spivey replied. "He'll never even know that it's there. I set it to go off by remote detonator, and we should be able to do it up to three thousand miles away."

"Cool!" Merkel replied. "Fireworks tonight!"

☙❧❧

We made plans to meet at Pod Four in half an hour. Before the meeting, I needed to check Nargas's schedule for the evening. If he was free, I was going to have to schedule a meeting with him. If not, I needed to figure out where he'd be, so I could interrupt him when our event happened. The strategy was pretty simple: If I had to meet with Nargas, then Spivey and Merkel would go to the main hangar and find a hiding place where they would wait. Washington would set off the concussion grenade in an empty corridor and then come through the door where Nargas and I were and announce that a bomb had been detonated.

When Nargas came into the hanger and entered his tureen, Spivey and Merkel were to let him depart from the hangar and then give him five minutes before hitting the button on the detonator. That should give him enough time to exit the exterior of the moon before the blast occurred. On the other hand, if Nargas was meeting with someone else, I would detonate the concussion grenade in an empty corridor and then burst into the room to announce that the Commissar should evacuate the artifact due to an attack supposedly intended for him. Washington, Spivey, and Merkel would hide in the hangar to do the deed.

So, I went to the commissar's office and knocked on the door. The same large lizard that I had met before was waiting for me. "I need to see the Commissar," I told him.

'The commissar is busy, Interrogator. Come back later.'

"Can I make an appointment to see him?"

The lizard removed his communicator and scrolled through its touch screen. *'He is busy tonight. Maybe tomorrow after his breakfast with the Chinese ambassadors.'*

"Too busy to see me? I have important news for him. Where can I find him?"

'He is dining this evening with important NWO leaders. He will be too busy.'

"Can you tell me where he will be dining? This is extremely important."

He lizard gave me an impatient look. *'The commissar always dines in the Imperial Suite, but you should not disturb him. He does not like surprises. I will leave word that you would like to speak with him in the morning.'*

I gave the lizard a look of frustration and then turned away. *I've got a surprise for him all right*, I thought.

☙❧

"So we'll execute Plan B," I told the others when we met at the pod. "I'll detonate the concussion grenade, and you guys will wait in the hangar to do the deed."

"Too bad," Washington replied. "I was hoping to be near the fireworks."

"You'll be real close to the nuke, especially if Nargas chooses not to exit the lunar artifact," I replied. "If you guys can, you ought to watch his progress from the end of the hangar. Be sure to wait until he is outside of the interior before hitting the remote."

"We can handle it," Spivey said. "I think the reptilians will call us heroes."

"They must never know," I admonished him. "You'll just get a promotion, and a medal of valor and nobody will know why. The paperwork will just say 'valor in the line of duty.'"

Chapter 25

Mack Smith sat in a chair across from an unknown grey and Johann Grauber, the leader of the NWO guard detachment. Beside Mack sat Bellatrax, the leader of the Reticulan greys. To the left of Bellatrax sat Assistant Commissar Anole. Commissar Nargas sat at the head of the table.

"Welcome back, Commissar," said Johann Grauber. The other guests all nodded.

"I regret having been away for so long," Nargas replied through a translation machine. "However, I am back, and there is much to do if we are to ready our forces for deployment to the Garden Planet."

"Are all forces expected to deploy?" Grauber asked.

"Yes. The lunar artifact must be completely empty within ninety of your Earth days. My message to our forces has mandated sixty days, because there will be inevitable delays."

"Then all of us must prepare to vacate our facilities?" Bellatrax asked.

"Yes, that is what Queen Igua has ordered."

Commissar Nargas could see logistical concerns on

the faces of those around the table. "I am confident that you all will be able to have your forces redeployed within that timeframe." Then Nargas swallowed a crustacean of some sort and changed the subject. "I have heard many rumors about the presence of two dissidents here in the lunar artifact. I know little about the interrogator who is here. We have spoken, but he does not impress me."

"We have all met him," Mack replied. "His name is Arreaux."

"Yes, that is the one."

"I know little about him, as well," Grauber said, "but he has been busy ferreting out potential assassins. In fact, he interrogated two suspects today, in the garage where your tureen is kept."

Nargas' eyes grew wide. "My guard did not tell me that my garage had visitors today!" He made a mental note to terminate the guard immediately after dinner. "Did the interrogation prove successful?"

"We are waiting to learn what he has uncovered."

The noise of a disturbance from the kitchen interrupted the conversation. Then the sound of an explosion erupted, shattering the glass panel in the swinging door to the kitchen. Smoke poured into the Imperial Dining Hall. Nargas and his guests leaped to their feet.

❦

I burst through the kitchen door about five seconds after the concussion bomb went off. I had planted it in a small refrigerator unit which had contained most of the damage, as I had hoped. "Evacuate the area!" I shouted. "That bomb was intended for all of you!"

Mack looked at me with surprise and darted out the main door, followed immediately by Bellatrax and the other grey.

"Is anyone hurt inside the kitchen?" Grauber asked.

"Nobody is in there. I don't know where they are. They may have been accomplices in this attack." I was lying. I had pointed to my stripes and ordered the six kitchen workers and the waiter to leave before I put the grenade in the refrigerator and set the delayed fuse. They left without question. Nobody fucks with an interrogator.

Suddenly Nargas grabbed me by the arm, looked into my eyes, and said, '*You're coming with me.*' I tried to pull away, but his grip was intense and vise-like. '*You will be my personal bodyguard.*'

"I need to find the perpetrators!" I argued, struggling against the grip of Nargas's claws. "I almost had those bastards when the explosion happened. If I hurry, I may be able to catch them!"

'*You are coming with me.*' Nargas insisted, putting a laser knife to my throat. I had no choice if I wanted to live. Nargas pulled me toward a wall with a mirror. He placed his finger on a small rectangular etching on the mirror. The mirror grew fuzzy and then disappeared, exposing the opening of an elevator. It was obviously a hidden Draconian escape route.

Before we entered the elevator, Nargas turned to his assistant Anole and told him, "Attend to the command center. Let me know when it is safe to return." Anole nodded, clenched his fist, and pounded his chest.

Inside the elevator, Nargas touched a symbol that looked like an asterisk, and we descended. When the door opened, we were in Nargas's hangar, directly in front of his tureen. He dragged me forward and up the ramp. The reptilian guard on duty saluted and stepped aside to let us pass.

Nargas cut him in half with a bolt of liquid light. I figured he was pissed about not being told about the guys that I had apprehended here earlier today.

As the door to his tureen closed, Nargas pushed me into a seat and told me to buckle my seat belt. I knew that I was going to be toast in no time. Spivey, Merkel, and Washington were in the main hangar waiting for Nargas to pass through on his way to his tureen. When they discovered that his tureen was no longer in its hangar, they would hit the detonator and send me to Hell with Nargas. This wasn't how I figured on being snuffed out, but there was no escape. I felt the tureen wobble slightly, and I knew we were exiting the moon.

I closed my eyes and waited for the end. I wasn't sure if I would see a bright flash of light, or if I would hear a brief roar of deafening noise, or feel an instant of pain. But, nothing happened. My mind shifted from fear of instant nuclear death to fear of having been ratted out by one of my supposed accomplices. Was it Washington, Spivey, or Merkel? Maybe all three? I could feel the sweat forming on my forehead.

Sudden motion snapped me back into the now. I opened my eyes. Through the skin of the tureen, I watched distant stars and the Earth flash by as Nargas flipped the tureen on its side and veered in a sharp semicircle, diving back toward the surface of the moon. Suddenly a large futuristic city appeared. Its glass skyscrapers were tall, stretching about a quarter of a mile above the moon's gray surface, in my estimation. Nargas piloted the tureen between two large towers, brought it to an abrupt halt, and then settled it quickly to the street below. The city appeared to have been constructed of some type of crystalline material, translucent if not transparent. But, it was deserted and appeared to have been that way for a very long time.

Now was not the time or place to ask about this ghost town, so I made a mental note to ask somebody about it later.

A beep from the pilot's control panel, followed by Nargas's hiss and guttural voice brought my attention back to the tureen's interior. Nargas turned and looked at me, and I heard a voice inside my head say, *'We have already received the All Clear.'*

I felt a small shudder and knew that he had already vaulted our tureen back into the sky above the city and toward the opening that led to the moon's interior.

"Maybe they apprehended the dissidents," I said.

'And maybe there are none to apprehend, Interrogator,' Nargas hissed. He rose and walked toward my seat. As he did, I unbuckled my seat belt and rose, prepared to fight to defend myself if necessary.

Nargas gave me a stern look, examining me silently. *'I am unsure of you,'* he told me. *'Something is not right about your presence on the lunar artifact.'*

"I assure you, Commissar, I am here to find the conspirators who wish to assassinate both you and His Excellency."

The commissar hissed at me and moved his hand toward the weapon buttons on his breast plate.

"If you terminate me, the way you have done to so many," I told him, "the NWO will ensure that you are relieved of your command."

Nargas pondered what I had said and returned to the pilot's seat. After buckling himself in, he turned and said, *'I will be watching you, Interrogator.'*

"And I will be protecting you," I replied. "If you suspect anyone, let me know immediately."

Nargas adjusted several switches and then pushed his control lever, sending the tureen into a spiral and sending me crashing into the curved wall behind me. He turned to look in my direction, sneered, and told me, *'Buckle your seatbelt.'*

I rose to get into my seat. As I did, he hit the control again, sending me smashing into the interior wall again. Motion on the interior walls caught my eye. We were circling the moon at an extremely fast rate of speed, making one pass around it in less than a minute. I crawled on hands and knees to my seat and buckled my seatbelt. Nargas flipped the control again, rising upward and away from the moon. I could feel my stomach hitting my ass. I realized that Nargas must have shut off whatever technology controls inertia on the inside of the tureen. It was like he was using technology to beat me up, sending me a message that I'd better watch out because he was bigger than I am. He hit the control again, and we reversed direction, shooting downward toward the moon at an incredible rate of speed. I blacked out.

When I came to, I was alone inside Nargas's tureen, and it was hovering silently inside its hangar. I unbuckled my seatbelt and staggered down the ramp. The lizard that Nargas had cut down was still a two-piece mess on the concrete floor. It was time to go talk to Mona.

I groggily walked through the door to the main hangar and found my way to the elevators. When I reached level 346, I got out and went to Pod Four to find Spivey, Merkel, or Washington. Nobody was there. So, I found the elevator that went directly to the nursery and stepped in.

When the nursery door opened, I saw an older lizard in a nurse's uniform sitting at a desk. My arrival caught her by surprise, and she put down her communicator. The picture on its screen was moving, and it looked like she was watching the old black and white Japanese version of Godzilla. She looked me in the eyes and told me, '*Get out of here! The babies are sleeping. Come back in the morning when we are open for visitors.*'

"It is important that I ask Commissar Nargas's guest some questions about the event this evening."

'*She is sleeping. Come back in the morning.*'

"Are you aware that someone tried to kill the commissar this evening?" I asked pointing to my stripes. I was getting used to doing that. "I need to speak with that woman to see if she has information that will lead me to the perpetrators."

'*I am not aware of any incident this evening.*'

"Have you checked your communicator for announcements?"

The old nurse sighed and picked up her communicator. She touched the screen a few times and began reading. '*It says here that there was a fire in the kitchen but that everything is okay now.*'

"It wasn't a fire. It was a bomb, and Commissar Nargas was the target. Now I have to speak with the woman."

'*Do you have a warrant?*'

"I am an interrogator," I said, pointing to my stripes again. "I don't need a warrant or clearance from anyone."

The old lizard sighed again. '*Okay, but don't you wake any of the babies, or you're going to rock all of them back to sleep.*'

I nodded and then crept quietly over to the cot where Mona would be sleeping. When I saw Mona, she was lying on the cot with her hybrid daughter in the crook of her left arm. Both were fast asleep. I hated to wake her, but I needed to tell her what was going down and what to expect. At least I hoped that it would be going down and I hoped that I wasn't already targeted for termination.

I knelt down and stroked Mona's cheek. In the dim light of the nursery, I could see that her natural chestnut brown hair was growing in. Although her blonde hair was still dominant, her dark brown roots were almost an inch long, giving her head the appearance of a racing stripe, or maybe a football helmet.

I stroked her cheek again. She stirred a little. "Mona! Mona, baby!" I whispered. "Mona, it's me, Danny. Your Danny."

"Danny," Mona repeated, rolling toward me.

"Mona, wake up!"

"Huh?" she asked.

"Mona, it's me…Danny"

Mona threw her right arm around my neck and planted a warm, juicy, and welcoming kiss on my lips. Yes, I thought, this moment was worth it!

"Mona, we're going to leave here tomorrow!"

"Danny, I love you so much," she said. "I've missed you terribly."

"Yeah, baby, I love you, too. But you've got to listen to me. Listen carefully."

Her expression became serious. She was now fully awake and cognizant of what I was saying.

"Mona, we're going to leave here tomorrow."

"How are we gonna do that?" she asked. "That bastard has me under constant surveillance."

"Tomorrow I'm going to blow the support beams off of this place. The whole facility is going to shake, and maybe the floors are going to buckle. This place is going be in shambles."

"How are you going to do that?" she asked.

"Don't worry about that. I'll explain later. The important thing is that when you hear the blast and feel the explosion, you and little—does she have a name?"

"I call her Stella."

"When you feel the explosion, you and little Stella gotta get out of here and find your way to the visitors' tureen hangar. It's on level three-forty-four. If you can't take the elevator, you gotta take the stairs, but you gotta get there as quickly as possible. Look for Mack. He's here, and he'll be evacuating as soon as you arrive. Do you understand?"

"Yeah, Danny, level three-forty-four and look for Mack."

I gave Mona a passionate kiss and squeezed her. "I love you, baby," I said.

"Watch it. You're waking Stella, Danny."

"Okay, okay. I'll back off." I released my hug and took Mona's hand. "Just remember what I said. When the explosion goes off, get the fuck out of here!" I squeezed her hand, blew her a kiss, and left.

As I passed the old fart nurse, she was back watching that movie on her communicator. I patted the top of her desk twice as I left, but she didn't even look up at me. Nothing like third shift workers, I thought.

Chapter 26

an! You're okay! We thought the commissar might have done you in!" It was Spivey. He jumped from his bunk and rushed toward me like I was a long lost brother.

"You'd didn't detonate the nuke!" I replied. "I thought you were going to hit the detonator when the commissar's tureen left the artifact."

Spivey threw his arms around me. "God bless that you're alive!"

"How come you didn't detonate the nuke? Was it too far away?"

Spivey let go of his hold on me and replied, "Naw, you was in that tureen, so we decided against it."

"How did you know where I was?" I asked.

"It was Washington. When we got to the main hangar, he figured that there might be another way into the commissar's hangar, so he went in from that side door and hid there while Merkel and I hid in the main hangar."

"How are Washington's arms?"

"Oh, he's sore, but he's gonna be okay."

"I guess I owe him big time."

"Merkel and I was waiting, but nobody ever came in. Then Washington came back through that door and told us that Nargas came out of the wall over there and that he was dragging you by your arm."

"That's about the size of it. Nargas took me for a ride in his buggy. He said that I was his protection."

"So we pow wowed when we knew that Nargas had you, and we decided not to detonate that nuke until we knew what happened to you. If he'd killed you, we'd really have been pissed, but we planned to hit that detonator the next time he took a trip somewhere."

"Close call for me, huh? So where are Merkel and Washington?"

"They were called for clean-up duty. Seems there was a fire in the kitchen of the Imperial Dining Room," Spivey snickered.

"What did you guys do with that detonator? I wouldn't want that nuke to go off when Nargas's tureen is in its hangar."

"I got it under my pillow. It's safe there. Nobody's been under my pillow since the tooth fairy quit coming."

I laughed and then turned serious. "Listen, Spivey, I'm pretty sure that Nargas has a breakfast scheduled with the Chinese tomorrow morning. That gives us another chance to strike."

"Whatcha got up your sleeve, Dan?"

"Can we set off a small nuke at the top of the tower? It should send a shudder down the entire tower and send Nargas scampering again. Only this time I don't plan to be invited aboard his tureen."

"It can't be too big, because we don't want to damage the supports, do we?"

"Exactly," I said, reassuring him. "Maybe one of those ultra-small nukes that won't leave a bunch of radiation, but will give this place a good shaking."

"Yeah, we can do that."

"Okay, let's go get one and tape it to a support beam!"

Spivey led the way, and I followed. We took the elevator to the nuclear storage facility at level 443 and walked in together. Only two workers were there, and both were cleaning up after a full day's work. Hell, it was approaching bedtime.

"Hey, Spivey," one asked, "What brings you here at this hour? You ain't on duty until morning."

"The interrogator wants to inspect our supply of smaller devices. It seems there was an explosion earlier this evening."

"We heard. A couple of lizards were up here around dinnertime. They were asking who might have access to the concussion grenades other than immediate staff."

The other laughed. "We gave them your name, Spivey!"

"You'd better not have!" Spivey replied seriously.

"No, we wouldn't have done that. They were asking about non-staff," said the first.

"And we forgot about the interrogator, too," added the other.

"That wouldn't have made no difference. He's immune to suspicion," Spivey told them.

At least until they find out that I'm not really an interrogator, I thought.

Spivey took me into the small device room. We selected a grapefruit sized nuke and then found the cabinet with the detonators. Spivey activated the detonator by touching its red and blue buttons simultaneously and then touched it to the nuke. After two seconds, the detonator beeped and flashed a red light. "It's activated, Dan."

"Maybe we should wait until it's taped to the ceiling," I said.

"Naw, it's perfectly safe. Remember that we have to push two buttons on the detonator before the nuke will go off."

"Yeah, okay," I replied. "You're the expert."

A voice from the other room interrupted us. "Hey, Spivey, we're checking out. See you in the morning." It was one of the two staffers who were working when we came into the nuclear storage facility.

"Yeah, no problem!" Spivey shouted back. "That's good," he said to me, "because nobody's gonna suspect anything when we walk out of here with weight in my backpack."

Spivey then opened a drawer in a workbench next to the detonator cabinet and pulled out a roll of black duct tape. "This will do," he muttered.

When Spivey and I exited the facility, we took the elevator to level 500 at the top of the habitation zone of the central tower. We decided that the best place to attach the small nuke would be on the flat surface of one of the large round support columns, where it would do little damage and would probably not compromise the structure. We wanted the central tower to shake, but not to collapse.

"Column number one is definitely the strongest," I reminded Spivey.

"Yeah, and there ain't no use in climbing up to the hanging walkway, besides, we wouldn't want to risk damaging it."

"Yeah," I replied.

The outside of column one was very smooth, but Spivey found that he could wedge himself between it and column eight and shinny up about thirty feet into the space feet between them by pressing his back on column eight and pressing his feet against column one. When he reached that height, he stuck two pieces of duct tape onto the grapefruit nuke in a plus mark configuration and slapped it against column one, rubbing the tape briskly with his hands. For extra assurance that it would remain adhered, he put several more pieces of tape on each of the four legs that were attached to the nuke. It was ugly, but effective.

After Spivey shinnied back down, we returned to the elevator and rode it back down to Pod Four. On the way, I asked, "So, Spivey, how can you tell the two detonators apart? If you put them both under your pillow, aren't you likely to blow the commissar's tureen when you intend to blow the grapefruit nuke?"

"I'll keep this one in my backpack."

"Okay. I guess that'll work."

It was now close to midnight Earth time, and both of us were exhausted. Merkel was already asleep when we found our way to our bunks, and we didn't wake him. Spivey whispered that he would fill Merkel in on the plans in the morning. We piled into our bunks. In less than five minutes, I could hear that unique wheezing snore that Spivey made every night. I waited another ten minutes to be sure he was really out, and then I quietly left my bunk and headed back to the elevator.

❧❧

The corridor outside of the nuclear storage facility was dark and quiet. It appeared that nobody was stirring in the tower except for one pretend interrogator. I pressed my hand upon the metal plate beside the door to the facility, and it popped open. *Security clearance Q is a good thing*, I told myself.

I closed the door behind me and found my way to the room where the suitcase nukes are kept. The door was ajar. I entered, shut the door, and hit the light switch.

Hundreds of devices lined the shelves, but I only needed a couple.

At the floor level, I found a shelf with a dozen or more containers that looked like bowling ball bags. I took two to help me to carry the nukes. A couple of shelves later, I found medium-sized nukes that fit inside the bags. They were rectangular and were colored with that familiar dull army green. I wasn't sure of their destruction capabilities, but I figured that two might do the trick anyway. I put them into the bags, and they fit perfectly.

Next, I found the detonator cabinet and removed one from its box. I resealed the box and put it neatly back in the cabinet, where its absence wouldn't be discovered for a while, I hoped. I took the two nukes out of their bags and placed them on the workbench beside the cabinet. I placed the detonator so that it sat neatly across both nukes, then I pressed the blue and red buttons simultaneously, the way Spivey had done. The detonator beeped twice. Both nukes were armed!

Then I opened the workbench drawer and pulled out a roll of duct tape. It was red. *Go figure*, I thought. *Red for 'kaboom!'* I turned out the light, walked through the main room, and exited the facility. The elevator door was still open, so I entered and hit the top button. Fifty seven floors later, the door opened at level 500.

I found the entry door to column seven and entered it. I shut the door behind me, turned on the flashlight that hung on my belt, and began climbing to the top. After a hundred steps, I noticed that the nukes were beginning to feel heavy to my arms, but I didn't stop because there was much to do and very little time.

The large crack at the top of Column Seven offered the best place to set off a nuke if I hoped to damage the central tower, so that was my destination. I continued my climb, exiting the main shaft at the location of the catwalk, and then continuing the upward trek to the crack in the ceiling above. When I reached to final plateau, I wedged one nuke-in-a-bag into a step, and then followed the narrow pathway up into the crevice. When I reached the flat spot where Merkel and Spivey had been sitting on our first trip there, I held onto a rock outcropping with my left hand and threw the nuke onto the plateau with my right. Then I returned to get the second, repeating the process.

Using my small flashlight, I could see that the plateau appeared the same as we had left it. The old mattress lay in a heap against one wall, and tiny pieces of evidence of someone's presence there at some time in the past were still around. However, I didn't think that anyone had been there since Merkel and Spivey and I had found it a few days before. That gave me a sense of comfort.

After a brief rest, I took a nuke in each hand and began climbing up into the crevice, holding the flashlight in my mouth so I could see the next foot and hand holds as I progressed. Basically, I lifted the nukes, set them on a small level spot, and then climbed up to that level before repeating the same steps. I climbed that way for an hour before deciding that I was deep enough into the crevice. Besides, the sides of the crack were beginning to close in on me, so I was nearing the end of my ability to climb.

I set the nukes side by side on a small ledge at waist level and then duct taped them to the surface. The duct tape was probably a waste of time, but what the hell, I had brought it and decided to use some of it rather than carry it back down. When I was finished, I descended to the entrance, taking much less time to reach that level than it had taken to climb up. I threw the roll of duct tape down the last ten feet and listened as it thumped onto the ledge. Then I turned my back to inch my way down safely.

When I reached the plateau, I saw that the mattress had been disturbed. *Fuck*, I thought. But before I could think "my ass is grass," a large one-armed lizard hissed and spit at me from the shadows to my left. I pointed my flashlight into his eyes in an effort to blind him. I could see that he was unarmed—by that, I mean that he didn't have a weapon that I could see. He roared and charged me. I ducked and rolled toward his right, where his arm was missing. He spun, and the jagged nails of his left hand narrowly missed ripping into my rump. I landed on my back and quickly pushed myself against the wall. He was now between me and the way out. This was not where I wanted to be, and I knew that I was in deep shit.

As he strode toward me again, I felt the floor with both hands, hoping to find something I could use to defend myself. All I found felt like dirt, so I picked it up in both hands and threw it into his eyes. He roared again and wiped his eyes clean with the back of his right hand. Then he spit, trying to clean his mouth. I realized that I must have found a pile or two of his feces, because my hands smelled like manure. I bent over, grabbed more in both hands, and threw it into his face again.

He roared and charged me, and I rolled again to his right and escaped. But safety was brief. I was near the ledge to Neverland and my only escape route. I turned so that I could climb down to the narrow pathway which descended from the ledge. I was too slow. In less than a second, I felt him grab my left arm with his, and suddenly I was launched like a stuffed toy across the plateau and against the jagged rocks at the back of the plateau. The wind left my lungs. My chest ached in pain. *Fuck, I'm finished*, I thought. I slid to the floor and feigned unconsciousness. As I lay waiting for his next move, I felt warm liquid running down my cheek, and tasted blood in my mouth.

I felt the lizard's large hand grab my belt. He lifted my body and flipped me over, plopping me like I was a piece of steak. He rummaged through my pockets, taking my wallet. He also found the detonator, which I heard fall to the stone floor beside my head. I guess he wasn't interested, or else he didn't know what it was. Thank God he didn't press any buttons, I thought.

I heard him rise, so I opened one eye carefully. He was studying the mess card that I carried in my wallet. He looked back in my direction, and then he stepped toward the ledge and roared loudly. He must have thought he was Tarzan. I seized the moment. Springing to my feet. I charged him, leaping into the air feet first and catching him in his gut with a side kick. My weight wasn't enough to send him flying off the edge, but he lost his balance and teetered, arm flailing to grasp something, and fell off the ledge.

I stood and peered over the edge, hoping that the lizard was enjoying a two hour free fall to the bottom of the hollow moon, but as luck would have it, he had managed to catch a small outcropping of stone with his hand, and was busily trying to get a leg onto the pathway so he could lift his immense lower body weight to safety.

I dragged the mattress to the ledge and pushed it over. He held on when it hit him in the head and then cascaded downward. I hurried to the side of the plateau and began feeling for something to pry his fingers from the rock. Nothing. Then I discovered my flashlight. Its button was in the ON position, so I shook it. It came to life, thank God for LED bulbs, and light filled the darkness. I frantically passed the beam across the floor. There was the detonator!

I picked it up and put it back into my pants pocket. Then the beam passed over an eight foot long piece of angle iron, probably something the lizard had dragged up to the plateau to use as a tool or a weapon.

I quickly picked up the angle iron and found my way to the edge again. The lizard had managed to get his foot onto the pathway and was wrenching his body upward. I knew that if he had had two arms, I would already be following the mattress, hoping that I would land on it in a couple of hours. There was no time to lose. I put one end of the angle iron against the sole of his foot then used the edge of the ledge as a fulcrum to pry his foot free. He let out a brief squeal as his body fell from the edge of the pathway, leaving him suspended again by one hand.

For a brief second, I felt sorry for the poor bastard. Disabled somehow, he had probably escaped going into the soup by hiding in this crevice in the roof of the moon. Now discovered, he had been defeated by a paltry human and was breathing heavily, fighting for his life.

But, what the fuck, he was a goddamn lizard and they'd just as soon eradicate all of us humans, so I did the right thing. I smashed the end of the angle iron onto the tips of his three clawed fingers. He screamed out in pain. I smashed again and again. Blood covered the rock that was in his grasp, but he did not release his grip. "Fuck!" I mumbled. Then I raised the iron as high as I could and brought it forcefully down into his face. His hand slipped from the rock and grabbed the end of the angle iron. The sudden weight of his body on the end of the angle iron ripped it from my hands, and I watched the lizard fall backward into oblivion.

As the son of a bitch fell, our eyes met for a second, and I heard him say, *Death to you, human!* Well, not yet, anyway, I hoped.

I waved back at him and muttered, "Enjoy your flight!" Then I collapsed to the floor of the plateau, breathing heavily, glad to be alive, and now aware that my forehead hurt like hell.

§

An hour later, I snuck back into Pod Four. Everyone was still asleep, which was a good thing. The bump on my head still hurt, so I washed it off with cold water in the latrine, and then crept back to my bunk. Spivey was snoring with his back turned toward me. I reached gently under his pillow and removed the detonator to the nuke in Nargas's tureen.

Then I replaced it with the detonator to the two that I had just taped to the stone outcropping, deep in the crevice above column seven.

As I rolled over to put Spivey's detonator into my pants pocket, he woke up. "Where've you been, man?" he asked.

I quickly pulled my hand under the covers to hide the detonator from his view and rolled back to face him. "I got into a pissing match with a lizard," I told him.

"Here?" he asked.

"No, I couldn't sleep, so I took a walk. Ran into him near the mess. I think he was stealing food. He cold cocked me and slammed me against the wall." I pointed to my head. "Look at the goose egg he gave me!"

Spivey lifted his head and squinted. "Can't see it too good, but it ain't too bad." He laid his head back down. "What's keeping you from sleeping, man?"

"Today's the day, Spivey," I said. "I keep thinking about the zillion things that have to go right for us to pull this off."

"What time do we make the artifact ring?" he asked matter-of-factly.

"I think that you guys ought be to be in the hangar at breakfast. When Merkel and Washington get up, we can discuss the exact time."

"Yeah, that's probably good. I'll give you the detonator that's in my backpack. You can set off the grapefruit nuke whenever you're ready. We'll watch for Nargas and be sure you ain't with him again."

"Thanks, buddy. I'm glad you're helping me with this."

"Me, too. I wouldn't miss it!"

"The second time's the charm."

Chapter 27

When will you inform Her Majesty that we have delivered the final shipment of gold?" the Chinese ambassador asked, dangling a whole cooked tree frog from his fingers and then popping it into his mouth.

"She has already been informed of your arrival," Commissar Nargas replied through his digital translator. "As soon as the quantity has been verified, you will be notified of the date and time of the official transfer of property ceremony."

"Good. We are looking forward to establishing our presence on the lunar artifact."

"You may tell your leaders that we anticipate relocating within two of your months, giving you access sooner than anticipated at our last meeting."

"Excellent!"

Unexpectedly, the room shuddered, spilling cups of hot liquid onto the table top. Then a dull rumbling sound became audible, and the ceiling above Nargas and the ambassador cracked, spewing dust onto the food.

"What was that, Commissar?" the ambassador asked.

Commissar Nargas leaped to his feet. "Come with me, Your Excellency," he said to the young Hitler who also had been enjoying the breakfast meeting.

Nargas and Hitler waited at the wall for a moment as it became fuzzy. When the elevator door opened, they entered, leaving the Chinese ambassador and his aide to fend for themselves.

ɛᴈɛᴈ

Mona heard the explosion and felt the floor of the nursery tremble and then buckle beneath her feet. A steady sound, somewhat like the Tibetan singing bowl that her sister gave her last Christmas, began to fill the room. She grabbed the bassinet with her free hand, steadying herself while she cradled Stella in her other arm.

Suddenly a pulsating alarm of some sort filled the corridor outside of the nursery. Screams and shouts erupted from the nursing quarters, and babies in the nursery began crying. The door to the nursery burst open, and an NWO guard shouted, "Evacuate! Evacuate!"

"Danny!" Mona whispered.

Mona had packed a small bag of diapers and clean clothes for Stella, just in case Danny's prediction came true. "This place is going to be in shambles!" he had told her.

She carried Stella to the cabinet where the liquid baby formula was stored, took a handful of bottles, and stuffed them into the bag. She threw the bag over her shoulder and then she and Stella escaped into the corridor.

She had only moved a few yards down the corridor when she felt a large clawed hand grab her shoulder. She turned, and the reptilian nurse's eyes met hers. '*Where do you think you're going?*' the nurse asked her.

"I'm taking my baby to safety!"

'*The commissar left explicit instructions that his issue was not to leave the nursery under any circumstances. You must give me the child.*'

Mona wrenched her shoulder from the lizard's grasp. "Can't you see that this floor has buckled and the nursery isn't a safe place for any of the children?" she asked.

The nurse pulled a hypodermic needle from her pocket and approached Mona with it. '*Don't fight me, human. The commissar will not let this hybrid child leave the nursery.*'

Mona offered Stella to the nurse. "Take her in two hands," she said. "You have to support her head."

The nurse put the hypodermic needle back into her pocket and reached for Stella. When the nurse had Stella firmly in her grasp, Mona released her. Then, without warning she reached into the nurse's pocket, pulled out the hypodermic needle, and plunged it into the nurse's eye, pressing with her thumb to ensure that its unknown contents filled the eyeball. The nurse roared in pain, releasing Stella as she grasped her eye. Mona caught Stella as she fell toward the floor and quickly brought her baby to her breast. As she did, the nurse fell to the floor, writhing in agony. Mona spit at her and continued quickly down the corridor.

The sound of the alarm pierced her ears as Mona made her way to the elevator, weaving between reptilians and NWO staff who were hurrying in every direction. When she found the elevators, she realized that they were jammed with panicked people, lizards, and greys, so she joined the hundreds who were descending the stairway to safety, if safety could be found anywhere in the central tower.

Several large lizards pushed by her, knocking her into the railing and causing her almost to lose Stella.

A grey fell past her from above.

"Bastards!" she screamed at them.

She regained her footing, continuing downward five floors, as Danny had told her, where she found the exit and followed the crowd, all hoping to find a seat on a tanker, transport, or shuttle that would be leaving the lunar artifact. As the mass of strange creatures surged into the Visitors Hangar, in the distance she could see tureens departing and people fighting to board others. Then in the distance to her left, she saw an old Nazi bell. *If Danny is going to be anywhere, it'll be in there*, she told herself. Fighting against the current of the masses, she pushed through person after lizard until she reached the open concrete floor.

Mona turned to look backward for a moment and saw Commissar Nargas and a young dark-skinned man enter a tureen. Nargas stopped at the top of the ramp and fired a bolt of liquid light at the crowd behind him. Several greys and a lizard were cut down, and the crowd drew backward, giving Nargas enough time to close the ramp. Then the crowd pushed forward, and people began beating on the tureen's door and shouting for help. Within seconds, the tureen rose to the ceiling. "That coward did the same thing to me at Livermore!" Mona cried out. "He's chicken shit!"

But the tureen that Nargas and the young man had entered quickly dropped back down to the floor. When its ramp opened, three fully armed reptilians marched down and drove the crowd back. Nargas and the young man followed, and were escorted by the guards to a Draconian elevator. The wall became fuzzy, and then the elevator door opened. Nargas and the young man entered and descended, leaving the three guards to manage the crowd of mixed aliens, many of whom entered the vacant tureen only to discover that its fuel cells were empty.

When she reached the old Nazi bell, Mona beat on its side with her open palm. "Danny! Danny! It's me! It's Mona!" Maybe he couldn't hear her. She saw a wrench on the floor, picked it up, and began beating it against the bell. The hatch opened, and a ladder descended. Mona climbed up. "Danny?"

"Mona?"

"Mack!" Mona cried in relief. "Mack, where's Danny? He told me to meet him here."

"Come inside, Mona! Let me close the hatch again!"

Mona did as Mack instructed, first handing Stella up to him and then climbing into the bell. Then she took Stella from Mack and sat in the co-pilot's seat where she could watch the crowd in the hangar via the craft's single monitor. Beside her in the pilot's seat sat a grey who she thought might be Grau. He was checking controls and preparing for lift-off. She watched on the monitor as hundreds of greys, reptilians, and NWO soldiers poured into the hangar area hoping to catch a ride on a departing tureen.

Many of the unlucky left the visitors' hangar and descended by elevators and stairs to the military hangars in hopes of finding a seat. Like the Titanic, there simply were not enough lifeboats for everyone who wanted to escape probable death.

As the visitors' tureens departed laden with passengers, the crowds began to disperse. It was then that Mona saw Danny, weaving through the dozens of remaining evacuees, and coming in the direction of the old Nazi bell. Twice he ducked as low-flying tureens whizzed at head level toward the exit doors.

"Mack! There he is! There's Danny!" Mona cried, pointing to the monitor.

Mack looked closely at the monitor. It was Dan!

"Watch out, Danny!" Mona cried out.

As Mack continued to watch, Mona took the .45 pistol from the holster Mack wore on his hip. "Watch Stella for me, Mack!" She hurried down the ladder to the hangar floor. Mack closed the hatch behind her.

As Dan approached the Nazi bell, he was suddenly attacked by a man wearing an NWO officer's uniform who had followed him into the hangar. The man came quickly from behind and threw a cord over Dan's head, attempting to strangle him by pressing his foot into Dan's back and pulling backward with his torso. Instinctively, Dan fell backward, smashing the man's head to the floor. Dan twisted free from the cord and grasped his throat to be sure that he wasn't bleeding. The man rose to his feet and charged, tackling Dan at his waist. As Dan fell, he raised his right foot into the man's abdomen and launched him upward, flipping him onto his back on the concrete floor.

The man pulled a gun, pointed it at Dan, and said, "I thought the wine I sent you would have done you in, but you're a tough bastard to kill."

"You've got me confused with someone else!" Dan said, holding his palms up as if they could stop a .45 caliber round.

"I lost my son at Livermore," the man shouted at him, "and I know that you're the bastard who nuked the place."

"I'm sorry that you lost your son, but lots of people died at Livermore. I didn't set off the nuke!"

"We had such plans for him. He was in line to be a colonel in the NWO by this year, and you ended it all for him!"

Dan could see motion coming quietly from behind the man, so he tried to buy some time. "What was his name...your son?"

"Lieutenant Colonel Charles Lee."

"Sorry, but we never met."

"You're gonna meet him now in Hell, you sorry bastard." The man raised his arm so he could line up the front and rear sights on his model 1911.

"Drop it, mister! Put the pistol down or die here and now!" It was Mona.

The man turned his head to see Mona holding her own model 1911 about three feet from his head.

"You don't understand, lady. This guy nuked Livermore and killed my son. I recognized him in Dulce and followed him to the Lunar Artifact on the same shuttle. He's harder to kill than a goddamn roach. But, he's gotta die."

He turned his eyes back toward Dan and raised his hand again. As the tendons in his wrist signaled that he was about to pull the trigger, Mona put two rounds into his head, Pop! Pop! He fell quickly sideways, a red mist filling the air behind him and his pistol sliding across the floor.

"Just in time, baby! God, I love you," I said.

Mona gave me a big hug and a kiss. "Did you really nuke Livermore?" she asked.

"You were there. You know I didn't. But I wish I had."

We hurried back to the Nazi Bell. Mack opened the hatch and lowered the ladder. I helped Mona up the ladder and then climbed aboard. Mack shut the hatch and told Grau that he could leave whenever he was ready. As the grey moved the controls at his fingertips, a vibration accompanied by the sound of electric arcing filled the cabin. But Mona didn't notice. She was in my arms.

Chapter 28

I just couldn't leave her behind, Danny," Mona told me.

"I know, baby," I replied. "She looks a lot like Melissa."

"Yes, doesn't she?"

I unbuckled my security harness and walked toward the pilot's seats so I could look at the monitor. "Where are we?" I asked.

"We're about five hundred miles from the moon," Mack replied, directing the external cameras toward the moon. Behind us, I could see half a dozen tureens hurtling in various directions from the dark side and exposing themselves to observers of the light side the lunar artifact, as the NWO called it.

Suddenly a light emanated from the moon. Its brilliance blotted out the monitor, turning it into a sea of white. After a few seconds, and as the light dissipated, I could see a fissure with dust and smoke pouring out of the upper right quadrant of the moon.

"What was that?" Mack asked.

"Probably three young NWO guards who thought

they were doing in the commissar," I replied. Grau raised his three fingers into the air and clenched them into a fist. He had a smile on his face. I guess he liked what I had to say.

"I feel kind of bad about it because they were almost friends," I told them, "but they were die-hard NWO types who couldn't wait to take over the Earth. They would have died for the cause, and I'd have never been able to convert them to see it our way."

"I guess they did," Mack replied.

"Did what?"

"They died for the cause."

"Yeah, I guess."

લ૭લ૭

Hamilton W. Herschel, descendant of William Herschel who discovered Uranus and the Martian ice caps, clicked the shutter again and again on his telescope's digital camera as moving objects appeared against the surface of the moon. If he had to describe what he was seeing, he would say that the objects reminded him of bees flying around their hive. Suddenly, a beam of brilliant light burst from the Mare Anguis crater at Latitude 22.43 and longitude 67.58 on the bright surface of the moon. He clicked the shutter again and again, as a plume of fire and smoke bellowed from a crack on the crater's floor.

Without taking his eye off of the telescope's eyepiece, he called out to his graduate intern, "Call NASA! Call NASA now! There's evidence of seismic activity on the moon! It's in the Mare Anguis crater."

"Really?" the young woman asked. "You've got to be shitting me, Hammie!"

"Yes! I mean, No! This is no bullshit! I'm making a photographic record of it the best that I can, but I can't do videos and stills at the same time. It might be a volcano. Hurry! Call NASA!"

The intern opened a directory, found NASA's emergency number, and dialed it on her cell phone. "This is Ellen Farrow. I am a graduate intern at the Palomar Observatory. Dr. Herschel asked me to call you. He wants you to focus your telescopes on the Mare Anguis area of the moon. He says there's a volcano erupting there.

"Bullshit!" came the reply.

"This is no bullshit," she said. "Once you verify this, you can name it the Herschel-Farrow Volcano. We were the first to see and report it. Dr. Herschel has taken dozens of photographs."

"Email me some, and we'll take a look."

"You might want to look at it for yourself. You won't want it said that NASA wasn't on top of this."

"Ellen!" Herschel said with urgency.

"Just a second," she said to the unnamed NASA representative." She turned toward Hammie Herschel. "Yeah?" she asked.

"Tell them that the fissure appears to be about—"

"Just a minute," she replied. "You can tell them yourself."

She climbed the stairs to the observer's platform and put her cell phone against Hammie's right ear.

"Is this NASA?" Herschel asked, still watching and snapping pictures.

"Are you Dr. Herschel?" the man asked. "I want to record our conversation." He fumbled for a few seconds and then said, "Okay, go ahead!"

"I don't remember the exact time, but my digital camera records the date and time on each picture, so we can verify the time later. Anyway, about half an hour ago I started observing moving objects leaving the moon in a variety of directions. I took dozens of pictures of them.

Then, maybe five minutes ago, there was a brilliant flash of light followed by fire and smoke emanating from the Mare Anguis crater."

"If you're right, this is the first seismic activity ever reported on the moon."

"As I look at it now, it's a fissure. It's approximately one-point-four miles long and point-fifteen miles wide. Smoke is still pouring out of it, but the fire appears to have diminished. I've seen nothing like it before. At first, I thought it was a volcano, but now I think…"

"Think what?" the NASA representative asked.

"It's more like a crack in the moon!"

౷౷౷

Grau directed the Nazi bell toward Mars, where we looked forward to safety and much needed R & R in Waam's Ummite outpost. I sat beside Mona and held her hand until she asked me, "Would you like to hold her?"

I'm not skilled at holding babies. In fact, they make me nervous. But I wanted to show Mona that I'd be willing to play the fatherly role, so I outstretched my arms, and she placed little Stella in them. Stella was so tiny that I felt like I might break her. I wanted to hand her back, but I knew that Mona wanted me to feel the joy of holding a little child in my arms. Stella's black eyes were intriguing, and I could see Mona in her face. I wanted to find revulsion in her, but she didn't look like the lizard I expected her to be, and I knew that she was Mona's baby. I found myself baby-talking to her like a great uncle or something. Weird, huh?

About two hours into our ride to Mars, the bell suddenly shook violently. Grau looked excitedly at Mack and made rapid gestures with his hands. "We are under attack!" Mack shouted. "It appears to be the commissar's tureen."

"How are our defenses?" I asked.

"We have shields, but he has greater firepower. I'm not sure how long we can take his assault. This is an old buggy."

I removed the detonator from my pants pocket and shouted to Grau, "See if you can maneuver away from the commissar. Get as far away as you can. I think I can take him out!"

Grau gave me a puzzled look. I showed him the detonator, and he nodded in understanding. Grau looked into my eyes and told me to buckle up. As I hurried to my seat, the bell shook again from the impact of a bolt of liquid light. Sparks flew from the control panel at the co-pilot's seat where Mack was sitting. I stumbled to the right and then to the left, and Mona caught my arm as I almost landed in her lap from the rocking bell.

Once I was seated and buckled, Grau hit a lever, and we suddenly spun to our right and dived. I heard a blast of liquid light glance off of the side of our bell. If it had been a direct hit, it might have killed our magnetic thrusters, so I guess it was a good thing that we dived when we did. Grau then rotated us in the opposite direction and jammed on the reverse thrusters. The commissar's tureen shot by us at hyper-speed. As it slowed to return for another attack, I raised the detonator and hit the button.

The monitor inside our bell turned white again, and then reddish orange before we were shaken violently by the blast. It was clear that we were too close to the commissar's tureen when the nuke ripped it apart. Grau had to fight to stop our bell from tumbling with the shock wave that burst through space. Fortunately, we suffered no damage, except maybe for some radioactive fallout that might have adhered itself to our shell. Fortunately, too, the bell was constructed of a steel/lead alloy, so those of us inside were protected from radiation poisoning.

"Is the commissar dead?" Mona asked me when quiet returned to space.

"Yeah, he's nothing but space dust now."

"Good! I hated that bastard."

"You and little Stella should be safe now," I said, putting my arm around Mona and kissing her forehead.

"Waam will be disappointed that he couldn't push the button," Mona reminded me.

"Yeah, I was supposed to deliver the commissar to him so he could avenge Doroo's murder. But I don't think we had any choice, and Waam will understand that."

"I think he'll be happy that Nargas has been terminated, anyway."

"I think half the guys in the NWO will be happy that Nargas is gone." I thought about that for a second and then said, "Well, at least those who survived the two nukes that went off inside the moon. I'm thinking that the NWO guard ranks took a big hit today."

The remainder of the trip to Mars was uneventful. Several tureens passed us along the way, but we couldn't travel as fast as they could anyway. Remembering our trip from Mars to the Earth, I figured we had a solid fifteen hours of traveling to do after dispatching Nargas. I slept most of the way. Mona, too, with her head on my shoulder, when she wasn't repositioning Stella in her arms. Or changing her.

Chapter 29

T ime to rise," Mack told us. "We'll be landing in just a few minutes. I'm sure that Waam will be there to greet us and you can tell him the good news about the commissar."

I sat up and rubbed my neck. I had been sleeping in an upright position with my chin on my chest, and my neck was complaining about the position it had been in. I unbuckled my seatbelt, stood, and then helped Mona to her feet.

"They need to install sleeper bunks in these things," she said.

"Yeah," I chuckled. "How's Stella?"

"She could use a changing and a fresh bottle of formula, but I'm all out of both," Mona replied. "Hopefully Waam's quartermaster will have something on hand."

"I don't know, baby. They probably don't have much call for diapers and formula on Mars," I said.

"My mom used to mix condensed milk with a little honey when she was out of prepared formula. Maybe the chef can whip something up."

"I'm sure we can figure out something," I assured her.

As we approached the Martian atmosphere, I waited to see if the Draconians would harass us like they did on our first arrival. I guess that I really expected them to do so, but they let us arrive peacefully. Maybe the loss of their commissar had them rethinking our capabilities. Maybe they were in mourning. Maybe celebrating. No matter, we simply descended slowly into the mouth of the Ummite fortification and flew to the docking station in the hanger.

"Anyone here to greet us?" Mack asked Grau.

Grau shrugged his shoulders, got out of the pilot's seat, and opened the hatch. He looked up at me as he descended the ladder. I could tell from his expression that something wasn't right.

Instinctively, I stepped in front of Mona and said, "Don't move, baby. Something isn't kosher." I looked at Mack and said, "Something isn't right with Grau."

Mack stood up from his co-pilot's seat and walked to the hatch. "Hey, Grau!" he shouted downward. Suddenly a large reptilian hand took him by the throat and pulled him through the hatch. I heard him hit the ground with a thud.

"We've got company, Mona, and I don't think they're happy to see us."

A fully armored lizard came up the ladder and leaped into the bell. He was followed by another.

"We're fucked," I told Mona.

The first lizard tried to grab my arm, but I leaped aside and kicked him in the groin. He didn't even wince. Instead, he backhanded me across my chest and sent me flying into the back of Grau's seat. I struggled for breath again, like I did when that lizard lofted me into the wall in the crack above column seven. It must be some special technique they've learned, or else I have a knack for flying chest-first into hard things.

I heard Mona scream, "Hands off of me, you bastard!" I knew she was being taken down the ladder to who knows what. Then I felt my ankle being grasped by a lizard's claws—I was now pretty good at recognizing what that felt like—and I felt my body being dragged across the bells' steel floor. As I was being pulled down the hatch, my head smacked against its edge. They really didn't care if I got banged up a bit. That wasn't a good sign. Suddenly I felt myself falling head first to— whomp!—the concrete floor of the hangar.

I heard a hiss and some garbled guttural sounds. I was lifted to my feet by two lizards, each one grasping me by an arm. I felt a scratchy hand take my chin. Still gasping for breath from the impact of my chest against Grau's seat, I opened my eyes to see who wanted to chat. It was Commissar Nargas!

"I thought you were dead," I gasped.

'*And I thought you were dead,*' he told me, '*but we will soon rectify that.*'

"How did you get here?" I asked, bewildered.

'*We drove the Ummites off of the Red Planet four days ago. His Excellency and I have been waiting for you since we evacuated the lunar artifact a few hours ago in a standard military tureen. I assume it was you who weakened the tower structure.*'

I saw Hitler standing beside Nargas. "It was me who blew your tower fortress to smithereens, too," I told Nargas. "I hope I killed all your scaly soldiers."

'*You terminated a few, but those who are still inside will survive. As your scientists discovered during their early atomic bomb experiments, we reptilians are immune to radiation.*'

"Danny! Danny!" Mona screamed. "What does he want with you?"

"I think he wants to fuck me."

Nargas tightened his grip on my jaw bone. I winced in pain. '*Keep it up, Earth Scum, and I will shorten your life span even more than the few minutes you have remaining.*'

Nargas motioned to his guards with his head, and they dragged me over the where two other lizards in full combat garb were holding Mack and Grau prisoner. When our eyes met, I smiled at the lizard who was holding Grau. "A year ago I ate a lizard egg omelet in Nicaragua. It tasted like shit." He released his grasp on Grau long enough to hit me in the gut. I barfed on his foot. He raised his hand to hit me again, but Nargas stopped him.

"You will have the honor of cutting him in half in a few minutes," Nargas told him. Or at least it was something like that, because I couldn't understand what Nargas really said. It just sounded like hisses and the gurgling of an upset stomach.

While Mona was held securely by a lizard, Nargas snapped a collar around her neck and attached a six foot leash made of some sort of cable. It was the same contraption that he had put on her at Livermore when I disrupted Hitler's migration ceremony. For Mona, I knew it was both confinement and humiliation to be treated like a pet dog. If she had had a pistol, she'd have put a couple of rounds through his brain. Hell, she'd have emptied her clip into him.

Nargas led Mona and two of his Draconian guards down a corridor and through a door. Hitler accompanied them. Once they disappeared, the guards who held Mack, Grau, and me forced us against a wall, where they shackled our arms to iron bars. Then the guards conferred for a few moments. One guard climbed onto a backhoe and used a post hole digger to drill two feet into the rock. When the hole was deep enough, another guard shoved a round steel post into it. Hanging about eight feet high on the post were two metal rings. I could already envision what was going to happen.

When their execution station was fully erected, they released Grau from the iron bars on the wall and dragged him to the post, handcuffed him, and pulled his arms upward by a cable that ran through the rings on the post. Once he was secure, the four lizards played some sort of betting game to see would go first. The winner then took aim and sent a burst of liquid light at Grau's legs, severing them at the ankles. Grau squealed in pain, and his body fell, supported now only by his wrists. The lizards laughed.

"Keep the faith, Grau," I called out to him. "It'll be over soon. Show 'em you can take anything they dish out!"

The lizard who punched me earlier grabbed me by the jaw and looked into my eyes. *'I'm saving you for last,* he told me. *Yours will be a very long death.'*

That made me feel much better.

The second lizard took aim and shot a burst of light at Grau, severing his right arm at its shoulder. Grau screamed again and appeared to pass out. *Thank God for that*, I thought. As I watched, Grau's body twisted like a piñata in a breeze from the weight of his torso and legs on his left wrist. His face was now sideways to me. Without warning, a burst of liquid light hit his head, and it simply disappeared. It was over for him. Mack's turn.

Grau's left arm and torso still hung on the execution pole. The shortest of the three lizards walked up to it and ripped the arm and torso off of the hand by pulling downward at the elbow. Blood splattered onto his hand, and he bent over and wiped it off on Grau's baby blue jumpsuit. Then he used his boot to push the bodily remains out of the way.

The other two lizards removed Mack from the rock wall and dragged him to the pole. Mack didn't make it any easier on them. He picked his feet into the air and tried kicking them in the face in an effort to break free of their grip. It was a useless exercise, but it was clear that he hadn't accepted his fate. I watched his struggles, thinking that when it was my turn, maybe I could do something to actually free myself. Maybe if I could blind them with my fingers or toes. But it wasn't looking good.

They strung Mack up by his wrists, as they had done to Grau. "Fuck you smelly bastards!" Mack yelled at them. "I hope my guts splatter into your eyes!"

Way to go, Mack, I thought. *I hope they do, too.*

Again, the lizards played some sort of game that determined who got to take the first shot at their new target. Then they separated, and the guy who had shot Grau the first time prepared to do the same to Mack.

"See you in Hell, Mack!" I shouted to him.

Mack smiled and cocked his head like a rooster that knows he's going to lose his head to the axe. I didn't think Mack had planned to go out this way. Come to think of it, neither had I. I just hoped that Mona would be okay, now that she was under Nargas's protection again.

As the lizard reached for his breast plate, a burst of liquid light came from my left and cut him in half. Surprised, the other two lizards ducked and sought shelter. The big guy fired a shot in the direction that the light had come. Then again. Then two bolts of light hit him from different angles. He was toast, severed into three pieces and heaped onto the floor. The other turned and ran. Three or four bursts of light flew past him, but all missed, and he escaped into a small corridor that led to safety.

Because of a small abutment in the rock wall, I

couldn't see who had attacked our executioners, but Mack's face lit up.

"Waam!" he cried, "I owe you my life!"

"Waam!" I called out when I saw him and ten huge Ummite warriors appear from the shadows. "It's about time!"

"I guess we got here too soon," Waam replied with a smile.

"You're alive," I exclaimed. "When I learned that Nargas had captured your outpost, I was afraid that he had killed you."

"We were lucky and were forewarned of his attack. Only three of our number were killed. We have come back today as a scouting party to see if we can retrieve some important computer files. And, of course, to save any hapless humans who happen to be hanging around."

"Enough with the funny stuff. We have to save Mona."

Waam pulled the iron bar behind me off the wall with the jerk of one hand, and then one of his men cut the metal cuffs off of my wrists with some sort of laser device. It got hot but didn't burn me. Another Ummite attended to Mack. In no time, we were hugging Waam, and thanking him for saving our lives. Then, I said it again, "We have to save Mona!"

"Where is she?" Waam asked.

"Nargas has her and her baby. He put another collar on her."

"So, she was able to be reunited with her hybrid?"

"Yes. It's a girl. Mona named her Stella."

"In which direction did the commissar go?"

I pointed to the corridor where I had last seen Nargas leading Mona by her leash.

Waam suggested that Mack and I should accompany him and his men because the one reptilian had escaped, and we wouldn't be safe where we were. He was right about that.

The Ummites were almost twice our height, and we had to jog to keep up with their gait. We passed the door that the commissar had entered, and then Waam touched a dark spot on the ceiling. A hidden door opened on the same side.

"What is this?" I asked.

"We installed secret passageways to enable us to escape in the event of an attack like the one we experienced four days ago. When we first built these passageways, I thought it was a waste of time. However, we are now using them for the second time in less than one week."

With liquid plasma guns raised in the ready position, Waam's men entered first, followed by Waam, and then Mack and me. The corridor was dimly lit and the two of us in the back of the pack made our way in the shadows of the tall fighters who led the way. When we came to an adjoining corridor, one of Waam's men rotated the barrel on his plasma gun so that it was bent ninety degrees, and then he held it around the corner. A small monitor mounted on the top of the receiver showed us that the corridor held no surprises. "The monitor gives us a visual, as well as an infrared scan," Waam told us. I made a mental note to get myself one of those babies.

We continued straight because our corridor paralleled the corridor that Nargas had entered. After we walked about fifty yards, the Ummite in the lead raised his hand. Waam stepped forward and pressed his eye against a scanner that was mounted eight feet above the floor. A monitor lit up, showing us the activity in the room on the other side of the wall. We could see two lizards sitting at a table, drinking from metal bottles. "Every room in our outpost has been outfitted with multiple video cameras," Waam told me. "Unfortunately, during their attack upon our facility, the reptilians destroyed the wireless router that would have enabled us to check each room from a single monitor."

Waam nodded to one of his men, who pushed on a metal panel, exposing a small opening into the adjoining room. He then stuck the end of his strange weapon into the opening and used its monitor to make some small adjustments. When he pulled the trigger, his weapon hummed quietly. Within a few seconds, the lizards collapsed to the floor, dead.

"Cooked lizard," the Ummite told us with a smile.

I looked at Waam quizzically. "Microwave cooking at its extreme," he told me. "It quickly heats water and bodily fluids by as much as two hundred degrees, essentially boiling the victim. It sounds grizzly, but it's a quick death."

"I want one of those," Mack said.

"Sorry, but this is a technology that we cannot trust humans to use ethically," Waam replied.

"But—" Mack began to say.

"They're lizards, Mack," Waam said matter-of-factly. "You know that we Ummites have taken a vow not to hurt humans. If we gave you this weapon, you would use it against other humans, and we would be the fundamental source of the harm. See? Giving you this weapon would violate our ethical code."

Mack nodded. He turned to me. "I still want one of those."

I nodded in agreement. Waam and his men began moving again, further into the depths of the corridor, and Mack and I continued struggling to keep up. After a couple of minutes, I could feel my heart racing, and I was happy when Waam stopped. Again, he placed his eye against a scanner that was mounted high on the wall. When the monitor lit up, we could see Mona, sitting in a hard backed chair but leashed to a reptilian soldier. Nargas was nowhere to be seen.

As before, one of Waam's men opened a secret panel and took careful aim. His weapon hummed briefly, and the lizard who was guarding Mona fell over dead. This time, as boiling liquids escaped from his body, his back actually appeared to be smoking.

When the guard fell, Mona stood up, looked around, and wrenched the cable from his hand. Carrying Stella, she hurried to the door to the room, opened it and looked into the corridor. She brought her head back in and returned to the chair. Within a few seconds, another guard entered the room and hissed at her when he saw his comrade on the floor. He left, securing the door as he went for help.

Waam pressed his hand on a panel in the ceiling above, and a section of the wall became fuzzy. As soon as it disappeared, we rushed into the room. Two of Waam's men took positions at the door, two others set up against opposite walls.

Waam and the others encircled Mona and me. We were embracing and kissing, and I was trying my best not to press too hard into Stella because I didn't want her to start crying.

"Get this thing off of me, Danny," Mona said, pulling at the collar that gripped her throat.

I unsnapped the leash, opened the collar, and threw them both onto the corpse of the dead lizard. "We're gonna get you out of here, baby."

"Nargas will be back at any moment, Danny," she told me. "He's got Hitler with him somewhere in this bunker."

"Yeah, but your safety comes first. We've got to get you and Stella out of here, and this place is crawling with lizards."

"How are we going to leave here? Who's going to fly us home?"

"Waam's here to help us. He knows all sorts of secret passages that the lizards don't know are here."

Mona suddenly became cognizant of the fact that the room was full of giant soldiers. She turned until she saw Waam and then gave him a hug, pressing her cheek into his belly. "Thank you for helping me again, Waam! You're always rescuing me from that bastard who killed Doroo."

Waam bent down and looked closely at Mona. "Was it Commissar Nargas who had Doroo murdered?"

Mona looked at me.

"I'm sorry, Waam," I said. "We've been so caught up in the moment that you and I haven't had time to debrief. But, yes, we learned on Earth that it was Commissar Nargas who ordered Doroo's death, and we just learned today that it was Nargas who led the attack on the Ummite outpost here on Mars."

"And he is here, now?"

"Yes," I replied, "he is." I needed to explain, so I told Waam, "Mack, Mona, Grau, and I managed to escape from the lunar artifact, and we came here to tell you what we had learned. On the way here, we were attacked by the commissar's tureen and managed to destroy it. We thought that the commissar and His Excellency were both dead. Unfortunately, when we arrived, they both were here to greet us, and they brought a group of reptilians with them. They took Mona with them and left the rest of us with a bunch of scaly goons who were supposed to execute us. You managed to spoil their fun, except for Grau, who was first on the execution block. You arrived a couple of minutes too late for him." I reminded myself to send a card of condolence to Grau's family. Then I remembered that he didn't really have one.

Stella began crying, so Mona walked away and began to sway and hum to her. Mack followed Mona to see if he could help in some way. A father of three kids, he liked little ones. Waam and I watched for a few moments, and then we got back down to business.

"It is unfortunate about Grau," Waam replied. "He was a good friend. However, we need to turn our attention to terminating the commissar before he leaves the Red Planet."

"I guess we can search every room in the outpost until we find him," I suggested.

"Or when they find that Agent Casola has escaped, perhaps they will come to us," Waam suggested.

I liked the way that Waam thought. The commissar seemed to have a thing for Mona, and she would be our bait. Of course, I didn't want to tell her that because she'd get pissed that I would put her in jeopardy of being captured by the commissar for a third time, if things went his way instead of ours.

It was time to vacate the room before scaly reinforcements arrived to figure out what had happened to the dead one. Waam signaled for us to leave. I took Mona's hand and led her to the door in the wall that opened to the secret Ummite passageway. Once we were all through it, Waam touched the spot on the ceiling again, and the wall fuzzily reappeared and then turned back into solid rock.

We started back down the corridor and then took a right. Waam checked two more rooms through the video monitors, but they were empty. We then turned to go back to the corridor that led to the exit. Suddenly we heard alarms go off in the main corridors. "I guess they've discovered that Mona is gone," I said to Mack.

"Don't panic everyone," Waam reminded us. "They don't know about these passageways, so we should be safe inside."

"They put one of those tracking devices into my arm," Mona said. "They may be able to find me pretty quickly."

Waam broke his flashlight against the wall of the passageway and picked up a small magnet that was embedded in its base. I didn't know what function it served. "Can you fasten this over the spot where they inserted the tracker?" he asked me.

I thought for a moment and then removed my shoe and took off my sock. I put the magnet inside the sock, and then tied it around Mona's right arm, ensuring that the magnet was centered over the tiny new scratch beside her elbow. "Looks like another trip to the doctor when we get out of here," she told me. She was right. This would be the second tracking device that she would have had surgically removed in less than six months—if we got out of here and back to the Earth.

We found our way back to the corridor that led to the execution room, and from there, Waam led us to the hangar where his tureen was waiting. As we approached the tureen, we heard noise coming from a distance away, and it was coming quickly. Soon shadows were dancing chaotically upon the walls near the entrance to the hangar. There was no doubt that it was lizards.

Eight of Waam's men knelt in the ready position, prepared to defend us. Waam and two of his men opened the ramp and prepared the tureen for take-off. Mack, Mona, and Stella were ushered inside. Suddenly the lizards were upon us, less than fifty yards away. They fired first. The burst of liquid light struck one of Waam's men, severing his leg. He fell in agony. Two of Waam's men dragged the wounded warrior inside the tureen.

I picked up the warrior's weapon and began squeezing its trigger in the direction of the approaching lizards. The remaining five Ummites joined me in protecting the tureen until it was ready. Light and sparks ricocheted off of the walls and off of Waam's tureen. Sparks flew everywhere. Another of Waam's men was hit, struck dead. Two of Waam's men dragged his body into the tureen. One shouted, "Come inside! Come inside! We're ready to go!"

The two remaining Ummites shielded me as the three of us backed up the ramp to safety. The ramp was immediately closed once we were inside. Waam shouted, "Shields are up!" We were safe, at least for the moment.

I felt the slight movement characteristic of the newer tureens, which told me that we were airborne and moving toward the exit of the outpost. We could hear the whining of bursts of liquid light which were being fired in our direction, and the strange sound of their being deflected by the plasma shields that now surrounded the tureen and protected us from harm.

Within half a minute, Waam said, "We are out and off the surface!" There was a pause, and then he told us, "The lizards are scrambling!"

At first, I didn't know what that meant. Perhaps they were running to and fro on the ground? Then Mona cried, "They're sending a tureen after us. It's going to be a rough ride home!"

Stella began crying. *God, I hate a crying baby! Especially when the tureen I'm riding in is under attack and everyone inside is shouting commands and responses at each other.* It was chaotic! And I was useless when it came to helping out. I mean, I knew nothing about flying a tureen or firing its weapons. I was simply a passenger observing a battle in outer space. This was a role that I wasn't used to playing. I wanted to do something.

Waam was adjusting something when one of his men shouted, "We have company!"

Mona and I stood to look out through the transparent

upper shell of the tureen. Gaining on us was a Draconian military tureen. It fired two shots, but our shields deflected the bursts of light. It pulled alongside us, like a British man-o-war preparing the fire a broadside. "It's Nargas!" Mona cried.

"Yeah, it's him, and he's got Hitler with him," I shouted to Waam. "And maybe six lizards in full gear!"

"Excellent!" Waam shouted back. "Sit down in the co-pilot seat, Mr. Arrow!"

Waam's co-pilot stood up and motioned for me to take his seat. Mona sat back down, and Mack buckled her seat belt while she held tightly onto Stella. Mack winked at me, so I knew that he would take care of my new family. I smiled at him, blew a kiss to Mona, and hurried to the co-pilot's seat, as Waam had asked.

Waam flipped up a rectangular cover on the control panel. Beneath it was a red button. "Hit that button when I tell you to do so!" Waam instructed. I nodded back to him. "Here we go!" he shouted.

Waam rotated a small his accelerator wheel on the control panel with his finger. Our tureen took off—as Mona would say, "like Snyder's pup"—rapidly pulling away from the commissar's tureen. We were screaming through space, directly at the sun. The commissar raced after us, firing bursts of liquid light. Fortunately, our shields continued to work.

Waam spun the tureen, rotating full circle to the right while continuing to streak toward the sun. The commissar kept firing, and bursts of light flew by, missing us completely. Waam looked at me. "Get ready." I put my finger beside the red button, but not on it because I didn't know how sensitive its trigger mechanism might be.

"Hang on!" Waam cried. He rotated the accelerator backward, engaging the retro magnetic thrusters, and pulling our tureen to a dead stop. The commissar shot by us.

"Now! Hit the button now!" Waam shouted.

I hit it twice and watched as two balls of liquid light sped from our turret toward the commissar's tureen. In front of the balls of light, space seemed to bend, the way that heat makes distant images wiggle and dance in the desert. The light itself had an orange glow, unlike the pure white light that the commissar had been shooting at us.

When the light hit the commissar's tureen, it ripped a hole through its outer shell. His tureen flipped on its side and then onto its back and fell toward the sun. About ten seconds later, a small burst of white light erupted when the tureen entered the sun's burning plasma. "Must have been the nuclear reactor exploding," Waam told me with a smile.

"Didn't he have shields?" I asked.

"This is new, shield-piercing technology that we retro-engineered from a tureen that we recovered ten years ago on Ceres, a dwarf planet in your star's asteroid belt. We have no idea of its origin, but its technology surpasses all that the Draconians have. It's a two stage weapon. First, it sent an electromagnetic pulse, which destroyed their electrical microcircuits, followed half a second later by the new liquid laser that penetrates almost anything."

"He didn't have a chance, did he?"

"No, he didn't have a chance. I like it that way, and Doroo has been avenged." Waam's face grew serious. "What you saw today—our weapon—must not be described or revealed to anyone. It is the only thing that will keep you humans safe during a Draconian invasion, and you know that's part of their ultimate agenda."

I nodded. "Thanks for letting me do the deed."

"Hitler was on board, and you know that I've taken a vow to harm no human, no matter how evil. But I also knew that you wouldn't think twice about it."

Waam was definitely right about that.

I left the co-pilot's seat and told Mona, "That bastard is finally out of your life, baby. He and Hitler are dancing with the devil in the fires of Hell."

"Did you see him die, Dan?" Mack asked.

"It was new technology, and he didn't stand a chance. If you're ever in a dogfight in space, be sure that you're riding in an Ummite tureen."

"I think I want one of these!" Mack replied.

Chapter 30

The trip back to Earth was peaceful once Nargas was out of the picture, and during the flight, I had time to think about the events of the past few days. The Chinese had spent a fortune in gold, stealing much of it from beneath the surface of other countries, and had delivered it to the Draconians in exchange for rights to the moon. It promised to give them an advantage over all other nations on Earth. I guess that was their attempt to dominate the NWO or to render it powerless. But now the interior of the moon was highly damaged, if not totally irreparable. Certainly, it would be radioactive into the foreseeable future, and they would not be able to establish a military presence there.

As for the NWO, it had lost its entire contingent of lunar troops, which should cause a major setback in its timetable for implementing Agenda 21, especially the release of a pandemic on the Earth. And now, with Hitler out of the way, the NWO would have to reorganize and select a new leader. Still nagging at me, though, was Hitler. When I saw him standing beside Nargas in the hangar of the Ummite outpost, he seemed uncharacteristically quiet and Nargas never addressed him as "Your Excellency." But, he was definitely the same young man who addressed the NWO troops on the moon. Or else he was a double. If it was the latter, then Hitler was going to pop up again sometime, and when he did, I was going to have to whack him.

And Mona had changed, too. Other than calling a lizard a "bastard," her language seemed less colorful than usual, as though she was selecting her words more carefully now that Stella was within earshot. *Motherhood seems to change a woman*, I thought, *and in very little time*. I hoped she still wanted to have sex.

❧❧

Six months after Waam dropped us off—Mona, Mack, and me, and oh yes, Stella, too—in a forest preserve outside of Quantico, about thirty miles south of DC, Mack came by to see us. He brought Stella an iPad, probably something that he bought with Bureau money.

"How is she?" he asked.

"She's only seven months old, and already she's walking and talking," Mona replied. "Her vocabulary seems to grow by ten or more words every day, and she already weighs forty pounds."

"They grow fast, Mona. If she's like the others, by the time she's eight, she should be fluent in three or four languages and should have mastered advanced principles of calculus. By ten, she should have knowledge equivalent to a master's degree in most subjects."

"I'm worried about that, Mack," Mona replied. "I want her to have a normal life, and that just isn't normal."

"There's nothing normal about her, baby," I said. "She was saying things to us in our heads by the time she was three months old. Speech came later, didn't it?"

Mona nodded. She had been on special assignment from the FBI since returning from the moon. Her job was to keep a daily log of Stella's growth, both mental and physical, and do everything that a human mother would do to ensure that Stella was fully adjusted to the expectations and customs of the human species.

But Stella wasn't human. Her eyes were noticeably larger and jet black, with baby blues where the whites should have been. And every now and then, maybe once every five minutes, when she blinked, her secondary eyelids closed from the sides. We were used to it by now, but we knew that we couldn't send her to school or take her to a playground where regular kids were playing because they would call her a freak.

We shared our concerns with Mack. "That's why I'm here," he said. "I want to make you an offer."

We listened suspiciously. After all, Mack was still FBI and there's always some kind of hidden agenda in whatever it is that the Bureau offers. They don't do anything that doesn't have something in it for them.

"Near Little Devils Stairs, Virginia, just off of the Skyline Drive, there is a special school where Stella would fit right in. She would be normal."

"You mean a school full of alien-human hybrids?" I asked.

"Yes, exactly. There are over two hundred little boys and girls just like Stella. Some look a little reptilian, but most look like normal human kids, except for their eyes, and their brain power."

"I'm not sure, Mack," Mona replied. "Did you pick that place because of its name?"

"It's a great opportunity, Mona. Some of these kids have remarkable powers. Who knows what Stella might discover in herself when she sees what some of the other kids can do. In a way, they sort of teach each other, like normal kids do, but the things they teach each other far surpass our simple human skills."

"I couldn't bear to be away from her. I'm her mommy, and Danny is her daddy. I'm not putting her in some boarding school where I can't see her."

"Did I say it was a boarding school?"

"Well," I replied, "we live in DC, and you're talking about sending Stella to Little Devils Stairs, wherever the fuck that is."

"It isn't *in* Little Devils Stairs. It's *near* Little Devils Stairs. It is a special community in a remote area, built by the CIA using black ops money. It has homes, and streets, and playgrounds, a church, the school, and basic shopping—you know, everything you could want: a grocery store, a drug store, gas station, library, and a special hospital, equipped to treat special kids."

"What, no Macy's?" Mona quipped.

I brought us back on task. "What's the catch, Mack?" I asked.

"We'll house you there for free, at least until Stella grows up and takes a job. By then, you should have saved enough money to be able to buy a nice home for cash wherever you want to live."

"And Stella?" Mona asked.

"She's special, Mona. We don't know what the future holds for her. She could become a great scientist, or a doctor, or an artist of some sort."

"Or a spook for the CIA—" I added.

"That's not the plan, Dan. The plan is to watch and learn from these kids. They can teach us a lot. Besides, I think the world is going to be theirs one day. I think as they begin marrying and multiplying, our kind of humans will just sort of go away, like Neanderthals did when Homo Sapiens arrived on the scene."

"Are you inferring that Homo Sapiens were planted

here by aliens the way that Stella and the Star Children have been?" Mona asked.

"We've had that discussion before, Mona. It certainly seems plausible. But I'm not saying it's so. Others believe it, though."

"We've got time to think about it, don't we?" Mona asked.

"Sure, take all the time you need, but I think if you watch how fast she develops intellectually, you'll realize that she needs to be where she can get the proper intellectual stimulation. In fact, and I hate to say this, but she'll surpass you and Dan intellectually in a very short time. She will love you for being her parents, but she'll find you boring."

Mona and I knew that Mack was right about that. Two weeks later, we agreed to go see the new community near Little Devils Stairs. Mack drove us there himself in a black Hummer, the same type of vehicle that the tall goons drove when they harassed Hal and stalked Billy Powers.

I had to admit, though, that the community was nice. As we entered it, we were greeted by a security guard at a checkpoint. The sign on the fence said *US GOVERNMENT FACILITY. NO TRESPASSING*. However, a quarter of a mile down the road, another sign greeted us with *VILLAGIO IBRIDO, VISITORS WELCOME*. It sounded Italian to me, so I asked Mona what it meant. "Village of Hybrids," she said. *Great*, I thought, *nothing like making a kid feel normal*.

However, once we entered the village, it was beautiful. The streets were wide and lined with flowering bushes. People were walking and biking in the downtown area, and in the residential areas, people were mowing lawns and watering plants. Welcome to small town America.

Mack pulled into the driveway of a small Cape Cod. "This is your home, if you choose to move here."

"It's pretty, Mack, but what are we going to do?" I asked. "I'm a private eye. There's no work out here for me."

"I have plenty of work for you to do. You'll be a government investigator, grade GS Thirty-Five. The pay and benefits are great. You can't beat the health and retirement systems. You'll be issued a car and a governmental side arm, probably a nine-millimeter Glock." This was sounding good to me. Hell, I had nothing set aside for retirement yet, and I avoided doctors and dentists unless I had the cash to pay them.

"Mona will still be with the FBI on special assignment," Mack went on. "She'll receive a two grade promotion and a car, probably a newer electric model based on Tesla's principles. They're pretty neat."

"Can you make it a Tesla?" Mona asked.

"No, but these vans are really nice and serve as excellent family cars."

Inside the Cape Cod, everything was new and energy efficient, especially when Mack hit the light switch and the walls themselves glowed with a white light that could be adjusted by simply turning a dial. I sensed that alien technology was being put to good use on an experimental basis in Villagio Ibrido, but I figured that I'd learn more about that later.

Over the next hour, we checked out the stores, the medical facilities, and the schools.

They were all clean and new, and the staff seemed especially welcoming.

At the school, we stood at the edge of the playground watching children swing and play tag.

One little blonde girl came over to us, clearly interested in Stella. "Would you like to swing?" she asked.

"Thanks, sweetheart, but Stella can't stay long," Mona told her.

"That's okay. Maybe next time. My name is Myra."

Stella smiled at Myra and Myra blew her a kiss. Then her secondary eyes blinked from the sides, like Stella's. That clinched the deal for Mona. She turned to me. "It's a little surreal here, Danny. Like, there's no pizza places, no hot dog vendors on the sidewalks, and no derelicts or street musicians, but this is a perfect place for Stella. I vote for accepting Mack's proposal."

I really didn't have a choice. I wanted Mona and Stella to have the best, but I couldn't afford a place as nice as the Cape Cod in Hybridville. Also, Mack was offering me a steady paycheck, which was something I had never enjoyed. For me, it had always been feast or famine, and I had never had the ability to sock much away for a rainy day. So, I agreed, and we both shook Mack's hand to seal the deal.

But I knew that the Bureau wouldn't pay me a steady salary without expecting something in return. I wondered how long it would be before they called in the favor.

෩෩෩

When we got back to our apartment that evening, I told Mona, "I always wanted a place in the country."

"Don't bullshit me, Danny. You're going to have to work hard to fit in with the locals. You've got an edge, if you know what I mean."

"I guess I do have an attitude. I'll do my best to control it."

"You'll have to learn how to garden," Mona told me.

"I'm not much for flowers."

"Me neither, Danny. We'll start with tomatoes and basil. I'll need them to make us fresh Italian sauce."

"I love your sauce, baby."

Mona sighed. "Do you always have to go there?" She kissed Stella, who at forty-five pounds and almost three feet tall, was resting her head in the cradle of Mona's arms while her feet hung from the edge of the sofa. Stella's eyes showed love for Mona.

Mona handed her to me, and Stella immediately started crying. I gave her back to Mona and Stella cooed.

"That's like most of the women in my life," I said. "When they find themselves in my arms, they cry."

Mona reassured me. "When little Stella takes her nap, I'll prove you wrong."

Epilogue

A month later, Mona and I moved into our new residence at 14 Sirius Avenue, Villagio Ibrido, Virginia, moving van courtesy of Agent Mack Smith, FBI. My hair had grown back fully, and I had shaved the beard that I had worn as an interrogator. Mona, too, had returned to her chestnut brown hair. The dye job was a pretty good match to her natural color, and I had done a pretty good job of applying the dyeing goop, if I do say so myself.

Before we moved, however, Mona and I did the right thing—we got married. It was a small ceremony with just our families, well just Mona's. Her parents were there and her two sisters, but little Wendy's husband decided to opt out of a wedding that was held at the picnic area behind the FBI Training Facility in Quantico, and we had no reception offering free drinks.

Mona's dad was irritated that she was marrying me, especially when he learned that we had a baby that was pushing fourteen months old, if you looked at normal growth curves. We told him that we had adopted little Stella.

"What's with her eyes?" her dad asked.

"Some kind of genetic anomaly," Mona replied. "That's why we adopted her. Nobody else would have."

∽∾∽∾

Mona was upstairs putting Stella to bed when Mack Smith called me on my cell phone. I had a feeling that it wasn't a social call.

"Dan, can we talk?" he asked.

"Yeah," I replied, "Mona is upstairs with Stella. It's been a long day. We finally finished unpacking our stuff and dragging the boxes out to the curb today. We're planning to turn in early."

"It's good that I caught you then," he replied.

"What's up?"

"I'm going to send you a link to a YouTube video that has gone viral. I think you'll find it interesting."

"Can you clue me in?"

"It's a guy who is promoting being born again."

"Like another fundamentalist preacher?"

"No, he claims to be a technologist who has developed a process to enable people to live forever, by cloning their bodies and moving them from their bodies to their clones as they age. He claims that his invention will bring about a new world where death no longer exists."

"That sounds too much like the Draconian migration process, Mack!"

"And the New World Order," Mack replied. "But you gotta see the guy in the video, Dan."

"Why's that?"

"It's Hitler!"

About the Author

Born in Massachusetts, Edward Baker traveled widely as a child because his US Marine father was transferred to new assignments across the USA on a regular basis. By the time Baker was twelve, he had crossed the United States three times. And at the ripe old age of sixteen, he actually drove a stick-shift Ford across the USA, following his dad, who was pulling a small camping trailer behind the family station wagon.

An English major at Elon College, Baker earned a master's degree at Appalachian State University and a doctorate in Educational Leadership at the Graduate School of the Sage Colleges. After thirty-five years in higher education, and after retiring as the interim president of a public community college, he turned his attention to his first love, writing, while continuing to teach undergraduate and graduate courses on an adjunct basis at a private college in upstate New York.

During the warm months, Baker and his wife Edna reside in their cabin on Galway Lake, New York. During the cold months, they "hole up" in their winter quarters in Saratoga Springs, New York. When he's not teaching or writing, Baker is playing with his four grandchildren or working on a long list of renovations and construction projects.

Baker saw his first UFOs as a young man while camping out at Green Lakes State Park near Syracuse, New York. He saw his second while living on the beach at Emerald Isle in North Carolina, back when it was still a wild and undeveloped stretch of dunes. His first Black Opal book, *Dan Arrow and the New World Order,* is based on these experiences and on current conspiracy lore, combining the UFO mystery with national and international politics and the rumored agenda of the legendary New World Order. Baker says that the Dan Arrow books are fun to write because they permit him to delve into seemingly unrelated elements that mesh together into a fabric offering many clandestine possibilities.